BEST LESBIAN EROTICA 1996

BEST LESBIAN EROTICA 1996

Selected and Introduced by
HEATHER LEWIS

Edited by
TRISTAN TAORMINO

CLEIS
PRESS

"The Snow Queen" ©1996 by Dorothy Allison. The first part of the trilogy, "The Snow Queen's Robber Girl," appears in *Once Upon a Time: Erotic Fairy Tales for Women* (Richard Kasak, 1996). "Festival of Sighs" ©1995 by J.M. Beazer is an excerpt from her novel *The Festival of Sighs* used by permission of the author. "Trade" ©1995 by Lucy Jane Bledsoe used by permission of the author. "The Little Macho Girl" © 1996 by Kate Bornstein will appear in *Once Upon a Time: Erotic Fairy Tales for Women* (Richard Kasak, 1996) and is used by permission of the author and editor, Lily August. "Touch Memory" ©1995 by Meg Daly used by permission of the author. "Salt" ©1995 by Mona de Vestel used by permission of the author. "And Salome Danced" ©1994 by Kelley Eskridge was published in *Little Deaths* (UK Edition, Millenium, 1994, US Edition, Dell, 1995). "Healy" ©1995 by Jennifer Natalya Fink has appeared (in earlier versions) in *two girls review* (1995) and *Global City Review* (1994). "Addict Girl #1: Drug-free Afternoon" ©1995 by Karen Green used by permission of the author. "Pumpkin Pie" ©1995 by Sandra Lee Golvin is adapted from her one-woman show "Pumpkin Pie: A Story of Cross-Gender Transcendence" which debuted at Highways in Los Angeles in 1994. "Yaguara" ©1995 by Nicola Griffith is an excerpt from the novella *Yaguara* which was published in *Little Deaths* (UK Edition, Millenium, 1994) and *Asimov's* (1995). "Semiraw" ©1995 by Corrina Kellam used by permission of the author. "Ghost Crab" ©1995 by Linda L. Nelson used by permission of the author. "She Falls to Pieces" ©1995 by Gerry Gomez Pearlberg used by permission of the author. "Bing" ©1995 by Jane Perkins used by permission of the author. "Dybbuk" ©1995 by Robin Podolsky was first published in *Diabolical Clits* (Vol. 1 #1). "Bird" ©1995 by Marian Rooney was first published in *Diabolical Clits* (Vol. 1 #1). "Confessions of a Blood Eater" ©1995 by Vanessa Scott used by permission of the author. "Chelsea Thirteen" ©1995 by Linda Smukler is from her forthcoming collection *Home in Three Days. Don't Wash.* (Hard Press, 1996). "Against the Grain" ©1995 by Wickie Stamps used by permission of the author. "Lucky Girls" ©1995 by Nancy Stockwell used by permission of the author. Excerpted from her novel *Lucky Girls*. "I'm Sorry" ©1995 by Trish Thomas was first published in *Taste of Latex* (1995). "Sinner" ©1995 by Alison Tyler used by permission of the author. "Seduction" ©1995 by Terry Wolverton was first published in *modern words* (Summer 1995).

CONTENTS

ACKNOWLEDGMENTS

There are two very important women who, for me, inspired this book: Pat Califia and Claire Potter. I would like to thank Charlotte Abbott, Malaga Baldi, and Michael Thomas Ford for their assistance on the project. Extra special thanks to Gabrielle Maloney and Philippa Rizopolous for their friendship and their editorial suggestions for the Foreword. The following people have given me unwavering love and encouragement throughout: Adrianne Bushey, Wendy Caplan, Michelle Duff, Shannon Ebner, Heather Findlay, Sandra Lee Golvin, Ron Lieber, Jonathan Munk, Judith Pynchon, D. Travers Scott, and Anna Lisa Suid. Kathy Blenk, Amanda Tear, Mark Thomson, and Winston Wilde have also given me so much from so far away. My work could not have been possible without tremendous support from Constance Jones, Jill Muir-Sukenick and the staff at Buttrick White & Burtis. Heather Lewis' work on this book has been thorough, incomparable and outstanding; as a mentor and friend, she has been a wonderful force in my life. And finally, huge thanks to Karen Brophy—gourmet chef, Reggie-wrangler, computer genius, girlfriend extraordinaire, secret sharer, dream warrior, and the one—for everything and more.

FOREWORD

"I'm not a lesbian."
"I don't write erotica."
"The characters in my story aren't all lesbians."
"There's no actual sex in my piece."
"There are men in my story."
"There's no lesbian sex in my piece."
"My writing is dark, gruesome, not everyone's idea of erotic."
"I don't know if my writing is erotic or sexy enough."
"I don't think this is appropriate."

If *Best Lesbian Erotica* sounds like something you've heard before, like something you can easily wrap your head and hands around, it's not. These three words are highly charged and hotly contested. They may not have a long history, but it's a dynamic one.

The infamous Lesbian Sex Wars of the eighties spawned a radical lesbian sex movement which has flourished for more than a decade. Social and political groups like SAMOIS, the Lesbian Sex Mafia, and various butch/femme networks were organized around sexuality; they gave women a place to talk and learn about lesbian sex. Today, there are community consciousness-raising groups of the nineties: new cybercommunication on-line through bulletin boards, discussion groups, web sites, and e-mailing lists (my favorites are Boychicks and Kinky Girls) which connect women worldwide to talk about sex. Magazines like *On Our Backs* and *Bad Attitude* paved the way for a string of others—*Taste of Latex, Frighten the Horses, Venus Infers, Brat Attack, Paramour,* and *Girlfriends,* which have all given opportunities to dozens of new porn writers. Many small and independent publishers have been successful with erotic collections like Naiad's *The Erotic Naiad,* Down There Press' *Herotica,* Alyson's Bushfire-Afterglow-Heatwave series, and Pat Califia's *Macho Sluts* and *Melting Point;* these books and others have appeared on gay and lesbian bestseller lists and created a space for themselves in their very own section in some gay and lesbian bookstores. These books, magazines, and new forms of multi-media communication have been crucial sites for the production of lesbian identity, sexuality, politics, and community. In addition to our own media, lesbians have come out of the mainstream media closets and erotica has come down off the bookstore "Anonymous" top shelves. Dykes and erotica are on the covers of national magazines, in the pages of Susie "Sexpert" Bright's *Best American Erotica* series, even on Hollywood's big screens.

Reading the submissions I received for this project, I was struck by the fact that certain conventions of lesbian erotic stories had become so standard. The is-she-or-isn't-she-a-dyke narrative of wonder and seduction. The one-night-stand-who-became-the-girlfriend tale. The "butch-flip" story of unexpected role reversals. The very existence of such conventions suggests that there is a recognizable (dare I say) canon of lesbian erotic writing with identifiable authors, publishers, and even themes. While this historical shift is thrilling, the codification of lesbian erotic writing has produced a known group of writers who, as the primary producers of the most widely accessible lesbian porn, end up in control of defining the discourse and agenda; even the Sexpert herself admits, "Eros is a universe, and we haven't even gotten off the launch pad."[1] We may have come a long way, baby, but we're not there yet.

For women, the articulation of desire is incredibly complicated, layered, and difficult since it is always entangled with power and politics, our bodies and our histories, and the culture-at-large. Writing erotica is like blazing through enemy territory: our bodies, our erotic lives, our desires and fantasies are undeniably complex, still uncharted, always open for debate, and relentlessly under siege. Writing erotica is absolutely a political and dangerous act. As the Christian Fundamentalist Right Wing *and* anti-sex/pro-censorship feminists promote obscenity laws, sexphobic legislation, and censorship, erotica is also *in* danger.

Members of the pro-sex movement have worked to counteract the restriction of sexual expression by creating women- and lesbian-produced pornography. But perhaps, over time, our definitions have narrowed rather than expanded. Just as feminists have fought to move definitions of sex beyond heterosexual penis-vagina intercourse, we must attempt to push the boundaries of erotica beyond simple description of sexual acts. Current writing tends to take erotica too literally. Erotica-as-sex-story has come to prevail when there is so much that is erotic outside of naked bodies and sexual acts: lust, memory, obsession, attraction, anticipation, longing, love, hate, transgression. Erotica (like sex itself) has also relied too much on fixed notions of gender and sexuality (e.g. men, women, straight, gay, lesbian, top, bottom, butch, femme, etc.) which are much more unstable than they claim to be and can make for over-simplified, uninteresting stories. Moreover, there is an assumed correspondence between a reader's identity and her tastes in smut, i.e. lesbians only read lesbian erotica and straight women only read straight erotica, which excludes the possibilities that our libidos are a lot more perverse. Nor is there a stable gender correspondence between writer and narrator. Like the labyrinth of gender, certain elements of erotic life still need to be fleshed out in our writing: the psychological aspects of eroticism; the subtleties, intricacies and erotics of power; and the significance of childhood experiences.

The interior, psychological erotic story, what psychologist Gina Ogden calls "thinking off," has been underexplored in most erotica. Sometimes I don't want the act spelled out for me. I want the door to possibilities left open. I want what's waiting on the invisible last page. Ogden proclaims, "Our minds and spirits are the ultimate erogenous zones."[2] That is where *my* erotic life exists a lot of the time: getting my brain wet and hard, making my skin *and* my head spin and sting with ecstasy.

Within lesbian erotic writing, a solid body of lesbian S/M erotica has developed as one of the sites for radical sexual writing. S/M writing illuminates some of the cerebral aspects of sex, alternative notions of sex, pleasure, and relationships, and the links between power and sex. Yet, I find that this writing is often full of "inside" terms and rules (like underground slavery worlds or elaborate dungeon etiquette) which only serve to distract and alienate readers. Or S/M porn focuses too much on the oversimplified master/slave dichotomy and the excesses of pain and pleasure, making the roles and the endurance of the unendurable the focus of narratives. The subtlety and intricacies of the flow of power and the exploration of difference are lost.

In this collection, stories focus on the complexity of characters, the powerful dynamics between them, the situations in which they find themselves and the ways in which they interact with each other. The narrators (and characters) in this book are not simply lesbians; sometimes they are little girls, horny boys, bloodthirsty women, or dirty old men. This fluid subjectivity creates an opportunity to delve into the layers of gender identity and explore what happens when an erotic encounter goes awry. Isn't safe. Melts boundaries of pleasure and danger. Is taboo. Blurs gender identities.

There is ongoing tension within the lesbian writing community about promoting positive, politically correct role models for queer youth. Safe, positive portrayals also serve to make queers more acceptable (or less deplorable) to mainstream America. Simply telling the truth of our experiences tends to be messier, uglier, and more complicated. Porn's godfather John Preston admitted about his "life as a pornographer": "Pornography has made me be honest, about myself and some of the most intimate details of my life and my fantasies. I think that's an important part of writing: being able to dare to put oneself on the page."[3]

The writers in this book *do* dare to put themselves on the page, with startling results. The majority of these stories are dark and violent. But the mood mirrors our histories, our lives, and our fantasies. For example, the effects of the AIDS crisis—how illness, death, safer sex panic and practice have creeped into women's heads, desires, bodies, and beds—still has not been explored as deeply as in gay male erotic writing.[4] Women also experience violence more frequently and intensely, and we bring those scars with us into our homes and our beds. Sometimes it can be in a constructive, positive, useful way; other times it can be destructive, negative, and disempowering. But usually, violence manifests itself as subtext, between the lines and the sheets, producing complicated and even ambivalent motivations, emotions, and desires.

The writing collected here also delves into other crucial aspects of women's lives. Memories from childhood—encounters with boys, girls, men or women; recollections of abuse, violence, fun, initiation; memories which are positive, negative, bizarre—all become part of our adult sexual lives, our erotic landscapes and fantasies, even if at the time we don't have a language to describe or process them. Likewise, men are involved in these stories in a way that the current canon tends to exclude them. For many lesbians, men were, are, or will be some part of our lives; they are also part of our sexual practices, relationships, identities and fantasies, and so they have a presence in our erotic writing.

According to some current definitions, lesbian writing is writing with lesbian content or lesbian writing is writing by lesbians. Because Heather and I included writers of all sexual and gender identities in this book, the writing here does not all include "lesbian content" as it is now defined, nor is it all "by lesbians."

So, you've got our version of the best lesbian erotica of the year. It's sometimes dark, sick, perverse, often strange, irreverent, unconventional, and always unique, compelling, provocative, and honest. For me, the best erotic stories closely resemble the people who make my skin flush hot pink and send my head into overdrive. They're fiercely intelligent, confident and intricate. They can sweep me off my feet or catch me off guard. They are tender and nasty and just a little bit dangerous. They are not always what you expect them to be.

Tristan Taormino
New York
December 1995

Notes

1. Susie Bright. *Herotica 3*. New York: Plume, 1994, xi.

2. Rebecca Chalker. "Sexual Pleasure Unscripted." *Ms.* Vol. 4, #3, 50.

3. John Preston. *My Life As A Pornographer and Other Indecent Acts.* New York: Richard Kasak Books, 1993, 21.

4. The best exploration thus far is Pat Califia's "Slipping" from her collection *Melting Point* (Alyson Publications).

INTRODUCTION

Heather Lewis

In the realm of human experience, my hat's off to anyone who can find an aspect more subjective than sexuality. Individual sexuality simply is, and ought to remain, as singular and distinct as a fingerprint. But singularity, of course, creates difficult terrain; engenders all sorts of attempts to deny and control. To see this applied to sexuality we need only look back to the eighties—our own porn-war years.

We're not in pitched battle anymore. We've retired to our separate camps. The nineties have been about cold war. It's an appropriate end to our heated fight because when all that heat fizzled out, when we were no longer at each other, constantly defending our positions, when the smoke finally cleared, we had to look at what we were up to back then—on both sides.

From our cold-war vantage point, what's striking about the two sides is their similarity. Each side had its own rules and regulations. Each side attempted to make their own sexuality, or lack thereof, okay for themselves by justifying and rationalizing it to others, academifying it even. So the outlaws made their own laws while the anti-porn activists tried to pass laws. The common goal was containment. And these attempts to contain sexuality—from both sides—had a chilling effect. What follows chilling, of course, is numbness.

As I read the work submitted to this anthology, it became hearteningly clear that the thaw has fully arrived. For some it's a slow melt, for others, things have cracked wide open. And certainly there were those who never went numb, just as there are those who'll remain perpetually frozen.

The truth of women's lives, the truth of women's individual sexuality? Maybe most of us knew all along these truths could never be muzzled, whether with a ball gag, or a gag order. This anthology confirms the power of those individual truths, confirms the power and singularity of sexuality.

My criteria for selection proved deceptively simple. I gravitated toward writers who confronted and then went beyond fear to tell complicated stories, and so obliged me, as a reader, to engage in a similar process.

15

The writers in this book challenged me to go beyond my own very singular fears and assumptions and wholly engage their stories, their truths. For me, this engagement is the heart of good fiction. For me, it's the whole point of fiction.

The best fiction transforms both reader and writer. To create this kind of fiction, a writer must remain unflinching and uncompromising. So in choosing the pieces for this book, I went with brave and honest writing. And I found, as usual, that the decision-making happened at gut level. When a writer scared me, or touched me, or made me think about something in a new way, I paid attention. Or, rather, the writing demanded my attention.

These writers got my attention because they did not hide truth behind language, whether pretty language or standard "erotic/porn" language. They discarded convention to move into the most forbidden territory of all—the mine field of an individual's singular sexuality—and, once there, they didn't tiptoe around, but tromped right through and let things explode.

By doing this kind of writing, these authors give a tremendous gift. The truths they tell are sometimes beautiful, sometimes ugly, sometimes heartbreaking. The range of subject matter and style is startling, but these writers share an ability to instill trust. Their courage and honesty compel our own; allow us to follow them with the knowledge that the trip through the mine field won't be without risk, but it will be worth the risk.

Some writers are no-doubt familiar—Linda Smukler, Lucy Jane Bledsoe, Gerry Gomez Pearlberg, Trish Thomas, Terry Wolverton, Kate Bornstein, Wickie Stamps, Robin Podolsky, Nicola Griffith, Pat Califia and Dorothy Allison—to name them all. They're here forging ahead on ground they've pioneered. Continuing to be brave and outrageous and truthful. They need no introduction, but continue to evoke gratitude.

It's the newcomers I want to introduce. So, to give you a brief map—I begin at the beginning, then take some detours to link similarly spirited material, and end at the end.

First up is Jennifer Fink. In "Healy," Fink explores the erotic possibilities of grade school paste when linked with the potent love for, and from, a caring teacher. In "Bing" Jane Perkins writes with language so simple and clean, and employs a wit so deft and dark, that before you know what's happened you've gone to that unbeatable place where your laughter catches in your throat, becomes a sob.

Meg Daly's "Touch Memory" also uses straightforward, spare prose to convey difficult emotions on a visceral level. At the same time Daly explores difficult and still-taboo subject matter. Alison Tyler's "Sinner" explores the taboo beneath the pseudo taboo of S/M, delving into the murky ambivalence that usually lingers there.

In "Salt," Mona de Vestel employs an economy and precision with her language that allows the reader to go to a near hypnotic state, and from there make linkages that might otherwise stay beyond reach. Hypnotic and otherworldly also describes Linda Nelson's "Ghost Crab"—where an island anti-paradise becomes the place a couple goes under to one another other. Nelson's sheer force with language, her mastery of the precise and poetic, dares her reader to follow her—in fact, demands it.

Vanessian Samois' "Confessions of a Blood Eater" also takes us to an utterly other place. No mere standard vampire tale; here, too, it is the precision and beauty of the language that separates. Samois' style employs a fervent energy reminiscent of symbolist poets, while somehow combining it with an utterly down-to-earth, even deadpan, realism.

Corrina Kellam's "Semiraw" is nothing short of terrifying. To say anything else would reduce it. Karen Green's "Addict Girl" is best described as a lesbian *A Clockwork Orange*—it's out there, way out there. Marian Rooney's "Bird" also goes way out, on a different, but no less dangerous, limb. And Sandra Lee Golvin's "Pumpkin Pie" uses juxtaposition to walk a structural tightrope.

Nancy Stockwell's excerpt from her historical novel "Lucky Girls" takes us on a totally different trip. Here, imagination and mystery, backed by evocative language, show the kind of breadth we can look forward to in upcoming novels. J. M. Beazer's novel excerpt provides a similar satisfaction. With seemingly effortless authority, Beazer serves up an immediately engaging story in a lush style that reminds you what you've been hungering for and letting you feast on it.

And, finally, Kelley Eskridge's "And Salome Danced." Simply read this one. You'll wonder where the hell Eskridge has been hiding, and grateful she's surfaced.

So there's my brief map. But I ask you to read this work the way these writers write—honestly, fearlessly. Discard your conventions and follow these writers. See where each one's take on sexuality takes you. Discard my map and tromp on through the land mines of this landmark book. See what explodes.

BEST LESBIAN EROTICA 1996

HEALY

JENNIFER NATALYA FINK

The thick, almost clay-like kind that came in white jars with a brush stuck inside the red top was the easiest to procure and the most similar to real food, sweet and gritty on the tongue like an undercooked vanilla cake. But Elmer's in orange tipped bottles, sipped straight down or half dried, licked off my coated fingers, Elmer's watery white in clear plastic bottles, leaving an aftertaste of chemicals that made me wild for more all day, Elmer's was not an experiment but a passion. In first grade, learning to wait my turn, to line up with the others, to pronounce s and sh distinctly, glue became my goal. Who knows when I first tasted its sweet unmilky flow in my high-pitched throat, but when I did I knew I needed it more than the four food groups we'd draw in bright pastels. White gobs of it, surprisingly unsticky when mixing with my mouth's fresh saliva, glue glorious glue my secret goal. Glue organized my schoolday. From collaging the Niña, Pinta, and Santa Maria to tracing the already well-known alphabet, every drab of knowledge might be an opportunity to sequester a sip or slug of it.

Are you hungry? Do they feed you enough in the morning? Mrs. Healy and her ever-changing eyeshadowed lids ask one day, taking me aside, showing me the secret drawer in her desk where she keeps her lunch which I am now welcome to if I am hungry. I don't cry. I concentrate on not crying, my cheeks hot pink, feeling shame like a song repeating in my ears. Caught. I am silent, eyes staring back at her green shadowed lids, hazel eyes filling with water, answerless. She frees me and I go to lunch with the others but my lust is doubly secret now, thrilled up with the new possibility of being caught glue-handed. Not of the consequences of being caught but of the being caught, of the kindness of interrogation.

Where glue is interrogation goes. After my private tour of Mrs. Healy's lunch (an apple, vanilla yogurt, and carrot and celery sticks in separate plastic bags) I grow extravagantly careless. I leave the drained-out bottles in plain sight on top of my desk, collecting the brushes stuck to the red tops for two weeks, then using them as the eyes of space monsters in our class collage of Apollo II. When she's eyeing me again during social studies, pencil eyebrows lifting up over the pearlescent lids, I become all smiley smart kid, arm shooting up, aching to tell the class the difference between horizontal and vertical. Inside the desk I finger the prize: four brand new extra large Elmer's, taken in plain view during art class. Fingering my booty in the back of the coat closet at home, I imagine Mrs. Healy taping me up, sealing my fingers and mouth together with some super superglue. And she did.

Yes, yes, Mrs. Healy.

Yes, yes, Mrs. Healy, I repeated after her, the s's sticking to my tongue. I still crave that game, crave the final s that grips tongue to mouth until you're so sticky with it she has to let you go.

I started speaking early, quickly, and in paragraphs. Nonetheless, the lisp saturated my speech so thoroughly that only my sister Jane could completely understand me. Even my parents couldn't quite decipher my lisping breathy prattle. Jane became my official translator. I spoke and their eyes would turn to her. Little girls grow out of these things, my parents reasoned.

Little girls lose extra syllables like baby fat, they told themselves.

In first grade at Northern Elementary School, I went to see Mrs. Healy after recess at one-thirty on alternate Wednesdays in the white and green trailer house attached to the main beige brick building. It was just that sort of seventies rural school: cows in the front yard fenced off from the playground, trailer house attached in the back for Special Ed. I remember nothing of how I unlearned my lisp there. I do know for certain that on each alternate Wednesday, Mrs. Healy wore a different shade of sparkly blue or pink or green eyeshadow all the way up to her thin arched brows. And the stick. She never threatened or hit with it; she simply pointed it at the hard s words on the pages of my reader. Her stick was too thick and long to be easily manipulated, so it would jostle all around in her hands as she'd point, its orange-varnished surface glinting with the light from the fluorescents overhead.

Yes, yes, Mrs. Healy.

Yes, yes, Mrs. Healy. Jane started the game, and "Yes, yes, Mrs. Healy" immediately became its official name. All of her games had official names. It was the summer I was obsessed with finding hidden dumbwaiters in restaurants and stripping down to my underwear in the cold empty auditoriums in the posh seaside scientific community where Dad had taken us so he could do his research. Jane was always Mrs. Healy. The other researchers' kids were younger than her and boys, and liked the idea of messing up Daddy's forbidden lecture hall. We were all Miss or Mister to her when Jane stood up there, hair pulled into a tight bun, white skin perspiring around her thin lips. With the long pointer, she'd stand at the lectern and assign us our tasks. Whatever she said, you had to respond, "Yes, yes, Mrs. Healy."

I was the projectionist. My job was to follow Mrs. Healy's motions with the slide projector, projecting the hot oval light slightly below her neck so that she wouldn't be blinded. She would yell, "Lights!" and I would twirl the projector onto her thin lips as I responded with "Yes, yes, Mrs. Healy," carefully shaping each s with my tongue and teeth. She glowed in that oval, the metal braces on her front teeth spraying the light back over us all as we waited for our next instructions. Hiding with my slide projector in the corner of the lecture hall behind the rows of blue fold-out chairs, I'd excitedly pull off my clothes, waiting for certain failure and its stick.

I liked my job pretty well, especially the part where I'd get tired and forget to say "Yes, yes, Mrs. Healy" and be called up by her in her white rage to take the stick. I'd close my eyes as the orange wood tickled the back of my throat where my tonsils had been, and think of the blues and pinks and greens of Mrs. Healy's eyelids as she pointed out the final s's. It never splintered but sometimes Jane would have to have a string of kids in a row take it: "Mr. Andrew! Mr. Scott! Miss Jennifer! None of you are addressing me correctly! Have you forgotten the rules?" and we would line right up, swallowing each other's saliva with the wood, not daring to spit it out in her presence.

Yes, yes, Mrs. Healy.

"Say it." Her rage was smooth, quick, absolute. The beads of sweat would gather on her part, a shallow river dividing the two halves of her brown-haired skull as she'd bend over us and the piss would squirt out of my thin gray underpants. Drying off in my corner under the oval projection light I would murmur "Yes, yes, Mrs. Healy" to myself, wanting it to never end, wanting to stand beneath her forever with the saliva of the other kids dripping slowly against my throat where the s's now emerge clearly when bidden at the end of each word.

BING

JANE PERKINS

I did it for the first time in a tent. It sort of happened; I didn't really expect it but I thought it was as good a time as any.

Me and my brother Randy and some people he knows are all camping out at the State Forest on Labor Day weekend, and Randy's friend Bing is there. He's the oldest guy here, twenty four. Ten years older than me. He's got a medal from Viet Nam.

He's not as big as my brothers, but he's bigger than me, and strong. He was the one who carried the huge pot full of stew from the picnic table to the fire—it must have weighed seventy-five pounds. And then after we finished eating, he was the one who took it to the stream, cleaned it, and brought it back again filled with water for drinking. He's the kind of guy who likes to help out. Not all guys are like that.

He has a trimmed blond beard and his matching hair is shoulder length, clean and shiny. He has nice teeth, just the tiniest bit buck, and he dresses like he cares about how he looks. Meticulous, I guess you would say. There's a crease in his jeans. I like that, it makes me think his house is clean.

I've had my eye on him since late afternoon, when I got here, but I was too busy setting up my tent and stuff to do anything except look at him and give him a little smile.

Things begin to happen after we eat our communal vegetarian stew

24

dinner, which isn't 'til after dark. I cut up the potatoes and carrots for it, bite-sized chunks. Not too big so you have to stuff your face with them, not so small that they'd get lost. I only eat a little because I don't want to get sick in front of anybody, which is what happens sometimes if my belly is full.

I start things off by opening up my face to him. I have this way I can make my face look shy and ready at the same time, to anyone who has the radar for it. Bing is definitely looking. And since he's sitting across the campfire from me, it's easy to play around with eye contact.

So we're all ten of us sitting around the campfire in the moonlight, passing around joints and Boone's Farm, talking about recent drug experiences. He doesn't bogard the joint; I respect that. Seems like his face catches more of the fire than anyone else's.

Wine goes through me quick, and pretty soon after dinner I have to get up to go pee. I don't like anyone knowing about my bathroom habits, so I find a tree that's a good distance away from everybody.

As I'm walking back, feeling just stoned enough to know I'm high but not stoned enough to feel happy, Bing comes up to me. We're close enough to see the campfire and hear it crackle, but far enough away so no one knows what we're saying.

"So you're Randy's little sister."

"Yeah," I say. An owl hoots and then something flaps its wings and skitters above our heads. He jumps a little. "What's the matter, scared of a little bat?" I ask him. I know he has probably seen a lot worse from being in Viet Nam.

"Only when I've got a pretty girl to protect," he says. "Don't want it to fly in your hair and get stuck there." "Bats don't do that," I say. "It's just a story, just like getting warts from toads." He goes, "Not only are you pretty, but you're smart. I like that in a girl." I don't believe he's telling the truth about either the smart or the pretty, but I pretend I am both of those things. I toss my hair like I've seen the cheerleaders at school do, and hope it picks up some of the campfire light and sparkles for him.

"Thanks." I say. "Thanks a lot." After a minute of him looking at me he says, "And you've got great hair. It's the color of golden fire with red embers."

"You must write poetry," I say. "A little," he says. "Maybe I'll show you sometime." I look down at the trampled pine needles on the path we're standing on and try to think of something more to say. I'm still no prettier than I was when I was a kid, but I've got a curvy shape now and if my face doesn't hold their interest, my body does. It's cold, I realize. I'm wearing a Janis Joplin T-shirt, didn't bring a sweater. One good thing, though, is that when it's cold my nipples stick out; Randy says guys like that.

"Randy's good people," Bing said. I can't figure out why Bing hangs out with Randy; Bing is six years older. "Yeah, he's okay." Since me and Randy got older and started doing drugs together, we've become better friends than when we were kids. I can't say I'm crazy about him, but at least we can spend time together without one of us ending up with a bruise.

"I saw you sometimes when I used to pick Randy up to go scuba diving, before I went to Nam. I never noticed how pretty you were."

"Thanks a lot," I say, thinking about how nice it feels if he really does mean it. I want to ask him what Viet Nam was like, have a real conversation like friends do, but I'm not too good at that in the first place. Besides the fact that the pot and wine make my words and thoughts scrambled and the cold makes my lips so tight nothing comes out right anyway.

I want to get warm, not at the fire but wrapped up in another person. He's thinking the same thing, I guess. "You look pretty cold. You want to come with me to my tent?"

I look toward the campfire and see Randy laughing and swigging more Boone's Farm. He probably doesn't know I'm gone, even. In a little while for sure he won't know, with the way he's drinking.

"Sounds good." I'm scared, though. Ever since that time with my dad, when he almost put himself inside me but stopped at the last minute, I've been thinking about going all the way with someone outside the family—but now that the time is close, I feel sick.

"Maybe I should go to my own tent first," I say. "I've gotta get something." Bing puts his arm around my shoulder. "You don't have your friend or something, do you?" Now's my chance to back down. "No," I say. "I've got everything you need," he says. He looks into my eyes and stays there. "Let's go," I say, and he takes my hand and leads me down the path that crunches with sticks as we walk.

His is two tents away from Randy's, which makes me feel protected in a weird sort of way. It's one of the most expensive tents from LL Bean. It's a big one—you can stand up in it if you want—but I'd rather just get started with things. I leave my clothes on, except my sneakers, and get inside the sleeping bag right away to get warm. I'm not sure if you're supposed to undress yourself or let the guy do it. He follows me into the bag, but he takes everything off first.

"I never get in a sleeping bag with clothes on," he says. "I'm surprised you do. I thought you were freer than that."

"I am," I say, "I'm just cold."

"This'll heat you right up," he says as he lights up a roach. It tastes dirty. "Don't have any more full joints," he tells me. Roaches are better anyway, they're stronger. We toke up and I get into another level of high, which pretty much gives me the courage to take off my clothes and not care about what he thinks.

I pull off my T-shirt and jeans while I'm still inside the bag and then I roll them up to make a pillow. I don't wear a bra or underwear, so the undressing is quick. My little nipples are hard as stones, and sure enough I can feel Bing looking at them.

"How you doin', baby?" "Good," I say, my teeth chattering. I like being called "Baby." He gathers me up into his arms and right away kisses me full steam ahead. I smell the campfire on his face and taste the sour smell of wine and pot mixing in his mouth. He sticks his tongue in my mouth and waggles it, pushes it down into my throat. I think I am supposed to be liking this more. I think if I touch myself maybe I can get some better feelings going, but I don't want to insult him or anything.

When Diane and I kissed, we would take our time and see what the other person felt like. We laughed a lot. With Bing I don't feel like laughing.

He kisses my mouth for a few more minutes and then he starts kissing my neck and feeling my breasts at the same time. I like that part. I pretend I am Bing and I am the one with my hands on the breasts, but I try not to think like that for long because it's perverted.

He moves on very quick. He gets more urgent, makes sounds like a dog when it's ripping apart a bone. Pretty soon he starts pushing his thing against my thigh in a rhythm, breathing heavy. His thing is very hard but very soft, like a stick covered in velvet.

"Grab it," he says. At first I am afraid I don't know how, then I remember how easy it was with my dad. I wish I could be more confident. I hesitate.

"Oh, man," he says, almost whimpering. "Grab it. PLEASE." I wait longer so he'll beg more. "Oh, she wants to tease." He grabs my hand really hard and puts it where he wants it. "Squeeze it, pig."

I have my hand on the head of it and keep it there, cupping it, feeling its size. My dad was wrong; Bing is even bigger than Dad was. Fatter and longer. I bet there's guys even bigger.

I am pretty awkward at it; I can't get the rhythm right. Every time Bing starts to act like we are in sync, my hand slips off or I let go when I am supposed to squeeze. I am worried that Bing is going to tell everybody I am a lousy lay.

He touches me down there and tries to stick his finger inside.
"You're not very wet, baby," he says. I know I am supposed to be from what I've read and feel embarrassed because I'm not.

He spits on his finger and tries it again. "God, you're really tight."

"I know," I say. "This is my first time."

"Jesus." He sounds mad. See, some guys don't want to be the first because they think you'll fall in love with them and it's a responsibility they don't want.

"I'm sorry," I say.

I hear Randy staggering down the path. "Smitty! Smitty!" He half whispers it, like he has something he really has to tell me.

Bing stops everything. His eyes are wide open and his heart pounds like a jackhammer against my chest. For someone who's supposed to have been so brave in a war, he doesn't act so brave in real life.

"She left," Bing calls out. "She told me to tell you she was going home."

"That bitch. How come her tent's still up? I suppose she wants me to take it down tomorrow. Lazy bitch."

I'll have to invent a good story by tomorrow.

"See you in the morning," Bing says.

"Yeah, if I can find my own fuckin' tent."

"Keep on walking down the path; two more to go."

"Ohh yeah. Hey, thanks, man. Sleep tight, bro."

It's a good thing Bing has my mouth covered with his hand, or else I would burst out laughing or coughing, I'm not sure which.

We wait until a few minutes after we hear Randy take a pee, burp, unzip his tent flap, then zip it up again. "G'night, bro," Bing says. "G'night man," Randy says from inside the tent.

It only takes a second for Bing to get hard again, so I guess he's okay with me being a virgin even though he has to work so much to get inside me. His face gets redder and sweatier as he pumps, his eyes roll up in his head. He stifles a loud grunt as he breaks through, ripping me apart, making me bleed.

As soon as I feel him inside I know it's a big mistake—I mean, I like having something inside me but I think it's better if you know the person. His body keeps heaving on me and finally he shudders and says, "Oh yes" and then comes out of me quick and shoots on my belly. He gets off of me and rolls over, out of breath.

I know you can't make generalizations on only two people, but both Bing and Dad said "Oh yes" before they shot.

I lie there next to him like I'm tied down with invisible cables and try to think of something to say. I smell eggy from the stuff on my stomach, but I'll hurt his feelings if I wipe it off. I spread it out thinner with my fingers so it'll dry there. It gets cold really quick, like oatmeal.

Even if I had thought of something to say, he's already snoring.

My head is on Bing's shoulder and I think about the kind of ring I want him to give me. I see opals and rubies before I drop off to sleep.

The early morning light colors his sleeping face. He opens his eyes, sees me, and closes them again. I dress quietly, unzip the flap as quietly as I can, and leave. He whispers, "I'll call you." I walk carefully up the path, quiet as an Indian, without crunching any sticks.

CHELSEA THIRTEEN

LINDA SMUKLER

I like our little white room in this soiled hotel and want an entire life to fit into our short five hours   the desk clerk irritates you by talking on the phone too long and when you ask I say choose the back not the street   our room dirty but with the light of Italy and I think I should take you right off but we talk and you ask do you like teenagers and I say no I like women and you look away as if your feelings are hurt   and in the time it takes to get you back I see the blonde of who you want me to see this afternoon   the pubescent thirteen-year-old   I see your thighs still long and boy-like   your small breasts   the pink in your cheek and your lips shell-like red   the inside of a conch   I want her as I want you   my little girl   want to put you on my lap   want you to sit on my cock   quiet now   want to rock you   hold you   take you home   lay you down on the leaves   watch you fight yourself shot through and taken no matter what you say

SALT

MONA DE VESTEL

I have become one huge gaping hole. A cavity that wants nothing more than to be filled. I move about with a franticness that only the starved and the consciously dying can feel.

I am standing by the counter of the Italian bakery counting the change in my pocket with one hand inserted in the folds of my jeans. Four more customers ahead of me before I can carefully express my desire to the chipmunk of a woman behind the counter. The protruding bone of her jaw is the most prominent feature in her face.

I can feel the pangs of hunger in my stomach. The gastric juices are ready, waiting, for the digestion of my hourly intakes of food.

"A half dozen of pecan chocolate chip cookies please."

She feigns a smile in my direction recognizing me from my last eight daily visits to this counter.

Eight days since she has left me.

Flour, sugar, butter, a pinch of salt, a pound of melted bittersweet chocolate.

A glass of milk.

A half dozen cookies.

One pint of strawberries.

Coke.

Eight days.

I can still taste her on the tip of my tongue.

"You're fucking me with your tongue," she had whispered.

Nine forty-eight PM, the door slams behind me. I am holding a chocolate croissant in my hand, crumbs falling on the front of my white unbuttoned shirt. I feel a tiny morsel land in the soft, warm curves of my breasts, caught by the fabric of my bra.

The phone rings. I drop the heavy leather bag I carry everywhere for security. The weight of these objects I never touch during the course of the day reassures me.

I bring the receiver to my ear: "Click." They hung up. Dial tone.

I place the receiver back in its cradle, my heart still beating in my chest from the anticipation of the sound of her voice on the other end.

I take the half pound of salted macadamia nuts into the bedroom and position them carefully on the edge of the wooden night table by my bed.

The image of juicy aromatic lime cut in perfectly thin slices against the white of a porcelain bowl. My mouth waters at the thought of the sour taste of lime juice and the warmth of her flesh against the fruit. Green on golden amber, warm on wet.

I sit on the bed and swallow my own juices.

The room is empty. The dirty clothes and various objects thrown on the floor, tipped over on the windowsill, only reflect the emptiness and absence of purpose they have in the quietude of night.

I unbutton my shirt and kick off my shoes.

The bag of salted macadamias is waiting.

"My finger ran along the curve of your breast, in a moment gone past."

I unzip my skirt and pull off the nylons holding my legs and feet captive.

No underwear. For the last eight mornings, I have forgone underwear, unwilling and unable to put on the silk and linen lingerie I was accustomed to wearing for her.

"Peppermint and the musk of your hair moistened by your sweat. You were not moving under the tight grasp of my arms and the weight of my breasts against yours."

One by one, I remove the pins restraining the weight of my hair in a tight bun. I feel the curls tumble around my face.

"Your hair caressed me, even in my sleep I craved the brush of you on my face."

I clear an open space on the bed among the piles of clothes from the day before and recline my naked body, eyes fixed on the ceiling. I reach for the bag of salted macadamia and continue staring in the space above my head. My finger rolls the granular shape of the salt against the smoothness of the nut.

"You offered me your flesh like one offers the pulp of a fruit to the thirsty."

I push the body of a salt-covered macadamia into my mouth and allow my tongue to run along the surface of its body until I can no longer taste the salt of it.

"I pressed your legs open with one of my knees and watched the green of your eyes come and go in quick, furtive blinks."

The motion of my jaw and the revolution of ground macadamia flesh in my mouth loses itself in the timeless air of the room. I lick the salt left over on the tip of my index.

After a long breath of air, I swallow the salty pulp in my mouth.

"The heat of you and the ease with which I entered you drew me off balance, like the vastness of a wide open space before the free-fall."

My hand is now searching for the remnants of a few nuts in an almost empty bag. The passing of time is revealed in the last grains of salt that remain on my fingers.

"The first time I entered you, you cried out like an animal trapped in the instinct of desire—trapped in the fear of its intensity. I watched you bite your lower lip and run your tongue along the surface of your still pale flesh."

I feel partial fullness settling inside of me. The weight of macadamia flesh and the parchedness of my lips fill me. I crave the coolness of a tall glass of water.

"You cried out and I muffled your cry with my own mouth like a bird feeding its young. I wanted to carry your breaths inside of me and fill your lungs with the air of mine. I saw a tear roll down along the surface of your cheek and ran my tongue to catch its fall. I swallowed you."

SHE FALLS TO PIECES

GERRY GOMEZ PEARLBERG

I. Outside

We're coming from a movie. A bunch of movies, actually. Lesbian Shorts. *The production value on these independent films is certainly changing for the better,* you remark as we make our way toward the restaurant. The new Annie Lennox song blares from a car stereo, *walking on, walking on broken glass.* Some kids from New Jersey out for the night, parked illegally, smoking cigarettes and drinking Millers out of paper bags. *Every one of us was made to suffer, every one of us was made to bleed.*

The ginkgoes are simultaneously molting and fruiting, their pungent yellow parachutes crushed all across Greenwich Avenue. The mix of leaves and fruit make for a slippery stretch of sidewalk, and you do a goofy little dance on it, sliding your feet this way and that, grinning your head off. You make me think of Danny Kaye and how I long to be your Lawrence Olivier, your famous secret—talented, British, and suave.

The attraction's as mutual as Mutual of Omaha's Wild Kingdom—it's one of those cobra-mongoose things, embedded like subtext in the way you look at me when you think I'm not aware, the way you practically flinch when I catch you in the periphery of my vision. Somehow or another we mesmerize each other, though I'm hypnotized as well by the need to keep my attraction under wraps. You have a lover, after all, and that makes you hazardous to my health. Still, I worry sometimes that I'll never get to find out who'd end up on top, who Mongoose, who Cobra.

35

II. Inside

The restaurant is filled with smoke. During the day, this kind of thing drives me crazy, but it's right tonight, a full moon night, and the scent, the haze, the ambiance is utterly erotic. I make this observation aloud, and you look at me like I've lost my mind. Maybe I have.

The Caesar salad arrives, a raw egg nestled in a curl of lettuce like a pearl in its deep green shell. The waitress begins tossing with a flourish. That's when it hits.

The first sign is subtle: the miniature chandelier hanging over our table begins a gentle sway. Absurdly, I tell myself the waitress must have bumped it with her head or that she's tossing the salad too boisterously—already a couple of choice Romaine leaves have crashed to the table. But a minute later, the whole room is rolling like a penny down an inch worm's back. Paintings are falling off the wall, silverware crashes to the floor, voices rise, glasses shatter in the kitchen, and underneath it all there's the dull rumble like something—an orgasm, perhaps—trying, unsuccessfully to gain momentum. After a time, it and all the other commotion subside. The room is silent for a moment, then thankful murmurs, the diffident laughter of relief, the playacting of normalcy as if it were ever possible to "return to normal," as if "normal" were a place. I've been in four earthquakes in the last six years—in San Francisco, L.A., Costa Rica, and Brooklyn—and following each and every one, my life took dizzyingly unexpected turns. This earthquake, in the West Village, is my fifth. And though five's supposed to be my lucky number, these days I take nothing for granted.

Was that a metaphor or what? You say, leaning across the table to take my hand. Romaine leaves are scattered between us like a photosynthetic still life. Our waitress has disappeared. The chandelier above us sways seductively. *They say unspoken feelings can cause all sorts of tumult, internal and ex,* you whisper, *but I never knew it could be like this.*

III. Deep Inside

You fit like a glove. A black latex glove you fit into me, twisting your finger like a cork until I whine. A boxing glove when you give me a hand, filling me with your skin till my ropes stretch to the breaking point, sweat all over the mat, my pelvis high in the air, jerking like the loser's head against a repeated sock to the jaw. An opera glove gliding white light inside my belly like a conductor's baton, hitting the high notes, shattering the champagne glass of my composure, then drinking from its hazardous remains. No shortage of tricks up your safe sex sleeve.

It's not until I spot your third and fourth sleeves—and the ambidextrous hands within them—that I realize, with a start, that something's radically out of whack. In a single moment one latexed hand rhythmically advances and recedes inside me, a palm circles my thigh, fingernails softly corrugate the small of my back, and a thumb makes its way across the inside of my mouth, rubbing the red lantern of my tongue till my genie begins to smokingly unfurl. It's a four-ring circus in what's normally a two-piece act, and as my busybox brain puts two and two together—literally—I feel a minor urge to panic at this biological breach. I'm awful close to coming, though, so I put my brain on hold, suspending disbelief as one must always do for perfect sex. A moment later I let slip with a jet stream orgasm that catapults my bed—and us with it—through the bedroom wall and into the middle of the chemistry lab next door.

IV. Deep

And there, while the dust settles, I study you in a post-orgasmic once-removed sort of way. To put it mildly, I am in a pleasure haze, or is it a dome? And it's a good thing, too, because I am watching you sitting on the edge of the bed literally putting yourself back together like a jigsaw puzzle: reshaping the two extraneous arms into thighs and pulling them on like hosiery; snapping them into place like doll's legs, ball and socket, with little flicks. Endorphins—and whatever other neurochemicals are making their way across my synaptic clefts—obscure my apprehension like a lunar eclipse. I know this pleasurable cloud cover will pass soon enough, but for now, I'm content to wallow in dysphoria, observing this phenomenal phenomenon, asking dumb questions like, "Hey, where'd you learn to do that? Can I try? Does it hurt?"

It doesn't hurt so much as relieve the hurting, you tell me, it's like a stag dropping antlers, there's the pleasant friction of nothing where something used to be. Except in my case, the antlers always return, like chandeliers to their golden ceilings, candelabras to their glimmering midnight wicks, their Sanskrit rivulets of wax.

What makes it happen is this: when you come like you're coming apart, I have a sympathetic response like the lightning bugs that incandesce in rhythm to the flashlight's beam. You think you'll never fool those fireflies with your double-A battery pack, but to the bugs, it's the ferocious pull of sex, a reply that cannot be denied, the "Who's there?" answer to that knock-knock joke. Resist though you may, "Who's there?" is gonna come seeping out of your mouth, those fireflies are gonna make their way to the flashlight's beam, and I'm gonna fall to pieces when my lover lets it rip.

V. Inside Out

What I want to know is, can you do it again? You can and do, but this time it's double the trouble, double the fun: eight pluperfect arms pouring from your rib cage and what their eight hands do to me, all the things that hands can do: they rub, tug, pull, assess, massage, caress, and plummet. But first your eight hands pull on eight latex gloves, black and white and black and white like some kind of sexual domino theory: eight consecutive snaps of latex pulled tight, eight little bursts of air from latex adhering to dampening skin, eighty knuckles grown smooth as stones at the bottom of a stream, hands like seaweed in crystalline shallows, retracting, pushing forward—slick and shiny and brilliantly alive. These black latex hands are the kelp that shelter the otter pups from rip tides. These black latex hands are the dark algae that oxygenate the earth. These white latex hands are the pearly bubbles, the bluish foam, the ghostly inner husks of sea mollusks as primitive and eternal as the brainless flesh that occupies them. And how they occupy me with their mindless sexual brilliance, their metaphors and similes and half-baked theories on the half-shell, their Domino sugar cubes dissolving in this unexpected chemistry, the chemical imbalance of lesbian passion taken to its logical extreme: the body, biodegraded by sex, literally coming apart at the seams, coming unhinged, falling to pieces, the sum of the parts becoming greater than the (w)hole, and *stranger things have happened,* you say, and you know, it's true.

AGAINST THE GRAIN

WICKIE STAMPS

When I hear her my lover's footsteps my mind, obsessed, as always, with its petty rules, ceaseless ambitions and senseless tasks, dissolves; my body rises from its chair; my legs, no longer riddled with their aches and pains, move quickly across the room; my hands, suddenly soft and tender, lift up. Reach out. I take my lover into my arms. Gently I run my fingers through her hair and brush it back off her forehead. I hold her close. At this moment there is no place to go, no relentless obsession to be fed. Quiet has settled in the air. A stillness blankets my frenetic mind. Momentarily, I am seduced away from my obsession with myself.

At other times my passion for my lover becomes a ground swell beneath my skin. Beginning with the subtlety of a breeze across my flesh it quickly pulls me into my body. It snakes into my veins. As my passion moves deeper, moves down, a wake of blood lashes out into my nipples, pulling them tight. Making them taut. Then my passion dives deeper again. It enters my breath. It lowers my voice.

My hands now become my eyes. Seeking. Touching. With forearms now strong my eyes yank off my lover's pants and pull her shirt up over her head. They push her down. Below me. I pause and stare at the body before me. I am shocked by my actions. I remember to inhale. And release.

My lover closes her eyes, spreads her legs and arches her back. I, kneeling before her, move my right hand in-between her legs, part her lips and gently slide my fingers into her. She moans. Softly. And pushes her hips down into the sheets. I push my fingers deeper into her. My lover arches her head so far back that her face disappears into the pillows. She turns her head to the side and exposes her neck. "So vulnerable," I think. I am reminded of all the small animals who, when attacked,

39

expose their necks to their predators, lay open their weakness, throw their enemy off balance. "So vulnerable," I think again as I, in response, move my hand deeper into her body. My jaw clenches; a snarl smears across my face; an ancient rage slowly, silently surfaces in the back of my eyes. I know it is her vulnerability that has provoked me. With my lover laid open before me, her eyes shut, her head tilted back, I, unobserved by any other than myself, slowly slip my hand from between her legs and raise it, in unison with its partner, upward into a prayerful position. I breathe in sharply, grit my teeth and force all of my fury into my hands. I clamped them around my lover's sweet throat. Her arms grab my wrists. Her legs flail about the bed. Desperately she struggles to breathe. I feel her trachea crush beneath my fingers. My hands know that I am playing out my destiny which demands that I destroy the ones who love me the most. My lover's body goes limp. I close my eyes and swallow hard. I am on the verge of vomiting.

Suddenly my body jerks. My lover opens her eyes, looks up at me and smiles. The scene in my mind of her—of our—demise washes through me. And my rage, which is merely my terror disguised, coils into energy in my fist. With control learned from centuries of practice, I lash back my desire to tear open the body before me. I remember to breathe. I pull back my hand, breathe deeply and slide my fingers into my lover again. Her cunt sucks me in. I coil my fingers into a fist and relish the heat and soft flesh that surrounds it. I choke back my tears. At this moment, I know that my lifetimes of loneliness are now past. I remember to breathe in. And exhale. My lover moans. Softly. Tears trickle down my face.

I am desperate now, trapped within a torrent of emotions I cannot endure. I look down at my lover who chooses this moment to slip her left hand between her legs. Mercifully I am swept out of myself and into her passion. I am desperate to please her now. Desperate to escape myself. I lay flat on my belly between her legs and match each thrust of my fist against her movements. Her desire is the only hope I know now. I wrap my left hand around my right forearm, and I keep pace with my lover's rhythm. Time is now measured by the sweat that trickles down my back. An icy sheen spreads across my flesh. I grit my teeth and force my body to keep pace with her need. I can no longer think. I can barely breathe.

My lover's fingers now ravage her clit. Her right hand clamps around my wrist. She, not I, now sets the pace of my fist. I close my eyes and obey her directions. My shoulders ache and my forearm burns with exhaustion. I am angry again. Angry at my lover's desires. Angry that I may fall short of her need. My mind screams at me to pull my fist from her cunt and stop this madness. At this point, when I know I have failed us both, we reach the crest of her desire. A final tremor plunges across my lover's body; it spills downward and crashes into a spasm around my wrist. Her body goes limp. We each breathe deeply. Slowly. In unison. She loosens her grip on my wrist. I rest my head on the sheets. As I lie there, my mind whispers to me that I will never feel the depth of passion my lover does. It tells me I will never experience anything but a sense of duty. But then my left hand slides down in between my own legs and I touch my wetness. It is at this moment that I know, once again, my mind has lied to me and, for one more day, for one more moment, my lover and I have deceived my self.

My passion for my lover is not lust. I know lust. Always short-lived, lust never lasts. A throbbing abscess in need of quick, sure lancing, lust is demanding, relentless, a persistent whore who offers fortunes and delivers nothing but mouthfuls of ancient, soured dreams. I know lust. Lust has had her way with me.

My passion for my lover is a place that I journey to. A place not within my body but between her flesh and mine, between my mind and her body, between our breaths. The place that goes against the grain of everything I was raised to be.

GHOST CRAB

LINDA L. NELSON

Pale and lashed to my ravenous water,
I cruise in the sour smell of the naked climate,
still dressed in gray and bitter sounds
and a sad crest of abandoned spray.
—from "Drunk With Pines" by Pablo Neruda

I.

My name is Jack. I like to surprise people. To name the bird by its song.

Several weeks ago, Helen and I listened through the fine, spring green skin of a tent as wild ponies thundered by in the dark, screaming as they swerved into the cold bay. I could smell salt, their thick soaked coats. I was lying with my eyes open, staring, wondering how the tent protected our skulls from being crushed beneath the herd's hooves.

We were on vacation. Our first.

Here in New York, where we live, I run a sex club for women. It's my job to create a space in which women can fulfill fantasies they don't even know they have. Which is sometimes difficult to distinguish from simply creating their fantasies for them.

You'd be surprised by how many there are of these. Women who don't know they have fantasies.

I like my job, and I work at it. It's the skill I've learned in order to survive. That's the nature of jobs, after all.

If this were the 1940s, you could call me a gigolo. It's a term toward which I have a distinct inclination and affection.

But I don't want to tell you about fantasies. Or how I fulfill them.

I want to tell you about the ghost crab.

II.

Helen didn't stir when I unzipped the tent, the zipper as icy and difficult to manipulate as my own sex-stiffened fingers. Her back was embedded in the damp floor, her lumpy silhouette engraved there by these fingers: fingers that had pushed into her over and over, scorching; fingers without ears to hear her cries or eyes to see her try to dig herself deeper into the dirt. I felt ungainly as I extricated myself from our shell, stumbling into my boots as I crossed the thick dewy weeds.

The ocean is darker today than I've ever seen it, more intent looking, Helen had said to me the evening before. We had just arrived, and before pitching camp had taken a walk across the strip of land from our bayside site to the ocean. We were standing next to each other, not touching, gazing out from a seemingly infinite vastness of Atlantic shore and sea and sun. It seemed to stretch for miles around the edges of her so that I couldn't breathe there was so much of it, a light so huge and red it could only be hell, a hell, distant yet imminent and not entirely threatening in its presence; and in the vacuum created by my empty lungs, I felt something sucking us forward into the future.

The darkly wavering orange fingered its bloody way deeper into dusk. I raised my right hand to press the bruise just beside my temple, knowing it was the same color as the sky there, behind me, in the already-dark; a baby eggplant withered in an unforeseen, early frost. Unable to make sense of how such a mark might belong to me, I instead found myself thinking that nature raises the same questions to each of us over and over. That night my question was: Do people respond only to victims? Always sunsets and never sunrise. Several terns had wheeled and wailed as Helen and I had approached. There is no way for us to empathize with cruelty. Human cruelty has its rewards, and as such it doesn't require empathy. The same can be said of success, or of winning. It is its own reward, to do something well. Cruelty is what sets the gods apart.

The simmering scent of bayberry leaves shifted around us. I had lost myself in these thoughts, during which time, Helen had left my side and settled herself upon the shoulder of a dune where the sand retained some warmth. She gazed out past me toward where the swells had sharpened and looked like sailors saluting and curtsying, dopey white caps askew across their crewcut foreheads. Her hazel eyes. The poems she carries with her, reciting stanzas from memory beneath her breath. All the reasons that I love her.

III.
She gets soaking wet, and then begins to hit herself.

The minute I touch her I feel it too. She's a swamp, sweaty, moldering, the kind in which you can lose your way, dizzy in the stench. The heat of decay just beneath layers of insects and leaves. Watching closely, I can see the surface shift, her pores open, peat exposed. A chemical odor rises off her like steam.

It's this, the scent, that stops me, even though she is so easy to slide into. She thrusts her hips toward my face, her wrists so thin, so much more fragile than mine as she tries to force my mouth to her gaping flooded center, but I don't allow this. In order to avoid giving her what I know she wants, to staunch the bile leaching from the back of my throat, I quickly—too quickly—thrust my hand inside her. She tears as I enter.

This is one of the ways I surprise people, including myself: who would have thought I'd be the one to lure Helen from Paris? It wasn't easy to break her family's hold. I had to go in the middle of the night, wearing my black peaked cloak, hoping my pale face would not cast too great a reflection upon the windows. They lived high above the city in the manner of falcons, in a penthouse looking across the Seine. I gagged her, grabbed her by the wrists, and pushed her down through the stairwells in front of me, thirty-six of them switchbacking left and right, her white nightshirt billowing behind her like a shroud.

I'm tall and strong; I used to be a basketball player. Once, when I was in high school, stoned on acid and Jack Daniels mixed with grape soda, I knocked out three cops who were trying to catch me.

They'd have locked me away for good, and I couldn't have that.

And all I know, even now, is that I must keep moving forward. There is nothing else I can do, with her crying and pushing against me at the same time. The blood, the tearing, her fists beating at my back, none of this matters. The only way a ballplayer keeps going, past the nausea, when muscles become one's own worst enemy, is to focus on bringing each heavy quad forward, forcing sneaker to grab waxed floor, down and turn and stop, up, stop, up one more time, up. Up. Up and in.

IV.

I only fuck the ones I can't put my mouth to. As if to carve out a mouth that someday I will find kissable.

Helen awakes every morning to a chorus of demonic mothers, hunched, crippled, angry old women telling her a woman is a cunt and nothing more, and our first morning in camp was no exception. And so having unraveled myself from the tent I drew water for coffee, water I'd been sure to fetch the night before while Helen scowled at me, wanting me to ignore my errands, to take her immediately to bed. I had sat her down on the bench by the gravel pathway and explained to her about hypothermia, and bears, and giardia, and dehydration; all the common, natural things that can kill a human being outside the city. By the time the water boiled above the unearthly blue flame, a gray light had seeped through the crack between earth and sky. The ponies, the rustling spartina made me restless. I had dreamed of listening to exotic ducks in the reeds plotting revolution over the tyranny of mallards.

Out there, far from cement brick crowds, the bodies pressed and rubbing against strangers all day long, a place inside me opens in just the way the water's surface becomes luminescent green and blue as if lit from within as the sky darkens. Only the wind relentlessly working at my skin and hair, employing sand and heat and hail and thorns as its weapons, can satisfy the ferocity of my desires; my lungs expand in the complexity of such air. Out there I can sit still for hours, my haunches taut upon packed sand, rhapsodizing.

In other words, I become romantic in the Great Outdoors.

It was in this way I discovered the ghost crab.

When neither the hot sweet mush I cooked nor the black coffee nor my insistent kisses could rouse Helen, I set out by myself.

I walked. Shuffling my feet ankle deep amid oyster and horseshoe crab shells. With my binoculars I could see hotels, aqua swimming pool slides, boardwalks and a ferris wheel at the north end of the barrier island which we'd chosen to explore, a thin sandy strip cut off from the mainland by a storm in '33. Like nearly all American places, it was named for the Indians who were resident when British colonists arrived to cheat and beat them out of land and food. As I stared through the binoculars at the resort, abandoned and boarded up for the winter, I was filled with fear. A fear of myself. A fear that I, like the British, will pursue all that I love and love it with great intensity to its extinction.

A scuttling just to my left caught my attention. There was a small hole there, a channel of sliding, glistening sand.

I watched the hole patiently. I had to know what it was, wanting, as always, to know by what creatures, friends and foes, I was surrounded. The creature, however, had noticed the jerk of my head in its direction and was refusing to resurface. Had I been a dog, I simply would have shoved my muzzle into its hole, scratching at the tenuously constructed abode with strong claws. But I was patient. Eventually the creature—my creature—reappeared.

Carefully, a fraction at a time, it emerged, hauling more sand with it. It was yellow—more yellow than a gold finch, a lemon, a tennis ball—yet translucent. I'd never seen anything like it, and still couldn't be sure I'd seen anything at all. As I watched it, counting its brown spots, I remembered John Audubon, who loved his intimate knowledge of wild birds so much that he trapped and killed one from each species, stuffed it, preserved it, named it. Measured and recorded each one for all time, to leave his imprint upon it, to create his own legacy.

I watched. It moved sideways. The way it slithered from under earth so dry as to make its legs seem viscous. Suddenly it appeared to be dragging a round, soft white belly, and I realized with horror that it was a giant spider. A creature spinning its sticky web around me.

I imagined the magnificent, ghostly thing turning swiftly and without warning in my direction; crawling, crawling, crawling on me. I forced myself to remain still. The next time it appeared I could see a large claw on its front left side, eye stalks raised to face me. Thank god it had eye stalks. It was some sort of crab, but I'd have to look up the name.

The power of knowledge. As I felt my breath growing more even, I looked up and saw Helen, angling each narrow shoulder forward as she lifted the corresponding leg, moving toward me. Her white blond hair was cropped close to her skull and she is so fine-boned she appeared to be a fledgling, a thin black shadow in the sun. Her blue jacket was zipped up completely beneath her chin. The power of all that I know. I looked up at Helen, the abrasions on her chin and brow, the scabbed over places where she did to herself what she would have me do to her. Her lips were slightly parted, looking at me, wanting forgiveness, and I remembered the night I pushed my fingers down her throat, thrilled at the way she tried and tried to swallow me, until she choked; her head moving forward to take more of me down her unwilling orifice, my fingers controlling and filling a space never meant for this. She allowed me.

Ramming first my fingers and then my cock down her throat, I had come, and come again, fucking her head, her face, this part of her so much her personality, so public.

Helen fell heavily beside me and began to sob. I can't believe I found you, I wasn't looking for you, she said while I froze, loving her fragility and hating that she couldn't see: my solitary observation of something rare, something difficult. Something so in tune with its habitat you couldn't be sure you'd ever seen it. I wasn't looking for you, she repeats. What if I was meant to find you! What if I am meant to find you, she muttered. Then she got up and looked down at the hole. Oh, a ghost crab, she said, and moved away without realizing she had pushed sand into the hole with the heel of her boot.

V.
I let her take my hand in her damp one and lead me back to camp.

Once there, however, Helen began to move with jerky, exaggerated motions around the picnic table. I recognized the actions, but could not think of how to stop what I knew to be coming. As fast as the tiny juncos flitting from bush to bush, she was over at my truck, pounding her fist into its side.

I watched as she ripped off her expensive waterproof wind breaker and hurled it down onto the rough pavement of the road.

I'm feeling hideously well-disposed toward you, she said. I thought she was perhaps baring her teeth. It was certainly a grimace. Hideously well-disposed, she repeated, which makes me circle myself in fear. I'll try not to make these feelings of affection dangerous.

I wanted to hit her then, and she wanted me to. She'd dented my car. Ruined the tunnel of the ghost crab. But I couldn't. To hit her would be to return myself to the sixteen-year-old I was before I became clever enough to assume the guise of bohemian artiste: strong and vicious and victorious; a welder of eighteen-story nuclear submarines; a cop beater. I couldn't put myself back in those ignorant hands. Yet the main reason I have never been able to hit Helen, my glorious, my beloved, is precisely because she wants it so badly. I consider it a form of noble cruelty to rise above this, to be withholding and self-righteous in the face of another's need.

Sometimes, during sex, I think perhaps I am your garden variety rapist. The woman shouts No, No, and I insist I know she means Yes. Because, of course, I know better than she what it is she wants.

It's my job to know.

And it's a rhythm, you see, and, as with anything one does well, with practice one hits that place, the sweet spot, where you no longer think of the ball as a hard orange shape rough and too large for your hands, or of the rim as an obstacle through which you must force the ball. In the sweet spot everything disappears but you, becoming part of the swelling roar which is crowd and praise and promise which is body which is high which is god. Which is you.

I left her by the truck and walked back to the table. She stood watching as I poured the morning coffee from a thermos, her beautiful golden hair brighter at this hour than the sun, a helmet of gold; little wonder we all want to possess her. Then she snarled at me, gyrating hips she says are too wide, one hand upon them, the other held out in vicious enticement. C'mon fuck me, fuck me baby, she crooned raspily. Fuck me, Jack. That's what a woman's for, isn't that why you won't call yourself one? Isn't that why you fall in love with women like me, and then leave?

She was hideous and she knew it. I knew what she wanted: for me to fuck her hole and turn her inside out through it, pushing myself through the other side of that waiting hole, that empty hole, that messy slimy leaky hole into the past, into a prehistoric burning place where we were all lizards, all water breathers, all equally dangerous.

I couldn't. The more she wanted me to hit her the more my skin pulled back to cling to bone, leaving only a warm spot hanging in the air between us. Three steps away, I watched as she balled her fingers into a fist. Her hands were red, raw looking, the way my mother's looked in the winter when she hung the laundry from ice-coated rope. Helen's hand rose. I thought she was going to hit me and I didn't know what I'd do. I learned to hit to kill, to punish, to escape. I don't know how to hit softly; there's no in between for me. You don't know how strong I am, I said, not for the first time. None of it was for the first time, and I couldn't tell whether she'd heard me. I was afraid of killing her with my fists in a way I'd never been afraid when fucking her.

The hand—could it have been her hand?—came up higher, its shadow ridiculously huge. Helen moved it as far from her body as it would go as if she was signaling something in to home, an airplane or a base runner or a puppy. It's such a welcoming gesture, this stretching out of a beloved's arms. It left the shadow of crucifixion painted long on the stones between us. Then she crooked her elbow slightly, as if to mimic a boxer's pose; I saw the fist accelerate, but not at me. It skipped against her jaw and slid off in the opposite direction and I thought oh, it's hard to hit yourself. You know it's coming.

VI.

I've never been fucked.

That was all she'd said to me our first night.
I've never been fucked before.
Which made me realize, albeit in my slow, circular way—since I'm not one to dwell on other's psychological motives—that this wasn't about horses or dogs or men or women. For years I had known this but never seen it, until that day of the ghost crab. That what I'd been after all along was to fuck the hideous into the beautiful, to use my fist to break apart the bonds of consciousness, to transform us from the limited flesh-eating creatures we are into something more grand. I longed for someone to take me there, to fuck me out of my head and make me theirs and, failing that, I offered it instead to each of my lovers. Always waiting in the alley, off to a side where they can't touch me, masquerading as a sailor, chinos tight to my muscled hips and flaring out at my ankles, whirling as I crank the chain tighter, setting out the anchor and reeling it in.

It's never about horses or dogs, men or women.
It's about the nature of being fucked.

TRADE

LUCY JANE BLEDSOE

I dragged the ringing phone, along with my cold brew, out to the front porch. Sometimes I don't answer the phone, I just listen to it ring. A ringing phone is kind of like a vibrator up against the ache in my chest. It's like holding possibility up against hope. And not answering the phone is sort of like masturbating instead of having sex with someone. If you answer the phone, or if you take a real partner in sex, you got to deal with who it is. But if you don't answer the phone, and if your partner is in your head, it could be Marlene Dietrich.

It was one of those long mild Portland evenings and my lilacs were in full bloom. I settled into the porch swing and popped open the beer. The phone continued to ring. Down the street I heard a couple of kids arguing over some dumb game. Across the street a woman was mowing her lawn. I like having folks around. Just not too close. I took the first long swallow of my brew. Then I addressed the ringing phone.

"I'm busy, Marlene," I said out loud. Then I called my handy boy. "James? Fax a mess of these lilacs to Ms. Dietrich for me. Thanks, doll."

I took a slug of my beer. Nothing could make me believe there was anyone on the other end of that ringing phone but Ma. Don't get me wrong. I love my mother. But she was getting to the age where I should be calling *her* every night to see how *she* was doing, not the other way around. Ma didn't realize that calling me every night was like sky-writing, "You have no lover, Esther. You're all alone."

I picked a lilac and stuck it behind my ear so that its fragrance assaulted my nose. Then I answered the phone. "Hi, Ma."

"Esther." The sultry voice spoke my name as if it were sweet fruit. "Do you remember me?"

50

I sat up straight. "Who is this?"

"Big old bulldagger like you, and you don't have no memory?"

A big old bulldagger? Well, I liked that. I waited for the woman to speak again.

"This is Sherry, from ten years ago exactly, this summer."

"Sherry...?" I was still adjusting to this not being Ma.

"Don't tell me you've forgotten me?"

"No, wait a minute. I got it. Sherry from the trail crew. Where are you?"

"Chowchilla, baby. Doin' time."

I couldn't believe her voice, so low and seductive. I'd worked that summer as a trail crew supervisor for the county. My crew was made up of juvenile delinquents from girls' and boys' homes. Besides building trails in parks, I was supposed to teach those hoods job skills. Sherry had been a fourteen-year-old kid with a blond pony-tail and crooked teeth. She had those long colt legs of a barely adolescent girl, and her arms were always bruised and scratched as if she spent her days pushing through blackberry brambles. "Oh. I'm sorry to hear that."

"Me, too, honey!" Her rich smoker's laugh sounded much more mature than the dirty, brash mouth I remembered. "Truth, though, it ain't any different from the girls' homes. It's what I'm used to. Got me a woman to look after me, too. She's cute but she don't have no money."

So she came out. Or maybe this was just a prison thing. I opened my mouth to speak, but Sherry went right ahead.

"You ever hear from that fag?"

She meant Arthur. "No. I never heard from him after the summer."

"He's probably inside, too. I don't think you ever realized how deep that kid was. Into all kinds of shit even back then. Don't matter how many books he read." She laughed. "I know you liked him better than me, the whole summer, but I was a lot more honest with you than him. You know, I'd give anything to go back to that summer."

There, in that last sentence I heard the voice of the Sherry I remembered, the fourteen-year-old kid. I'd thought of her a lot over the years, convinced that she'd made it. I liked to think of her as a take-no-shit lawyer or doctor somewhere. To be honest, I counted her as one of my few successes. Even if I hadn't done much with my own life, I'd helped that kid back then.

"Do you remember," she asked, "that time by the river?"

"Sure." My voice cracked. "I remember."

"I guess you knew I was jailbait, huh."

"Well, I...uh, yeah."

"Or didn't you want none. Too knock-kneed for you? You probably had your pick of the girls. Grown ones, I mean. My, you were handsome. Bet you still are. What do you look like, Esther? Still tall? Still have those deep brown eyes? Still passing?"

I snorted into the receiver. "Come off it, Sherry."

"Give a girl a break. Tell me. What do you look like?"

"I'm the same. Six foot. Yeah, same eyes. Got some lines around them now. People still take me for a guy all the time, but I can't say I'm intentionally passing anymore. I've gained a little weight."

"Mm *hmm*." She said this like she'd just taken a bite out of a thick steak and her mouth was still full. "I bet it looks good on you, too."

"Why're you calling?" I asked.

I could tell I'd been too brusque because her voice got small. "I don't know. I just thought of you."

"They let you make phone calls from prison?"

Sherry didn't answer my question for a long time and in that pause, I remembered the real Sherry. She was an accomplished and frequent liar. But when you caught her in a lie, there was this grace period where she'd tell you the full truth. First, she'd be silent for a long time like this. I always figured she was planning her next lie, then she would surprise me. Her voice would open up, her demeanor would loosen, and you could just tell she was telling the truth. Those post-lie grace periods always softened me.

"Actually," she said slowly. "I just got out."

"Congratulations." My voice was taut as I pulled in the reins, tightened my control of the exchange. I guess it was the butch in me getting off on orchestrating that resignation in her.

"Well, my girlfriend's still in. She's doin' a life sentence. Killed a john. So, I'm sort of free." The tears in her voice shook me. I bet she ran her tongue over those crooked teeth, just like she used to. And probably twisted a clump of that blond hair around her finger.

"You'll do fine," I said perfunctorily. This thing was going too far. What if she was in a pay phone down the block?

"Do you think so?" she asked in a voice that was more than manipulative. She wanted a real answer. "I guess I called you first because you gave me that second chance."

"What are you talking about?" Very gruff.

"The first day on the trail crew. You found me in the bushes fucking that kid."

"Sherry." She was reaching now.

"Yeah. He was definitely a bad fuck."

"That's not what I meant."

"I still remember the look on your face when I told you why I fucked him."

The sky was thickening with the purple of dusk. Someone passing in the street was smoking a cigarette. Crickets were making a racket. And I felt as if the telephone were a giant suction cup. Like I could be slurped up into the receiver and through the telephone lines to wherever Sherry was. Part of why she felt so immediate was that not much had changed for me since that summer. I do better at holding down jobs. I've managed to buy this little house. But, as I've paid two shrinks small fortunes to tell me, I've got intimacy problems. Like, I can't seem to sleep with the same woman more than two times. Sherry was the opposite. She marketed intimacy like it was stock. Still, loneliness looks the same from either end of the pole. I guess we recognized that in each other, even back then, even with twenty years difference between us.

"Talk to me," Sherry begged. "Jesus Christ, Esther. I just got out of prison. I'm here on a goddamned street corner in goddamned Chowchilla, California and you're going silent on me. Talk."

She sounded like somebody's femme, all right.

"What do you want me to talk about?" I could hear the resignation in my own voice.

"Me. Tell me what you thought of me that first day. The truth." I was silent and she said, "Please."

I tried to sound indulgent. "I knew you were trouble right away. At lunch that first day you worked all the other kids on the crew. Loud-mouthing, flirting, demanding attention." I paused, reminded myself that Sherry was a whole state away, then said, "You had more sexual savvy at fourteen than I had at thirty-four."

Sherry giggled. She liked that.

I went on. "I remember that first lunch real well. Arthur was sitting away from the group, reading. He never ate lunch. It was like the books nourished him."

"Bullshit," Sherry interrupted. "He was fat. He probably stuffed his face before and after work."

"He wasn't fat." I enjoyed Sherry's jealousy. "He was chunky. And he had that mess of brown curls. With his chubby cheeks he looked like a cherub. Sure, I liked him. I liked that he did all that reading. He was a smart kid."

"He was a kiss-ass. I'm telling you, he's doin' time right now. You bet your ass. Intelligence don't have nothing to do with staying out of trouble."

"That's probably true."

"It *is* true. And Arthur *was* a kiss-ass. He always acted like he was your assistant and you fell for it. Oh, he'd pass out the tools or he'd run that little errand. Shit, he was just getting off to smoke a joint. He was selling dope to all the kids."

"No he wasn't."

"He was, Esther. But I don't want to talk about that fag. Talk about me."

"Okay, so I'm telling you about that first lunch. I was dead broke. I remember exactly how my peanut butter sandwich tasted—like sawdust. And it was all I was going to have until my first paycheck. So after I finished it, I lay back in the sun—right there in the forest dirt—and thought about buying a mess of sliced turkey, dill pickles, mayonnaise, mustard, dark rye bread. I was gonna make my future lunches feasts. Fresh peaches and slices of watermelon."

"What's this got to do with me?"

"Everything."

She giggled. "Okay, go on."

"So when it was time to go back to work, I realized that you weren't around anymore."

"What did you think?"

"I thought, shit. I've already lost a kid."

"Yeah, but did you worry extra because it was me?"

"No, Sherry. I'd known you about four hours."

"Mm," she said. "Go on."

"I went back to the van. You weren't there. So I started crashing around in the woods until I came to this pretty little meadow. And there you were." I remembered seeing her two bare bony knees pointing to the sky. Humping away between them was a thirteen-year-old boy with his jeans bunched around his ankles.

"He was definitely a bad fuck," Sherry mumbled.

"I can't believe that's the part you remember."

"I'm incorrigible. But go on."

"I told you to pull up your pants. There was fear in the boy's eyes, but you were cool. You were even a little scornful as you slowly pulled up your jeans." I added, "You weren't wearing underwear."

"You noticed that?" Sherry asked.

"So I fired you both on the spot."

"But I was there at the bus stop the next day."

"Yeah, you were."

"Were you glad?"

"No."

"But you let me in the van. You let me stay on the crew."

"Yes."

"Why?"

In the sky to the west the last streaks of light were orange. I felt nauseous, maybe from the motion of the swing. I took the lilac out from behind my ear and tossed it into the bushes. The smell of those lilac blossoms could be overpowering. I wasn't going to tell her that it was her aggressive vulnerability that I liked. Maybe not liked. Just understood. So I said, "I don't know."

"You made that contract with me."

"Yes."

"Did I ever break it?"

"No, you didn't."

"You took me seriously."

I remained quiet.

"You're so suspicious of me. Every time I say something nice to you, you clam up. I remember, you wrote out the work you expected of me for the summer, including my attitude requirements." Sherry laughed and finished it with her smoker's cough. "Then you looked me dead in the eye and said, 'Read this and sign it only if you intend to honor it.' " She sighed. "Honey, as if there was any question! I loved the idea of spending the summer adjusting my attitude for you."

"Cut the shit, Sherry. You were a kid. Fourteen." I remembered that moment so well, too. I felt frightened by how seriously she took me. She spent a long time reading the contract, then she carefully signed her name at the bottom, a big round adolescent girl scrawl. I signed mine below hers and dated it.

"I still thought you were a guy then."

I swallowed. "You thought I was a guy most of the summer, up until that time by the river."

Sherry laughed. "In your dreams, girlfriend. Most of the kids never figured it out, I'll give you that. They didn't even know Esther was a girl's name. They were such ignorant fucks. Anyway, we shook hands over that contract. Then you asked me why I'd screwed him, though you didn't put it that way, and that's when I figured out you were a girl. Remember what you said?"

"Sure. I said to you—" My voice was husky. I stopped and cleared my throat. " 'You don't know that boy. Why?' I expected you to fake vulnerability, get all coy on me. But you just looked me in the eye and said, 'I traded it for his piece of cherry pie.' "

"Is that why you told me the part about the peanut butter and turkey and dill pickles, all that, 'cause you understood?"

"I guess so," I conceded. She was ahead of me again.

"That time by the river." Sherry's voice was soft. "I wasn't lookin' to trade nothing."

"Sure," I said, grasping for the upper hand. "You haven't made a move in your life that wasn't calculated to get you something."

My sarcasm backfired. I could almost hear her smile. I as much as asked her to prove to me she'd been sincere.

"That's cold," she said gently. "Listen to me. That day I found you on our lunch break. You'd left everyone and gone to lie on that big flat rock by the river. I stood in the brush and watched you for a while. The sun was pouring down on you and I remember thinking that it was a spotlight just for you. You looked hot in those Levi's, your work boots, the big flannel shirt. And you had your hard hat off. Your short hair was wet with sweat and you were staring up at the sky. The river was really loud and I could feel it like a roaring in my chest. I knew you were thinking about some girl or other." Sherry paused. "And I wanted to be that girl."

"You were fourteen years old."

"Listen to me. So I went out and I lay down on the rock next to you. Remember? The rock was hot from the sun. You had your hands folded on your chest and your eyes closed. I reached over and touched your lips with my fingers. I remember thinking that I hoped you didn't notice that I bit my nails. You jumped as if my fingers were branding irons and yelled, 'Hey, cut that out.'

"'I love you,' I said. And you knew I wasn't lying then, didn't you?"

I couldn't answer for a long time. I felt as if I were on that rock again, on my back, with that little girl lying beside me, the sun flooding my pores. The power of being fourteen, of believing with your entire heart and soul that there was a world waiting for you somewhere. Sherry believed I was that world. "Yeah," I said. "I knew you weren't lying."

"You got to your feet and said, 'Listen, Sherry. I'm old enough to be your mother.' And I yelled out, '*Mother!* You said 'mother!' "

Now I laughed. "Yeah, you were pretty excited. But I knew I'd said *mother*. I wasn't going to lie to you then."

"Well, I already knew anyhow."

"No, you didn't."

"Honey. I did. Then I jumped on you and threw my arms and legs around you like an octopus. And I planted a big kiss on your mouth. Oh, you don't know, Esther. I wanted everything from you.

"But you pried me off and said, 'Come on, we're pals.' I said, 'How good of pals?' You said, 'Real good.'

"That's when I saw Arthur a few yards away, standing near a tree, leaning on a hoe, watching."

A shiver ran down my spine when she said that. I saw him, too, in that same moment, and I can still picture him perfectly. His eyes were like brass plates, flat and bright at the same time. And even from that distance, I could see him trembling. He was a spooky kid.

Sherry continued. "He still thought you were a guy, the ignorant fuck. I got so angry at him standing there watching us. I just lost my head."

"You sure did." I laughed but Sherry didn't.

"I would have killed him if you hadn't stopped me. I really would have. I hated that kiss-ass way he had, that stand-at-a-distance, read-books-to-impress you bullshit. I knocked him flat in a second. I wrenched that hoe out of his fag hands and stood with my legs spread right over him lying there on his back. I was gonna split his dumpy head open. But you came up behind me and grabbed the blade of the hoe. I freaked because I didn't know you were there and I could have hit you.

"Then, when he thought he was safe because you had hold of the hoe, he started saying, 'Just because you want to fuck the boss. Just because you want to fuck anyone with a dick. You probably fuck your brother. I know you fuck your father.' I was screaming, 'You fag! You fag!' Esther, he thought you were a guy. And you said in a big, bad deep voice, 'Sherry! Let go of the hoe.' Which I did. If you'd said, drive that thing through your own head, I would have. I remember saying to you, 'He harbors unnatural feelings for you! He's a fag.' You looked confused for a moment. Then I pulled out my ace. I told Arthur, 'She ain't a man. She's a woman.' Oh, the look on his face was rich. It was fuckin' price-less. But Arthur, he was smart all right. He waited one beat, then he said, 'Well, then I guess that makes you the dyke.'

"I jumped on him all over again. This time I was strangling him with my bare hands. His eyes started bulging. But you jumped on my back and put your arms around me to hold me back." Sherry was quiet for a long time. Then she said, "That was the only time you held me. Ever."

Even over the phone I could feel that scrappy strength in her arms and legs and back. Her muscles buzzed with it. I knew as I held her that that buzzing was the same thing as her faith in a world waiting for her somewhere, a world that understood Sherry. And the way she responded to my touch, I knew she thought I could show her the door to it.

Sherry went on with her story. "I almost liked Arthur in that moment after our fight because he asked you the question we both wanted to know. He said, 'Which one of us would you want, if we weren't too young?' You just stood there gaping at us. Like we blew your mind.

"Esther, you still there?"

"Yeah, I'm here."

"Tell me now. Which one of us did you want the most?"

I wound the telephone cord around my finger. I was thinking of Arthur, the way he was on the cusp of something more than childhood but less than manhood. He hadn't yet become desperate about grabbing masculinity to his chest. It wouldn't surprise me a bit if Arthur were in prison. He, of all the kids, knew how beautiful he was. And because he knew, he would be the first to destroy his beauty, before anyone else could. Sherry, she was more of a fighter, a fast-talking liar. Yet there was a brutal honesty in her acceptance of ugliness that attracted me powerfully.

"I ain't jailbait anymore, Esther. I just want to know. For fun. Which one of us would you have had if you weren't our boss and if we weren't fucked up kids? Come on, just say 'Arthur' or 'Sherry.' "

"I gotta go," I said, feeling something vital wither inside me. "But thanks for calling."

"Sure, baby." She sounded tough again. I knew I had disappointed her. Slipping back into hustler mode, she said, "But, hey, listen. Maybe we can get together some time, you know, just you and me. What'd ya say?"

An old bulldagger like me, I guess she figured, wouldn't mind a little action twenty years younger than myself. "You know," I said, "I don't think so."

"Cool, that's cool," she said. "I understand. You got an old lady. I respect that. But listen, I'm in a little bit of a tight spot here. See, they give me a handful of change and dump me on the street. I'm gonna be up front with you. A money order, twenty, fifty, hey, hundred if you can spare it. I know you're doing good, Esther. You're always doing good. And you know my choices. I mean, I could—"

"Sherry, okay," I interrupted. "I'll send you a little money." I wrote down the address she supplied. I felt like that boy who got fucked for his cherry pie. But I wasn't willing to let it stand as just a business deal. "Sherry," I said. "Hold on before you hang up. I got these lilacs in my yard. I'm gonna fax you some."

She was silent a long time. "I'd like that." Her voice was clogged with tears, real ones.

"Yeah," I said. "I'm gonna."

"Esther. What am I gonna do? What am I gonna do now?"

I knew I should say something about staying off the street, staying clean, finding a job, that kind of thing. But all I could think to say was, and it came out in a whisper, "I don't know, Sherry. I don't know what either of us is gonna do now."

THE FESTIVAL OF SIGHS

J.M. BEAZER

The time is 1985, the height of the Reagan era, and Kelly Bramble is a sophomore at socially conservative Noble University where Trilby Williston, an "enthusiastically straight" ex-debutante from a blue-blooded North Carolina family, has become the object of Kelly's romantic yearnings. In Noble's snobbish atmosphere, Trilby's background makes Kelly insecure about her own upper-middle-class Connecticut family, especially when Kelly is painfully aware that her whole family's nuts: Her brother Roland, for example, believes he can talk to birds. Kelly herself occasionally experiences visions, and she's not sure whether she's clairvoyant or crazy. But her biggest worry is her too-close relationship with her brother Gray, a proclaimed hedonist who is one year older than she, flamboyantly gay, and a junior at Noble. Their close childhood bond turned incestuous, culminating in a kiss when they were in high school. It's now two years later, and they've reestablished a semblance of their old bond only by refusing to discuss this one indiscretion.

When Kelly admits her hopeless crush on Trilby to Gray, he offers to help Kelly catch her. Kelly and Trilby become friends, but Trilby misinterprets Gray's efforts as a sign of his own interest in her. Trilby comes on to Gray at a party, and he indulges himself in the opportunity to make out with a woman who physically resembles his sister. Trilby exaggerates when she tells Kelly about this incident, claiming she and Gray had sex and are now "an item." Kelly tracks Gray down at his club and, dismissing his protests that he only kissed Trilby, almost succeeds in strangling him. When Gray tells Trilby he and she are decidedly not "an item," Trilby turns to Kelly for consolation. Trilby had been planning to invite Gray to spend spring break with her on Tortola, where Trilby's mother has a villa, but after this "break up" with Gray, she invites Kelly instead.

"Oooh, Mr. Arabian Nights is coming up from the beach!" Trilby whispers. She leans in close to my cheek, the brim of her straw hat grazing my eyebrow. "Honey, I need to make that phone call right now!"

She slides off her bar stool, landing with a graceful hop on her bare feet. As she pauses to adjust her hat, I turn and squint into the field of sharp, white sunlit beach, my eyes blinded until they adjust from the shade under the thatched roof of the bar. A slender young man with glossy, jet-black hair jogs up from the beach, cradling a Kadima paddle and pink rubber ball in his right hand. Trilby tightens the knot of her sarong over her waist, hikes her bandeau up over her breasts, and winks at me—one of those forms of unspoken communication, like lip-reading and social touching, I've never been able to master. "Nothing like a scrumptious bit of beefcake to wash the taste of that awful brother of yours out of my mouth," she says.

"That's the first intelligent thing you've said about the creep." My smile is guilty—why? I'm not Gray's keeper. But she's already turned and taken aim at her new mark. She starts strolling around the curve of the bar, a high-gloss, heavy oak counter in the shape of an elongated oval donut. Her slim hips are wrapped snugly under the magenta-and-purple tropical print of her sarong, its purple fringe brushing lightly back and forth over her thighs. She walks purposely toward the pay phone, timing her steps so she passes her Arabian prince just as he leans against the bar. She smiles and speaks to him—God knows how she can think of something that wouldn't be transparent. Or maybe she doesn't care if she's transparent. Maybe the point is to be as transparent as possible. He draws his head back, startled, but flashes a white, toothy smile, apparently pleased to be approached by this slim American girl. Smiles are in no short supply around here.

I turn to the beach. I don't mind watching her pick up strange men. Just as I didn't mind it when she sobbed on my shoulder about Gray. That firestorm of jealousy and rage is nothing but cinders now. From the moment I visualized her and Gray naked in bed together, she was ruined for me—like that old, sexist concept of "damaged goods." But I know that's irrational. After all, Trilby had done it with dozens of guys long before she ever set eyes on Gray—or me—and my knowledge of those encounters never "ruined" her for me. Why should it make a difference that one of them was my slutty brother? *She* hasn't done anything wrong, after all. I never had any claims on her. We're friends, that's all. In truth, she was ruined from the start.

I let my eye travel over the beach. Why shouldn't I check out the women, just as Trilby's been surveying the male population? Although of course I can't enjoy her easy assumption that the people around me share my sexual orientation. Two dark-haired women, perhaps in their early thirties, are sunbathing on a pair of towels, one reclining on her side and reading a hardback book. She looks French with her navy-and-white-striped one-piece bathing suit and petite build, her legs deeply etched with muscle definition and supple, like frog's legs. Her hair is cropped in a short pageboy—very Louise Brooks. Her friend, stretched flat on her back in a sleek black maillot, exudes a similar St. Tropez look. Could they be lesbians? They emit an aura of European sophistication, like the decadent lesbians of the 1920's: Radclyffe Hall, Djuna Barnes, Vita Sackville-West. But I'm letting my imagination run away with me. They're probably just sisters.

I turn back to the bar. Trilby's smiling like a fiend at the Prince, her head inclined deferentially to one side in that nauseating straight-girl way. But then she turns away, continuing on her way to the phone, and he leans forward to signal the bartender. Something must have misfired.

I pick up a cocktail napkin off the stack next to the basket of tortilla chips, noticing it's a perfect square: ideal for origami. As a kid I used to spend hours folding up little paper animals whenever Gray wasn't around, blotting out the bouncing-loony bedlam of home by concentrating on lining up the edges of the deep-hued paper, smelling the paper's opium fragrance while making crisp, perfect folds, then escaping into a miniature rainbow zoo. I open the napkin and neatly crease it along the diagonal.

Trilby finishes her pretend phone call in the minimum time necessary to fake a busy signal. She pauses at the bar as the bartender brings the Prince a pair of margaritas, the bowl-shaped glasses rimmed with salt and filled with a translucent, greenish fluid that makes me think of antifreeze. A pair of drinks—maybe that was the problem: He's got an Arabian princess back on his beach blanket. He smiles and nods at Trilby as he lays several large, multi-colored bills on the bar. In response she tucks her hair behind her ear and signals the bartender. Looks like she's getting us a third round of frozen daiquiris. Fine by me. I usually like a healthy vacation—running, swimming, tennis—but I might as well spend this one tanked, now that Trilby's ruined.

I quickly fold the napkin into a flapping bird, but it's too droopy and white to cheer me up. I crumple it and toss it on the bar. When I glance over at Trilby again, the daiquiris have arrived: two martini glasses brimming with a mound of pastel froth—pink for her, pale green for me—each mound pierced by a turquoise parrot-shaped swizzle stick. The edge of her glass is trimmed with a strawberry, mine with a slice of honeydew melon. Trilby crinkles her eyes at the bartender as she pays him, lingering a moment to check out his butt when he turns to the cash register. She shines one of her aren't-I-a-devil smiles at me, and I can't help it; it fills me with sunlight. I love her childlike sense of mischief in everything; the way she takes nothing seriously.

Picking up each glass by the stem, she makes her way back around the curve of the bar. Over the pink and green of the glasses, her cheeks have the rosy freshness of a bridal bouquet, the wholesomeness of that endless succession of brides rolled out, like cars off an assembly line, from under the white steeple of Winter Harbor Congregational each weekend back home. Her hips shift like a geisha girl's inside her close-fitting sarong, and the little smile dancing at her lips suggests she's conscious of the effect. Without lust or embarrassment, I admire the aesthetics of her breasts, perfect spheres that soften the hard triangular shape of the glasses in front of them, their roundness immured in the staunch, we-mean-business purple nylon of her bandeau. The gathered trim following the undercurves has a girl-next-door quality, but the flesh nestled inside it, round and alive and quivering ever so slightly as she walks, subverts any impression of modest girlhood.

"He doesn't speak English, can you imagine?" she says, sliding a hip over the bar stool. She hands me the melon daiquiri and takes off her hat, fluffing her curls with the other hand.

"Rotten luck," I say, plucking the slice of melon off the rim. "Thanks." For a moment I think I've caught of waft of Gray's aftershave, but it must be someone's suntan lotion.

"And he's Spanish, from Spain!" She takes out her parrot swizzle stick and sucks it clean. "Not Arabian at all."

"Moorish blood, no doubt," I say. She throws the swizzle stick with a little stabbing motion at the bar, as if she were hurling a nearly weightless javelin. It drops with a little click on top of our collection from our previous rounds: a pair of pink mermaids, a green monkey, a yellow giraffe.

"You'd think a Spaniard would know English." She takes a pensive sip at her drink, her tiny pink tongue darting out to lick off a drop of pink froth off her lips.

"It could be nationalistic pride," I say. Or he could've been lying.

She leans in close to my face. "He had the most beautiful long lashes," she says, her eyes so close I see the tiny, fluttering dilations of her pale grey iris around her right pupil. I'd already noticed Trilby maintains a shorter social distance than I do, and I try to accept it naturally—it's a welcome intimacy, and it would seem unfriendly to lean back—but it always makes my breathing turn shallow and inhibited. I don't want to breathe right in her face: I mean, how can you ever be sure your breath is okay? "You don't think he was a matador, do you?" She laughs, realizing the silliness of the remark.

"Too much work," I say, leaning back. "I peg him as an international mooch."

"You're so funny." She says it with a half-smile, her sidelong look telling me she means odd, not amusing. Swiveling around on her stool, she props her elbows behind her against the bar, holding her drink in front of her with both hands. "Well, if not him," she says, "who else, I wonder?" She lets her gaze pan over the beach.

I turn as well, the dazzling mosaic of sunbathers, beach chairs, and sun-sparkled water swimming a little until I anchor my eyes on a large, lime-green umbrella in the middle. Good work, daiquiris, I say to myself, noticing the absurdly pleasant little smile that tickles about my mouth, the shouts and laughter of children humming in my ears. I get an impulse to check out my two Frenchwomen, restraining it only by swiveling back to the bar.

Trilby suddenly follows, stopping her motion by catching hold of the bar. "What about that boy in the pink-and-purple jams?" she says, crossing her forearms in front of her on the bar. "Doesn't he look sweet?"

I barely glance over my shoulder; she nods toward a neurasthenic-looking blonde sitting under an umbrella. "Looks English to me," I say, thinking, why bother having sex with someone who lives on another continent? When there's no hope of a long-term relationship? Can she really just *like* it—having sex with guys?

"An Englishman—that's dreamy." She scrunches herself closer, her forearms squeezing up against her breasts. They're just below my line of vision, but I can feel them moving up and down as she breathes, gently pushing out against the fabric of her bandeau. She likes that position: I remember her resting against her forearms that way the first time I talked with her. She was leaning against the railing on the terrace at Holly Club during one of their house parties, her breasts squeezed against her arms. We were both champagne-tipsy, swaying back and forth on the railing in time with the Japanese lanterns that swung to and fro over our heads in the breeze.

"And what about his friend?" she asks. "Doesn't he look like Tom Cruise?" Next to the Englishman, a stocky guy with a hairy chest reclines on a blanket, picking at his toes. Yuck.

"I thought you liked them slender and willowy," I say. Yeah, like Gray.

"Not for *me*, silly." I stare at her, and she drops her head back and laughs. "A double date! Don't you think that would be fun?"

"I—I don't know," I stammer.

"Now, don't you go trying to wiggle out of it! It would be a blast!"

"Maybe back at school."

She groans, her expression faintly inquisitive as well as disappointed. Great, now she thinks I'm weird. And then she launches into trying to find out which boys I've presumably been drooling over at school. I protest that I'm too busy studying and finally manage to distract her with one of her favorite topics: the attractions—butt, shoulders, and feats of crew-team daring—of Casbah Phillips, her favorite post-Gray prospect back at school. I'm more familiar with this source of pain, and I almost convince myself it feels nice just to be two girl friends together, sitting cheek-by-cheek in the shade under the shaggy straw of the bar's thatched roof, tittering into our daiquiris over "girl things."

She sits up straight suddenly, gazing at the center of my chest. "Oh, make a wish!" she says, reaching forward with slender fingers.

I look down as her fingertips graze the thin, freckled skin over my sternum. It's my necklace: The clasp has worked its way down to the bottom, where it rests against the pendant. In one of those girly games from high school, whenever your necklace clasp drops down like that, you're supposed to make a wish while your friend restores the clasp to the back of your neck.

She's drawing my hair behind my shoulder with one set of cool fingertips and lifting the clasp with the other, her touch excruciatingly gentle on the side of my neck and in the hollow between my clavicles. I try to act normal, but I've stopped breathing. My hair out of the way, she holds the pendant in one hand and swings the clasp around with the other. The chain slices lightly over the flesh on the opposite side of my neck. I try to dig in my heels against the riptide of confusion surging through my mind. Why am I still wearing this necklace, an old Christmas present from Gray? Why must her lips, so grave in their concentration, hover so close to mine, calling up a fleeting image of turning my head and pressing my mouth against hers? And what are these little wishing games, anyway? Just an excuse for touching people?

"Are you wishing?" she asks, holding the clasp over the back of my neck. It's all I can do to nod, and I'm not wishing at all. Anything I could wish would be impossible; besides, I don't believe in wishes. She drops the clasp, gives me a little pat on the back of my neck, and turns for her drink. That strikes me as an excellent idea. I reach for my glass, down its contents, and look around for the bartender.

"Oh, goody, let's do have another round," she says.

My stomach feels like the home base for a flock of thirty homing pigeons, all of which have just arrived flapping and cooing to their roost. Jesus, let's say it one more time: We're friends, that's all. Why can't I get these things to register? I was beginning to imagine I'd pulled the feeling out by the root, but now I see it was like a tick and I succeeded only in pulling off its body, leaving the head under the skin to grow back. I should've burned it off with a smoking match head—with a blow torch. It's infuriating: Do I really want to kiss a girl who has "Gray was here" scrawled all over her body? The thought of putting my mouth in the same place he—Ugh, I can't even think it.

She puts down her drink and looks at me with a sad, puzzled expression, like a teacher poised to ask you why you've stopped coming to class. "So there's really no special someone who's stolen your heart away up at school?" she asks.

I've been biting my lower lip, and now I let it pop free, surprised and annoyed to find I'd created only a temporary distraction. "What, those self-important pigs at Noble?" I say. "Gimme a break."

She laughs. "They are awful puffed-up, aren't they?"

I screw up my eyes at her. "Funny thing to hear from you! I had the distinct impression you liked them."

"Now, what gave you that idea?"

I stare. "You tell me all the time how you sleep with them."

"Oh, you are an innocent!"

"You sleep with them even when you don't like them? Why?"

"Got me," she says. "Bad habit?" She picks up her hat and starts to fans herself, although the air is breezy and cool. "Seems to me that I, for one, have never been treated too kindly by men. Boys, I should say."

"Then why do you put up with them?"

She shrugs. "Have to sleep with someone, don't you? Everyone says so."

"Trilby, that's horrible," I say. She smiles indulgently, fanning away. "That's like a societal rape! Like our stupid, sick culture's brainwashed you into having—"

She laughs. "You're the one who sounds brainwashed, honey. With all your feminism." I'm too busy hanging open-mouthed to challenge her. She puts down her hat. "I've just been confused I think."

"Sure sounds confused. I mean, I don't get it. Do you just like the physical feeling of it? So you're willing to put up with their being assholes? Just because it feels good?"

She looks down, twirling her mermaid swizzle stick against the side of her glass. "Why, Kelly Bramble, are you trying to tell me something's lacking in your own sex life?"

My sunburn flares hot across my cheeks: I've never told her I'm a virgin. But I sense she's taking the offensive—something in the way she's looking down. "Now you're the one trying to wiggle out of something," I say, even though I'm only half sure it's true.

But her cheeks turn even rosier and she ducks down over her drink. "Gray is so right about you!" she says. "You do have ESP."

"What?" I blink, confused. It's Gray who's always been uncannily perceptive. And what exactly have I guessed?

"Well, as I say, my whole life I've had it pretty rough from men. Even my father—especially him. So sometimes I think..." She looks up from her twirling, her grey eyes still and placid, holding my gaze. "I think maybe it would be nice with a woman."

My eyes feel like they've dropped inside my head, but I try to look nonchalant. "Sounds like you've been talking to Gray," I say. Him and his "sweet sapphic delights."

"Well, yes, he did say a few things," she allows. "He has such a way of making things sound pretty! And I think it's true we're all basically, well, bisexual—don't you think? I mean, haven't you ever...?"

The fire in my cheeks churns like a furnace. Did Gray tell her about me? I wouldn't put it past him. "Well, of course—" I reach for my drink—but it's empty. Instead I pick up another cocktail napkin. "I mean, I agree," I say, folding the napkin in half, "I think we're all bisexual, more or less." Some more than others. I keep my eyes down and crease the napkin again, not even sure what figure I'm making. Should I just tell her? "And of course with Gray dancing around me my whole life, the possibility was always right there before me." I've folded the napkin into a double-layered triangle—the base for a Japanese lantern. "Although with my sister and everyone always telling me how he has such a huge influence over me—" I decide to go with the lantern, folding up each corner into a diamond. "—I wanted to be sure I wasn't unconsciously copying him." I press the side corners of the diamond toward its midline, tucking one layer from the top corners inside each fold as I go. "But after a while, I knew it wasn't just him. When I thought of all those crushes, going back to grade school...."

Her giggling makes me look up. Have I said too much? "Honey, you are the living end!" she exclaims. "The way you are always analyzing!"

I'm on the verge of telling her. But do I even count as a lesbian, when I've never acted on it? I tuck in the last of the corners and, holding the folded octagon up to my lips, blow into the hole at the top until it puffs up like a balloon. I can't help noticing it resembles a small, white breast. "Look, a Japanese lantern," I say, holding it out.

Her gazes shifts back and forth from me to the lantern, her eyes a sad, watery grey. Then her mouth drops open into a wide smile. "That's *so* cool!" she says. "How'd you do that? Show me—show!"

I show her how to fold the lantern and, over our next round of drinks, the flapping bird, dancing penguins, Christmas star, husky dog, cootie catcher, and polar bear. Soon we've created a small menagerie of paper figures arrayed across the bar, filled out by the animal swizzle sticks. When I look out at the beach again, the ragged shadow of the roof has stretched its fingers far over the sand, and the shouts and laughter rising up from the beach have been replaced by mothers calling for their children, people packing up to go.

We should probably go, too, and get ready for dinner, but we've got another round of drinks coming. Besides, I'm too content where I am, surrounded by paper and plastic animals, tucked in next to her breasts. She's humming to herself, bouncing a pair of dancing penguins and a nun before her on the bar. I think she's feeling the daiquiris.

"Actually," I say, "I haven't been totally candid with you." She looks up. What a stupid way to start: Now it's like she's holding her breath. "The thing is, well, I've known for a long time now that I'm a—" Get it out, girl. "—lesbian."

"Really!" Genuine surprise, I think. But maybe not.

Then the bartender is standing in front of us with our drinks: my usual impeccable timing. I feel exposed, like a clump of beached seaweed gathering flies in the sun. I seem to move in slow motion as I lift each frothy, overfull glass by the stem, holding the cocktail napkin against the base; carefully placing each glass on the bar. But the bartender beams down at me inexplicably, like a benevolent priest, his smile watermelon-shaped and dimpled, like Gray's. Did he overhear me? Could he be gay? Or is he just trying to earn a big tip?

"Well, I think it's great," Trilby says when he goes, placing a hand on my forearm. "I think we should all be free to be whatever we are. Whatever God meant us to be."

"Well, yes..." I guess it doesn't matter I don't believe in God. She removes her hand; I'm a little relieved. I take a gulp of my drink—it's a bit stronger than the others, which is all to the good. "Runs in the family, I guess." It takes her a second to get it.

"Oh, you *will* have to tell me all about that fascinating world. That brother of yours would only hint at it—when he was speaking generally, you know." Why did she add that? Is she trying to cover for him that he told her about me? She giggles, adding, "He called it '*le demimonde lesbien.*' "

"Sure, I'll give you the whole scoop," I say, for some reason unable to admit I know next to nothing about it. Two tense visits to a bar, and a lot of reading—and I know reading doesn't count. But it's too complicated to come out to someone and then explain how so far, you've been a lesbian only in your head.

"I would never have guessed about you," she says, smiling. She means it as a compliment. "I remember seeing a pair of them at the beach at Nice, and I tell you, they had the short-short hairdo's and the hard faces and these thick, muscular bodies—just so mannish! Scared the bejesus out of me."

"Oh, well, that's certainly a look," I say stiffly, feeling guilty for all the butch lesbians in the world, even if I haven't met any of them—or any other kind of lesbian for that matter. What does it say about me that I could fall for such a woman? Gray's right: It's not simply bad luck; it reveals a deep flaw in my character. "Some people find it attractive," I add, fingering a dancing penguin. "But you see all kinds. Like at the bars—" All two of them I've visited. "—you see lots of women who look like anybody else. Some even super dolled up—you know, that hair-sprayed flight-attendant look, or like they're taking a break from a particularly grueling event in the Miss America pageant."

"Ooh la, la, lesbian bee-auty queens!" She practically yells it, swiveling back and forth on her barstool, her hands holding on to the seat.

I pick up one of the parrot swizzle sticks, take aim as she rocks back and forth, and stick it in her hair. "Ooh, I feel pritt-tee!" she sings, raising a cupped palm behind the swizzle stick and rolling her eyes upward in a Mary Pickford impression. "Oh so pritt-tee!" I grab a mermaid and stick it in the other side, giving her a lopsided pair of antennae. She grabs one of the monkeys to retaliate, nailing me on the top of my head, singing "pritt-ee, and wit-tee" as best she can while laughing. I pick up the cootie catcher and try to nip her nose with it, calling out, "Watch out! Lesbian cooties!" She grabs the cootie catcher between her lips, crumpling it, and we descend into a war of decorating each other with swizzle sticks and origami, laughing and pushing at each other, throwing napkins and scattering tortilla chips. She tries to stuff a polar bear into the center of my bikini bra; I jump back off the stool.

But she's right there after me and quickly succeeds in stuffing the bear in between my breasts. I reach for a Christmas star, but she runs out onto the beach. I chase after her, stumbling on the sand, which gives her time to break into a full run, her sarong sliding down off her bathing-suit bottom and dropping to the sand. She barrels down the beach, and I run after her as best I can on four-plus daiquiris, the sand rising up and down in front of me like rolling waves at sea. She reaches a row of cabanas, white with green-and-white-striped awnings, and stops to look over her shoulder, prancing back and forth a few times.

I catch up and grab her by the arm. She twists away, turning, and grips me by both shoulders; after a moment's wrangling, I let her toss me down on the sand. She drops down on top of me, her eyes ashy and intent as she gazes down at me, her lips grave with concentration. "Honey," she says, "I'd really like to muss up your hair."

Then she's lowering her lips, and they're brushing against mine. The weight of her body relaxes against me, and then we're kissing and kissing, and her mouth is unfolding, so open and soft and warm, her tiny pink tongue dancing out to meet mine. I open my mouth wide and pull her tightly against me, and she squeezes her body against mine, her fingers raking across my scalp through my hair. I can't believe we're here, that this is happening, and I want it to go on forever, cupping my palm warmly against the full undercurve of her breast through her bandeau, her mouth a soft, open o. But then she draws her lips away and raises her head, her eyes half closed, still ashy and intent. She sits up and looks deliberately over her shoulder—no, no one has come by—and then back at me.

"Now we'll all go back to the house," she says, still fixing me with that ashy stare. She jumps up. "Race you!" she calls out, breaking into a run.

* * *

Mrs. Williston's closet is filled with lingerie. A white satin robe, adorned with feathers at the wrists and hem, hangs from one hook; the hangers hold a half dozen silk teddies in assorted colors: black, vermillion, pink, maroon, teal. No white, I notice. I wouldn't be caught dead in lingerie, but if I ever wore something lacy, it would have to be white or ivory, for sure. I don't like silk or satin for anything; even the idea of satin sheets seems slippery-slick and sleazy, reminiscent of those Total-Woman women from the seventies, eagerly anticipating the arrival of their husbands so they can greet them at the front door wrapped in cellophane. I like cotton; flannel in winter. But I guess that's part of what makes me such a sexual dud.

I push the closet door back to half-closed, just as I found it, and catch sight of my face in the mirror as it swings in front of me. Despite my sunburn, my eyes look pale in the dim light, and I can't seem to stop my eyebrows from rising up in the center, furrowing my brow. I walk past the vanity, touching the deeply engraved silver backs of Mrs. Williston's hairbrushes.

Trilby's in the shower. On the way back up to the house, she acted as if that kiss had never happened. I have to assume it was the product of the booze and a moment's excitement; that we're still going to dinner and the movies. Just as well. At most she'd probably just want to use me for an "experiment." I shouldn't let her.

But I'm not sure of anything—what I want; what she wants—and that's why I'm still in my bathrobe, floating like a displaced ghost over the rose-colored carpet in this unfamiliar room. I blow-dried my hair before putting on my clothes, hoping she'd finish in the shower before I'd have to commit myself to getting dressed, but now I've run out of delaying tactics. The water shuts off in the bathroom, but then I hear a couple of clicks and the whine of her blow drier starts up.

The bedroom is cavernous. With those daiquiris still buzzing around in my brain, the ceiling seems miles away. Even looking straight ahead, I feel an endless semi-darkness swirling in the rafters above me. The house, a symmetrical, three-story pile of pink stucco, ascends to one central gable, with the bedroom located just under the central peak. You could fit the entire living room of my suite between the foot of the king-sized bed and the vanity. Gray would drool over it: a Spanish villa stuck defiantly on an English Caribbean island. Serves him right he's stuck in Winter Harbor, that worthless strip of tinsel.

I wander over to the windows, a set of three casements divided with iron leading and hung with gauzy white curtains. Pushing a curtain to the side, I look down into the magenta bougainvillea growing in a heavy mass against the wall of the house. I unlatch the casement and push it open, leaning my head outside and letting my eye travel across the breathy green of the lawn to the cliff that drops down to the sea. The sun has sunk behind the house, leaving the garden blue and cool in the evening shadows. I draw in a breath of balmy, island air, enjoying the slightly rank smell of seawater.

I bring my head back inside, leaving the casement open. The bedroom's decorated in the French Antique style I think, based on my vague recollection of Gray's innumerable books on design. Flanking the bed are two elegant little button-back armchairs with plush, coral-colored cushions, the carved wood on their flimsy-looking legs matching the pattern on the vanity and dressers. It's a little creepy here. Too quiet and dark, and even up in the bedroom I'm aware of the furniture shrouded in sheets downstairs, the way the house broods over the sea like a vulture. Even though it's my third night here, I still feel as if I've slipped under the velvet cordon into a room on the National Heritage tour.

The blow drier stops its whining, and I hurry over to the bed, where I've laid out my clothes. If Trilby rushes out of the bathroom bubbling on about how we have to dash right out if we're going to eat a civil meal before the movies, I'll look awfully foolish sitting here in my robe, panting with my paws up in front of my chest like her pet springer spaniel.

But just as I'm pulling on my shoes, I hear the bathroom door unlatch.

"Why on earth did you get dressed?" She's standing in the doorway in her white terry-cloth robe, her cheeks pink with the heat of the shower. If she weren't smiling, her eyes would look so wide and wet I'd think she was on the verge of tears. "Oh, you nerd!" she says with a laugh. She crosses the room, pushing me back on her mother's bed. "After I worked so hard getting you here?"

Before I can respond, she sits on top of my hips, leans forward, and kisses me on the mouth, her lips forming the same wet and open *o* as before. "Getting" me here? Why is everyone always miles ahead of me? Did she invite me down here with the premeditated plan of seducing me? Does she have a secret agenda of racking up as many Brambles as possible?

She sits back with a bounce, making me feel like Winnie-the-Pooh with Tigger sitting on his chest. From inside her robe, I catch a waft of talcum powder and White Linen cologne. "You're the absolute opposite of that brother of yours," she adds. I try not to wince.

"I didn't want to presume," I say. Maybe Gray did let it slip that I'm gay. Maybe all her "maybe-I'm-bisexual" talk at the bar was just a way to coax me into admitting it.

"Oh, you're an idiot!" She leans down and kisses me again. "You'd think you were a brand new virgin!" I cringe inwardly, wondering if Gray also let slip this second little detail. But she's started untucking my shirt, nodding upwards to signal I should lift my arms over my head. I comply at once, wondering what's happened to my pride. Experiment. But who am I kidding? With the scent of talcum powder tickling in my nostrils, I'm not about to refuse her.

"And when you're the one who has to show *me* the ropes!" she adds, giggling as she lifts my shirt over my head. It feels as if a small hamster is turning somersaults in my stomach. Are we really going to do this? On her mother's bed? When I have no idea what I'm doing? But I tell myself it'll be all right. I've imagined doing it so many times, in such precise detail. And reading about it must be good for something—maybe? Gray would tell me to be bold; just go for it. For Chrissakes, stop thinking so much!

I smile as soon as my head reemerges, enjoying the feeling of my hair flopping down on the wrong side of my part. *Honey, I'd like to muss up your hair.* A warm wrenching grips the center of my stomach as I remember that moment—the moment when it first dawned on me she was actually feeling desire. For me, of all people.

I bring down my hands, tucking them between her arms and gently pulling open the lapels of her robe. My eyes zoom in and find her breasts: beautiful full globes, just as I'd imagined them, the skin a warm and creamy ivory, the color and consistency of buttermilk batter. I press my palm against the outer curve of the right; the skin gives with the springy softness of angel's food cake. She lifts her head and arches her back slightly, her robe falling away from her body while her breasts shift their weight back against her rib cage. They're perfectly round, like a pair of biscuits.

She rolls forward again, sitting up on her knees and placing a palm on each of my shoulders. Two blond curls bounce in front of her cheeks, and she grins devilishly as I massage both her breasts. She slides a hand under my back, hunting for the clasp of my bra. "Darn these darned clothes!" she says in a sorrowful voice.

I help her get rid of them, reaching down to unbutton my jeans as she finds the clasp of my bra and unhooks it, immediately sliding her hands under the thin nylon and passing them over my breasts. I worry they're too small to be satisfying, but her touch sends a shimmering like the Northern Lights over my skin. It seems next to impossible to wriggle out of my jeans, especially when her thighs are hovering just inches above my hips and she's slipping my bra straps off my shoulders. Our awkwardness busts her up, and she keeps laughing as she brings one knee over my body to kneel by my side. I sit forward and yank down my jeans and underwear together, the motion of my thighs and hips letting me feel the slipping and sliding of the inner lips of my vagina against each other, the sense of hollowness opening out immediately above. Already wet and open.

"I know: I'm hopeless," I say, pitching my clothes to the floor.

"Totally!" she laughs. Her bathrobe hangs precariously on the edge of one shoulder, and for revenge, I sit forward and touch it off, with my other hand gently pushing her down on the bed. I roll down on top of her, kissing her on the mouth and pressing my breasts against hers—*warm, soft breasts together*—my hips snuggling up into hers. I spread my palms flat against the sides of her buttocks, sinking into the thin, marshmallow-soft layer of flesh that seems to float over the muscle underneath.

Two female bodies, joined together in perfect symmetry: How many times have I've imagined it? Now that I'm here, I want to stay like this forever. But she arches her torso underneath me, and I let her roll me off to one side. Scooting herself back on the bed, she lays against one of the long, king-sized pillows, her grey eyes again taking on that ashy intentness. I sit back to take in the full view of her body: the generous curve of her breasts; the bumps of her rib cage above her slender waist; those marshmallow-lined hips; the brushy, reddish-gold patch of hair at their center. She clasps her hands behind her head, her back arching slightly again, her breasts lifting up. Their fullness bulges outward, and they seem to sway back and forth at me, their tiny, raspberry-pink knots pointing up and out. I want to throw myself down and submerge one of them in my mouth, kissing it, sucking on it, but I'm too embarrassed— even though I know it's something lesbians do. Then I remember how I know that: from Gray's copy of *The Joy of Lesbian Sex.* I can even visualize the illustration, damn him, and I hear his inane "explanation" for why he bought it: "Oh, but what I've always *truly* wanted is to be a lesbian!"

I blink the image away, and in a moment I'm caught up in those raspberry-pink knots again. Sensing she's got me mesmerized, she broadens her smile, revealing the hard, glossy white of her teeth. The smile is carnal and knowing—it makes that hamster wriggle uncomfortably in my stomach—and she lets her body sink more deeply into the pillows, at the same time drawing her left thigh outward. She slides it over the bedspread with maddening slowness, showing me, little by little. My eyes are riveted to the dense froth of reddish-gold fuzz as it spreads and widens, the dark cleft at the center slowly becoming visible under the tangle of brushy gold, emerging as a slip of soft, rose-petal pink, glistening in the dim light. It grows still wider, revealing a deeper pink nestled inside, and just barely visible at the center, a dark slit suggesting the stillness of a deep black pool beyond it.

How many times have I dreamed of it? Sinking down and letting my nose, lips, chin fall into that black pool, pressing my entire face into that softness? She starts gyrating it, circling around in tight, yearning gyrations, and in my head I hear myself murmuring, *pussy, pussy, oh, puhh-ssy,* just like I've imagined it all those other times, alone in my bunk bed at school, when I've moaned it aloud to myself. Needy—feeling that raw, animal need—after a certain point not caring if anyone heard me. I hear myself let out a small whimper; it embarrasses me, but it also feels sexy. I don't care; I let it come out again, just one little whimpery moan, and her gyrations grow stronger and wider.

I should do more than stare. *Shit, what do I—?* Just do what comes naturally. *I want it; I want it.* I don't care that I don't know how. I'll figure it out. That's when I sense someone watching me, and a waft of Polo aftershave tells me Gray's in the room. Without looking, I see him peeking out from the half-open door to the closet, the white feathers of Mrs. Williston's satin robe puffing out by his waist and shins.

—Go away! Jesus, he's going to ruin it. Can't I ever get away from him?

Her stomach is visibly trembling. I'm thinking I should ask her if she's okay; if she's sure she wants to go ahead. I'm not sure *I* want to go ahead. What if I'm too tense to have an orgasm? Or if I get carried away and start making weird noises? Maybe the noises I make when I mastur-bate are not like anyone else's. Trilby will think I'm this bizarre creature; maybe she'll go telling other people at school. That's paranoid.

—I'll say! rises up from the closet; I ignore it. But still I hesitate: What if I go so out of control I start twitching, like the way one of my legs some-times jumps when I'm falling asleep? What if I start having convulsions?

—Not too inhibited, are we, dear?

He's not really there, I tell myself.

—Oh, yes I AM! Wouldn't miss this for the world!

Trilby's eyes flick open a hairbreadth; I catch only the slightest widen-ing of the glossy black line of her eyelashes before they re-close. She's wondering what's taking me so long. I take a breath and lean forward, gently but deliberately placing my palm against her inner thigh where the flesh bellies out at the top, my fingers curling over the curve. I glance up at her face, just to make sure it's all right. Her eyes are closed, her head dropped back against the pillows and her lips parted. Just below her upper teeth, the small mound of her tongue somehow communicates deep relaxation.

I lower my head, my face not a half-inch from her brushy patch, my breath stirring a few strands of coarse hair on one of the upper tufts—it makes her groan. Heat radiates toward my lips and chin; the smell is close, humid, and marshy, and my nostrils drink it in—do I like it? I think so. It's not like fish, anyway—God, those jerk boys screaming about it in the playground. No, it's both savory and sweet, bland and salty; it makes me think of a warm and comforting dish, like chicken pot pie. I want to sink my nose and mouth into her soft folds right away, but I hold off, slowly letting out a breath through pursed lips, listening to her whimper, like a puppy left in the study for the night. Yes, better go slowly and let her anticipate it.

I blow out another breath, moving the air current down and up the sides of her velvety slip of pink. Her inner thighs lie serenely recumbent on either side of my face, and as I gaze into the folds around her dark slit I imagine it pulsing almost imperceptibly inside, open and not quite closed. It makes me think of the cliffs on either side of the gorge at the Satan's Nook Nature Preserve, the pulsing of the little stream over the rocks and weeds where it emerges from underground. While hiking I've often thought of how the U shape of the gorge echoes a woman's out-spread thighs: the two mountainous facings of rock rising up on either side of the waterfall, the winding stream descending to the pool below. I would entertain myself matching everything up: the moss-covered hill above the ravine like the fuzzy mound formed by the pubic bones and hair; the bumpy stones at the head of the waterfall like the nubbly folds over the clitoris; the silent black pool at the foot of the falls like the dark opening into the vagina. But the idea strikes me as too silly for words, mortifying me, and I shove it out of my mind.

—*Goodness, you ARE a nerd! The girl's right.* A glance to my right confirms that Gray's seated himself in the coral-colored armchair next to the bed. He's dressed in a Panama hat, ivory linen suit, and long white-silk scarf, the entire ensemble glowing bright against the cushions. His elbows are propped against the chair's upholstered arms, his fingertips pressed together in front of his chest; one ankle rests against the opposite knee. He settles into his El Grandissimo posture, his eyes feathery, a smile of perfect contentment playing over his lips. He seems to survey the scope of his plantation and possessions: his acres of coffee trees, his thousands of cruelly exploited laborers, his collection of rare Caruso recordings, his prized blue hyacinth. Oh, and of course his children, his mistress, his wife.

—*I can't believe your nerve. Crashing a lesbian—*

—*Oh, lighten up. What can it hurt if I stay?*

—*This is my very first time. You're gonna ruin it.*

—*On the contrary, I can only enhance it. Besides it looks like you need coaching.*

—*Go to hell.*

—*That would be premature.*

—*Then go to the bars—wherever. Just get the hell out of my head.*

—*Can't do it, lovey. You know very well I have no say in the matter. 'Crashing' indeed. Yes, I see you realize it's true.*

—*Fine, go ahead and watch. I'm not letting you distract me.*

—*No, no, that would be dreadful! Just concentrate on your pleasure and the lovely Miss Trillicious. Pretend I'm not here. A mere figment of your imagination.*

He raises his right hand, flicking the scarf over his head with a flour-ish. The motion sends his body floating up out of the chair, spiraling smoothly through one full turn before it settles itself back on his seat.

Damn him—I can't keep her hanging any longer! She's gyrating furi-ously, her moans both fierce and whimpering. I move my mouth in toward her glistening slip of pink, insinuating my tongue into the very top where the folds join together. She growls, her hips thrusting up to meet me. My eyelids droop shut as her blending softness closes around my tongue, and I burrow my face more deeply into the soft folds of flesh, feeling the prickly lining of underbrush against my cheek, nuzzling further down and finding the creamy liquid core inside, savoring the taste—*finally, finally; been waiting so long.* My tongue descends with her hot, creamy waterfall; rippling over the hidden, mysterious bumps like soft, warm pebbles and ridges—*soft together, slaves together*—sliding down inside the downy, black pool at the bottom. I don't care; I *like* connecting it with the gorge. Gorging myself on her gorgeous gorge—*mmn, mnmmm, pussy, pussy, pussy*—slathering my nose, lips, chin, and wide-open mouth with soft, slick, gooey goo; losing myself inside that melting blackness.

Inside it's still and silent. That's just the feeling, though: She's actually set up a steady stream of moaning, and she's gyrating so intensely my head rises up and down, my neck bending back with each upward surge. But I still feel as if everything is silent and motionless, like the swirling stasis of an ocean thirty fathoms deep, the dark luminosity and the resounding stillness of a void gurgling with hidden life. It's as if my entire body is submerged in soothing darkness; as if I'm scuba diving, the water bathtub-warm, my legs gliding through the blackness, flippers bending back and forth under the gentle force of the water.

She brings her arms down and grips the back of my head, pressing my face firmly into her crotch. I start playing up my slurping and smacking noises; she responds with even stronger thrusts and gyrations, raking her fingertips through my hair—*yeah, eat that pussy! Do it, do it*—and I swirl my tongue all around, listening to each subtle shift in her response, guessing what would feel good to me if I were the one getting done. I fall into a rhythmic pressing with my nose and chin, my tongue slipping into her pocket of flesh and back out again, the warm, melting silkiness enveloping me like clouds of Turkish Delight, sucking me further inside.

Suddenly I want to be on my knees on the side of the bed, like the woman in that *Penthouse* spread from so long ago—sneaking into Roland's room and sliding his stash of magazines from between his mattress and bedboard. I want to be the brown-haired woman on her knees, her nose and chin completely submerged in the fleshy mounds protecting the blond woman's dark slit. I can see the blond woman's white stockings and garters; her airbrushed light-brown fuzz; her arched back and the vacuous, open-mouthed bimbo look on her face. The image gives me a charge: There's something in the neediness and slutty abandon in the forward thrust of the brown-haired woman's neck; something in the health and strength in the blond woman's thigh muscles, so sleek and well-toned, and delicately veiled with sheer white nylon. I want to be the slut on her knees.

What if I did that? Just slid my legs down the side of the bed and knelt in front of her? Worshipped at her shrine.

—*That's EXACTLY what you should do!* Out of the corner of my eye, I see Gray's chair has turned into the white-wicker peacock fan chair from the veranda back home, his white-linen suit glowing phosphorescent green, as if the fabric were interwoven with fox fire. He's removed his hat and loosened his tie, and a blue hyacinth shifts from one clawed foot to the other on his shoulder, bowing and bobbing next to his ear.

—*No, I couldn't. She'd think I was a masochist. I'D think I was a masochist.*

—*So what if you are?*

—*Just because you are? Jesus, look at me: getting off on sexist male pornography, on a pair of co-opted fake lesbians serving as a stage set for male titillation. Probably supposed to be bisexuals, in fact. Gee, what a good little feminist I am. I ought to subscribe to* Penthouse *openly; stop being such a hypocrite.*

—*Oh, puh-lease. You're going to drive me away.*

Before I can encourage him to do just that, Trilby loosens her grip on my head. "I want to do you," she says. Breathless, panting, reaching down to stroke my hair and ears.

I draw my head back, the night air gently cooling the slickness smeared over my mouth and chin. —*Finally getting your face smeared, eh?* "Really?" I say, just as breathless.

"Oh, yes!" she says. She tosses her head from side to side, her eyes closed. I love seeing her curls tossed every which way on the pillows.

"You don't have to, you know."

She opens her eyes, her eyebrows tilting upward in the middle. "But I *want* to. Silly. What are we going to do with you?"

"But I don't want to stop," I say, giving her a pout.

That carnal smile again. "Who says you have to, honey?"

—*Sixty-nine! Ooh, do it, doo iit!*

"You mean, like both doing it together?"

She laughs. "Uh-huh. I want to hold you."

—*Go for it, girls! We want the beast with two backs!*

"C'mon," she says, beckoning. I sit back on my heels and crawl up to the pillows by her head. Feeling a little self-conscious, I swing one knee over her head so I'm straddling her face—what if I'm funny-looking down there? She's never done this; what if she doesn't like the taste? But she grips my thighs and firmly tugs them downward. I'm scared of bumping against her face, but she keeps inching me down, and then I feel a charge of pleasure: She's touched me with the tip of her tongue.

"Mmm," she says. I settle myself down gingerly over her quivering tongue.

—*Jesus, you'd think we were loading fine porcelain—packed with nitro glycerin.*

"Mmmmmm, mmnmmm," she murmurs. I lean forward and lie the length of my body against hers, wrapping my arms around her waist and pressing my breasts into the warmth of her abdomen, feeling the soft bedding of her breasts under my hip bones. I tuck my head between her thighs, searching again through the gold brushy tufts for that slip of pink wetness. Our bodies flow together as if caught up in a wave, and only then do I become aware of the intense sweetness of her tongue dancing inside of me—a part of me that's dissolved away into a dark, liquid pool. Her mouth and tongue merge with that pool, just as my mouth and tongue merge with its mirror image inside her. And then I'm lost in those swirling black pools of pleasure, the rolling motion of their waves.

In the back of my mind, I see Gray's glowing figure rise out of his chair. I panic—is he going to climb into bed with us?—but instead he starts one of his modern-dance routines, turning with his arms outstretched, one end of the silk scarf in each hand. He raises one arm and then the other, swirling the scarf around and over his head, then releasing it and letting it sail up toward the ceiling. The hyacinth, perched on one of the rafters, flaps its wings as the fabric floats past. Then he runs a dancer's run past the windows, gliding through the moonlight that spills from the windows onto the floor, the light cooling the incandescence of his suit to pale blue. He sweeps up the curtains as he passes, letting them fall slowly in his wake, the breeze lifting them once before they float down to rest against the sill. Circling once more around the room, he returns to the windows, and with a leap he passes through them, down into the garden below.

Except it isn't the garden, it's a forest of fir trees, their long, downward-dangling branches encased in ice. Through the trees, in a small clearing, I see a group of women dancing around a maypole wreathed with ice-covered pine branches. They're dressed in white fur hats, cloaks, and boots, with small gold bells fastened at their wrists and the toes. Each woman holds one of the white silk ribbons that stream down from the maypole's top; in the other hand, each holds a white candle. They weave in and out of sight behind the firs as they glide past one another, left and right, around and around. The fresh scent of fir needles and mountain air is all around me, and behind the jingling of their bells, I hear music and singing rising out of the forest.

I push the vision away—I want to be here, with Trilby—and as it swirls away into the darkness, I feel our bodies flail against one another, the intensity almost too much to bear. Trilby's body surges upward, building on a slow but powerful wave I know will take her over the top. The intensity in her body pushes into me, and my body is overtaken by a gurgling and then cascading rush of pleasure. The music, which never entirely faded, explodes into an ecstatic chorus of spirits: Bells are ringing, trumpets sound, and everywhere is a riot of white and gold and green, paisley and brocade; a blizzard of fir branches and white fur coats and twinkling candles. At the same time, my body squeezes itself against hers, pressing out the juicy, burbling waves of pleasure over and over again, drinking in the waves of sweetness flowing out of her, filling myself with it, squeezing and squeezing, wanting more and more.

Sometime later, I notice a shaft of light radiating through a half-open doorway, illuminating a column of dust and projecting a triangle of gold onto a rose-colored carpet. It resembles the light that sometimes shines from the hall into my bedroom at home, but I can't make sense of the carpet: It should be those wide, bare floorboards. I raise my head, and the sight of Trilby's yellow curls, spread out into a thin mesh over her cheek, brings me back. We're lying upside-down on the bed; I don't remember her turning around.

I roll onto my back, and Trilby follows my motion, nuzzling her head into the curve of my neck and shoulder. My body feels as if it's nearly full of seawater, waves of kelp-green rolling up inside and lapping against the inner walls as if it were a sea cave. I lie as still as possible and listen to the waves moving up from the middle of my thighs and passing under my hips, abdomen, rib cage, neck, and head. Eddies of backwash curl under my breasts and into my ears; rivulets stream down the length of my arms into my fingertips.

I lift my head to gaze at her cheek: the delicate ice-pink skin; the mist of fine, white peach fuzz. Such an extraordinary creature: It's an honor to lie next to her. I reach to touch her hair, and my fingers brush past my cheek, bringing the fragrance of her arousal to my nostrils. I stop my hand and press it against my nose.

Rolling onto my side, I catch sight of our lower bodies in the mirror on the back of the closet door, hip over hip, legs intertwined. The curves flow into one another, now following, now opposing, like sand dunes shifting across the desert. We're symmetrical, like the house around us. To me, the symmetry's much more beautiful than a mismatched pair of male and female bodies. But I guess I'm biased.

—*Rubbish! Of course it's more beautiful! Same goes for two male bodies.* I look up and find Gray perched on the headboard, his hair a little roughed up, but still dressed in his white-linen suit, one leg draped gracefully over the other knee. The hyacinth bobs on his shoulder, gently gnawing at one of his ears. *I mean, will you look at this sight? My cute little pomegranates.*

—*Jesus, I can't believe you're still here. Haven't you ever heard of privacy?*

—*Oh, stuff it. I'm going to watch over you.*

—*Like hell you are.*

—*Tonight at least you'll come to no harm. It's my way of saying thanks. I'll stand guard, like a faithful St. Bernard, while my two little hedgehogs are sleeping the sweet, downy—*

—*We don't need your protection. There's a security system. Connected to the police department—*

—*Oh, bosh. The police could take forever. And some perils may already be lurking inside the house.*

—*Yeah, one may be here in spirit. Which reminds me, don't even think about getting into this bed.*

—*Banish the thought! It would ruin the aesthetic effect of two luscious, pink baby buntings snuggled together under the quilts. One who's just lost her virginity.*

—*I'm glad at least you think this counts. Not that I care what you think, jerk. My first time ever, and you had to spoil it.*

—*Didn't look too spoiled to me. No, let me commend you on your lovely interpretation of the timeless blushing-maiden-turned-wanton-and-wild-animal theme. Certainly gave ME one of my most—*

—*Will you shut up?! I want to be alone with her.*

—*Yes, yes, of course. Don't mind me.*

—*I hate you. I hate myself for letting you stay.*

—*Goodnight, pumpkin. Sweet dreams.*

SEDUCTION

TERRY WOLVERTON

Night drew a filmy curtain of darkness over the city, a veil of cinder that blotted the stars. Kendra unbolted the door to the crumbling warehouse, and the sky disappeared, giving way to a thin, watery light cast on walls of scarred concrete.

As the young woman led the way up five steep flights of musty stairs, Lee grumbled, "I'm too old for this." Inspired as she tried to be by the undulation of Kendra's ass ascending before her, she found the setting put a damper on her lust. Her knees ached from the climb, and the squalor of the dank old building did not fuel the aura of romance.

The loft they entered after Kendra released three locks was large and filthy, full of decrepit furniture scavenged from curbside and strange configurations of objects arranged in a manner that was meant to be artistic. Perhaps there had been a time when Lee might have found the scene exotic, the proverbial walk on the wild side, but now it only wearied her. She longed for the neutral luxury of her hotel room, its gleaming tub outfitted with Jacuzzi jets, the chocolates left on the pillow like a lover's departing kiss, crisp sheets turned down, inviting.

That's where she'd intended for them to end up, after a quiet, elegant dinner in the Village, but Kendra had refused. "It'll be so uptight, so straight!" she'd whined in protest. "Come to my place—it'll be more fun."

It was a tactic Lee had used herself, a fatal blend of reprimand and promise that had proved effective in countless situations. Now here she stood in this grimy loft on the edge of what was once the Bowery.

Sound was blasting from some walled-off corner at the far end of the room, the same robotic, vicious beat Lee remembered from the club the night before. She cocked an eyebrow in question.

"That's just Arturo," the young woman explained with a breezy wave in the direction of the noise. "One of my roommates. Don't worry, he's cool."

At this news, Lee slumped into a chair, raising a swarm of dust from the hideous polyester spread that draped it. The frantic bass called forth an echoing throb behind her eyes.

"Isn't that a riot?" Kendra giggled, pointing to the bedspread's lurid pattern. "Nimo got it on Orchard Street for three bucks." There was marvel in her voice for someone who could glean such treasure with such economy.

Lee could only imagine how this gamin would regard her own Malibu hideaway, its careful landscaping, its lavish Southwest decor. She had paid hundreds of thousands of dollars to make her home exactly the way she wanted it, but these kids could only have disdain for such display, reveling instead in the tacky, the banal.

"Just how many roommates do you have?" she questioned, trying to keep the sourness from her voice. They might as well make love in Grand Central Station, for all the privacy afforded by this loft.

"Four," Kendra answered, slithering onto the arm of the chair, pressing herself next to Lee. In lieu of a shirt, the girl was wearing a long-line bra, recycled from a thrift shop and dyed black, the bra cups cone-shaped, pointed as missiles. Perched as she was, she afforded an enticing view of her cleavage. "It's the only way we can swing the lease. You'll probably get to meet them. Except for Trina; she's the video artist, remember? But she's out in San Francisco for a week."

Lee made a halfhearted stab at an expression of regret over the missing Trina; Kendra must have spoken about her but Lee remembered nothing. She was determined to maintain a semblance of charm, though a dark mood stalked her, shadowed her nerve endings with bared teeth and hungry eyes. She needed to regain the upper hand. Lee Bergman had accomplished her first seduction at the precocious age of ten; the object of her attentions, Delores di Carlo, had been twelve at the time, with a body that had burst abruptly into maturity only months earlier. Lee had had forty years of practice since that sweet initiation, and in that time had rarely met refusal.

Fingering the soft hollow at the base of the young woman's throat, Lee inquired huskily, "Where's your room?"

Kendra met her gaze and, with a breathless "This way," led her in the direction of the screaming sound. At the far end of the loft, both corners had been walled off; Kendra headed for the room that was not Arturo's.

A bare bulb in a wall socket illuminated the bleak space and its random contents. Lee had tried to prepare herself for the aging mattress on the floor, but when she saw it, sheets knotted in a lump and some-what less than clean, her spirits wilted. Aside from the mattress, there was a trunk, from which spewed an assortment of underwear; a portable clothing rack hung with various confections in leather and spandex; some piles of books, mostly art criticism and translations of French philosophers; a portable CD player; and a rough-hewn crate that served as nightstand and dressing table. Next to the bed, half-hidden by the tangled blanket, lounged a long, thick dildo the color of licorice, attached to a leather belt.

"Do you think he could turn that down?" Lee yelled to be heard above the roar of music. Her tone was frayed, but she tried to sugarcoat it, adding, "I want to feel like I'm all alone with you."

Obedient, Kendra left the room, and a moment later the wall of noise dissolved. When she returned she reported, "He was just going out anyway," and gestured for Lee to have a seat on the mattress. She made no effort to straighten the sheets or clear the clutter from the room.

Still, the silence was a balm, and Lee felt herself relax into it. The secret to seduction, she believed, was in knowing *where* to begin. She reached for Kendra's hand and pulled her to a sitting position on the bed, then nuzzled close behind her. She slid one elastic strap from a slender shoulder, the shoulder without the tattoo of a black widow, and kissed the skin where the strap had left a ridge, teasing it with her teeth. She traveled up the neck to the earlobe, tasting the salty tang on her lips and tongue, leaving gooseflesh in her wake.

Lazily, her fingers worked to untwine the skinny braid that snaked down the middle of Kendra's back, discarding the rubber band, untwist-ing the strands until fine ringlets hung to mid-spine, their jet color harsh against gold-tinged skin.

"You gotta let your hair go natural," Lee advised as her fingers wound through the curls. "I bet you're incredible as a blonde."

Kendra whirled to face her with a derisive snort. "You sound like my fucking mother."

It occurred to Lee that, since she was probably about the same age as the lady in question, she might do well to avoid the comparison. Still, as she ran her palm across the fine black bristles of short-cropped hair that covered most of Kendra's scalp, she couldn't help but muse, "I swear I just don't understand why girls don't wanna be *pretty* anymore."

"Where did it ever get us?" Kendra sneered, and swung her body off the bed. She began to peel the tight black skirt down her hips and over her thighs. She paused, glancing up. "Do you still wanna do this, or what?"

There was a hollowness in the young woman's question, a cheerful indifference that brought a stab of fear to Lee's belly, an icy finger of apprehension protruding into her spleen. She was quick to suppress it, shaking it off with a bemused toss of her head, nodding and coaxing, "C'mere. Let me do that for you."

Kendra allowed the skirt to drop around her ankles and carelessly stepped away from it, leaving behind its collapsed cylinder like a deflated tire abandoned at roadside. Lee's spirits brightened as the girl came toward her, a vision in the old-fashioned brassiere—one strap still slipped from her shoulder—and blood-red fishnet tights.

Kendra knelt on the mattress while Lee expertly released each of the twelve hooks that fastened the undergarment. As the corset fell away Lee caught the flash of silver—the hoop that pierced clear through the young woman's left nipple.

She found herself reluctant to examine it too closely; it made her a little squeamish even to think of it. Still, Lee cupped the breast in one hand and murmured, "That must have hurt."

"Yeah," Kendra agreed with a glint in her eye, her voice laden with feeling that Lee could not quite interpret.

She pulled the slender body on top of her own and tried to bury her uneasiness in the abandon of lovemaking. As Lee stroked the length of the girl's thighs, Kendra seemed cooperative enough, yet she remained strangely unmoved, some part of her elusive, distracted, almost inattentive. Lee liked it best when a femme was active in her response, not trying to gain control but fully participating in taking all Lee had to give.

But she didn't mind a challenge; she saw it as an opportunity to ply her considerable skill. Perhaps the young woman just didn't care for foreplay; maybe it was time to get down to serious business. Lee settled Kendra onto her stomach, then eased the fishnet tights down over the delicate hips. It was then Lee noticed the cluster of welts that covered the pale skin of the girl's ass, a crisscross of raised slashes, with the hue of an angry blush. With a finger she traced the path of one large weal and asked, "What happened to you?" She could not keep the horror from her voice.

Kendra half-turned, raised up on one elbow, and gazed at the older woman with curiosity. "I was at a party," she explained with patient matter-of-factness. "I guess things got a little out of hand. Usually the 'cats' don't make any marks at all."

As she spoke she fished under one of the pillows and produced the "cat"—a cat-o'-nine-tails. Its leather-covered handle was attached to nine leather strips, each about a foot long and knotted on the end. She proceeded to demonstrate its use by lashing lightly at her inner thigh.

As she observed Lee's dumbstruck expression, a sneer of amusement began to pucker Kendra's face; it was dawning on her that she had the power to shock this seemingly unflappable butch, and the fact induced in her both delight and contempt.

"It's how I like to fuck," she continued. "I thought you knew. I like it hard or I can't feel it."

A fissure was opening in Lee's chest, a tear that pressed with the weight of boulders and yet revealed a stupefying emptiness at its core. She longed to flee, lift herself up from this makeshift excuse for a bed and escape into the Manhattan streets, leave this fiasco behind. But Lee Bergman did not run from women, nor did she ever admit defeat in the lovemaking department.

Instead, she crafted a knowing smile onto her lips, and eased her body beside the young woman's. "So you like it hard, huh baby?" A cruel purr rose in her voice. "Well, I think we can do something about that."

With a forceful tug she turned Kendra over onto her back and wrenched apart her thighs. Savagely she pinched each nipple, willing to bruise, as the body beneath her began to writhe. She taunted, "Tell me how much you want it, baby," determined to make the girl beg.

Beg she did, and for a while Lee was caught up in the game of it, the sheer mastery she felt as she donned the brutal persona required to fulfill her part. She envisioned herself growing large with it, taller, her features more angular, chiseled, and ruthless.

But Kendra wanted more than just the play of dominance. It was not enough to be obedient to Lee's commands, for her wrists to be shackled with handcuffs, for her vaginal walls to be pummeled by Lee's taut fist, striking inside her again and again like a piston in a powerful machine. She wanted more than rough sex; she wanted clamps to squeeze her nipples to the color of raw meat, and the blister of hot wax spilled from candles against her tender skin. She wanted pain, sharp and immediate; nothing else seemed real to her.

"Harder," she pleaded, her voice breathy and raw with need.

"Hit me," she begged, and Lee raised her arm, palm wedged to strike. It was in the hand's trajectory from sky to the side of Kendra's face that the earth once more cracked open, and Lee felt the emptiness swallow her like death.

The hand did not make impact; its arc aborted, it swung dully to Lee's side and hung useless as she said, "I hate this. I'm sorry. It's just not sexy to me."

It was chilling, the ease with which Kendra recovered herself, the veneer of indifference returning to her eyes. "Wanna get me out of these," she suggested, nodding at her cuffed wrists, her voice vacant and flat.

Lee complied, her hands trembling a little as she fumbled with the key. She had the urge to talk about it, as if words might forge a rope to keep the connection, however fragile, but Kendra was closing like a fist, her jaw set, her gestures brusque, traveling away from her as if at the speed of light. The young woman did not look at Lee at all as she rolled beneath the sour sheet, pulling it tight over her body in a gesture that did not seek company.

Lee stood awkwardly, a bit unsteady on her feet. "I'm sorry," she said again and then, after her words were met with silence, "I guess I should be shoving off."

"Yeah, too bad," Kendra shrugged one shoulder, her face a brittle mask. "I thought we'd have some fun."

Once Lee reached the street, the sky was full of mist. It clung to her clothes and swirled gray above her head. She did not want to think about what had happened, wanted it to scab over quickly like a wound and leave no scar. She told herself the dampness of her cheeks was no more than the wet caress of fog. In vain she searched the dank, deserted streets for a taxi, then began walking briskly toward Chinatown, where she knew the streets would still be full of lights and traffic, and morning would still seem a long way off.

Sinner

ALISON TYLER

Wilt thou forgive that sin where I begun,
Which was my sin, though it were done before?
Will thou forgive that sin through which I run,
And do run still: though still I do deplore?
—John Donne

"You are such a naughty, sinful, little fuck, aren't you?" Jacqueline spits at me over the phone line.

I can picture her face as she says it, the sneer to her lips, the cold flame that burns in her eyes.

"Answer me, Alix."

I hold the phone with trembling fingers, but I don't respond.

There's a sigh, a hiss of air through clenched teeth before she continues, and now I know that she's shaking her head as she talks, shaking her dark hair in an ebony ring around her. "I could tell everything from the guilty tone in your voice. I knew the whole story before you even said her name."

Jacqueline's normally lazy drawl has become dangerously menacing. It's got an edge to it that lets me know just how pissed she is. "I'll be over in twenty minutes, Alix. You be ready for me. You be ready."

"Yes..." I start to say, but she's severed the connection, cut me off as cleanly as a sharp knife slicing through Jell-O. I've got as much backbone as Jell-O, so the image is appropriate. With my hand still holding the phone, I replay the conversation in my mind. Her words echo hollowly as I hang up the receiver.

I turn to stare at my reflection in the mirror over the antique hallway table, stare at the image of a sinful little fuck, sinful to the very core.

And Jacqueline knows it. She knows everything.

I play with the letters and coupons that litter the cracked marble table top. There are a few faded pastel petals from the last batch of wildflowers I bought at the Farmer's Market, and I scoop them up with a "Smog Alert" flyer and walk to the kitchen to throw them away.

Twenty minutes. Twenty minutes to transform myself. An impossible goal, so why even try?

In the kitchen, I lose myself for a long moment in the late afternoon sunlight that filters through my rice-paper blinds. The light makes shifting designs on the blue and white tiles around my sink, hazy shadows that are somehow comforting. I pull the cord to raise the blinds an inch or two, and stare out through that pale sliver at the grass that needs cutting.

Purple hyacinths, more weeds than flowers, are just beginning to poke their graceful grape-shaped blossoms through the grass. I stomp outside and pick a handful, then return to the kitchen to fill a vase with water. Who am I trying to appease—who would be fooled with a silly bouquet? Not Jacqueline. Why even try?

(Ten minutes until she comes.)

I bring the blue glass vase to the hall and place the flowers in front of the mirror, staring for another long moment at myself without seeing. Then I squint, staring harder, working to break through the fog that clouds my vision, and trying to picture myself through Jacqueline's eyes.

My hair is straight and golden brown, cut sharply in a bob that hits the line of my chin, razor-shaved in the back beneath the soft tresses. The style is exactly how Jacqueline likes it, feminine enough, with a bit of toughness to give me spirit, to let my real soul show through. My bangs hang in a perfect line over my forehead, the same as they have since I was in second grade. My eyebrows are blonder than my hair, and my eyes are green—bottle green when I'm serious, darker emerald when I'm afraid. Now they look as darkly jewel-toned as I've ever seen them.

Afraid of my lover?

Yeah—a laugh escapes me—I'm not ashamed to admit it. I should be afraid. Jacqueline is gonna.... No. Don't think about it. Don't worry about it. It's inevitable, so worrying won't do me any good.

My features are sharp, finely cut as if from stone. I have my father's strong jaw and straight nose, my mother's aristocratic high cheekbones. Bones from my ancestors that create the shell in which I reside. I have no real responsibility for my appearance, had no say in the matter. I control only with what I do to the surface, with the window-dressing, so to speak.

No makeup today. Nothing to give Jacqueline the impression that I was a flirt—which I was. That I was a sinful little fuck—which I was. No sense in adding insult to injury—my injury, of course. She'll escape this clean and unharmed. I'll be the one to wear her mark, her brand, her purplish bruises, like lipstick kisses, bleeding up and down my thighs, my ass, my lower back.

A shudder, a twinge, then I'm fine again.

Still in a daze, I go up to my bedroom to change, to rearrange the clothes that cover my slender body. Clothes are simply surface adornments. Jacqueline will see through any of my choices, and she'll strip me soon enough, regardless. But I do my best to choose the appropriate attire. Jeans are too rough. A sundress too "little girl" innocent. I settle on something that she bought me herself: a long silk skirt of periwinkle blue and a halter top that barely reaches my waist. When I move, when I turn at the sound of the door chimes ringing downstairs, the shirt floats over me, gossamer-thin and light, like the sunshine filtering through my blinds.

Back down the stairs before I'm aware I'm moving. To the door with nothing in my mind to say. Not, "I'm sorry," since she'll detect the lie in my voice, and she'll be ready with her classic answer: "You're not sorry now. But you will be." Not, "I love you," since she already knows it. And, anyway, Jacqueline and I don't love each other like that. Not in the classic sense. So there isn't really anything to say.

I open the door and bow my head, waiting.

Jacqueline enters without a word, backing me down the hallway, backing me with the simple, brute force of her power until I have reached the closed door to the living room.

"Little fuck," she says, a whisper-hiss, a sigh, the sound of skin sliding on skin in a dimly lit hotel room in a pensione near the East Village. "Little whore," she says next, a beat later, a rung louder. She uses both hands on my shoulders to push me through the door into the living room, and then grabs hold of my wrists and captures me, leading me like some dumb animal forward and to the couch.

I'm shoved down on my knees in front of her, while she seats herself serenely on the edge of the old red velvet sofa. My mind races with images: Jacqueline spanking me over this couch, dragging me over her lap, my legs kicking out and slamming against the wood rim with each blow; Jacqueline fucking me on this couch, my wrists tied and set on a pillow over my head; Jacqueline caning me on this couch, bending me over the rail and keeping me steady with her words alone.

Her left foot is placed roughly in my lap; on my right shoulder, the weight of her right foot, in its heavy boot, rests casually—a simple, though unnecessary, reminder of her power.

She shakes her head, her long black hair brushing against her cheeks. She and I both have eyes that change, a litmus test of emotions, easy to read for those who know the equivalency chart. I have noticed many times how dark her eyes are when she's angry, but this afternoon they seem darker still, coal-black, hollow or deep, glossy, like the polished malachite beads that traders use. Her skin is pale, but without the frosted look that many Mistresses have. My beautiful Jacqueline's is warmed from within by the heat of her power. It glows through her, it echoes inside her, and the fragments of light pour from her skin, her eyes, and burn me.

I bow my head to my chest, waiting.

"Just slumming, was that it?" The toe of her heavy workboot nudges my ear, prodding me. "Just out for a trick? A ride? A game?" Her words are switchblade sharp and they cut me; her tongue is fire-tipped and it licks at the edge of my wounds and makes me tremble. "Why do you do it, Alix?"

Again, so that I know, so that I can hear the taunting in her voice, the name of the song that she dedicates to me. She calls me her nympho, her bottomless pit, her fuck-toy. She says that I search the streets for love to fill an empty heart, that I use sex when I cannot find love, and that it works just as well. For a moment or two.

The sheets in the Hotel Meridian are powder blue and they crinkled like tissue paper when I lowered my lover to the bed. The pillows are thin, but I propped two under her finely-boned hips to raise them high enough. I wanted her to rise off the bed and meet the synthetic cock that was strapped to my waist. I plunged it inside her without checking first, but I knew she'd be wet. I could see it in her golden eyes. Could taste it in her kisses. Could smell it in the perfumed air that surrounded us both.

"Why did you do it?" Jacqueline says again. "Why do you need to confess. Why do you need to tell me? Huh?"

The cock teased her, and the feel of it, just gently pressing forward, made her moan and sigh, her eyelashes fluttering against her flushed cheeks. I worked her hard then, suddenly needing to see the change in her face as I thrust inside her, deep inside her. I pressed up on one knee, giving her the full length of the cock all at once. It's never felt like a part of me before. It's always been a tool I've accepted as necessary. A means to the end. But today was different, today I could feel her on it, could feel the trembling vibrations work through her body and into mine.

"Why do you need to confess?" Jacqueline asks again, the slightest bit louder. I can sense the displeasure in her voice, but I still do not answer her.

The girl was young, even younger than me. She was desperate with longing, it wracked her body, that need, brought her so quickly to the first climax, and then to the second, leaving her breathless and still hungry. How I loved her for that freshness, that purity. How I hated her for it, as well.

"Why, Alix?"

Because that's the part that makes me whole. Not the whoring, not picking up the girls in the Cafe Monet or in the shadowy alleys that back into the river. Not even watching their eyes light up when they see a handsome, finely-boned butch girl looking their way. Not peeling off my worn leather jacket, my faded jeans, the rough-shod boots I wear as if on a dare. Not even the cock that I pack inside those tight jeans springing free when I release it. Not any of that....

"You need the part that comes after, don't you?" Jacqueline asks, though she knows it's true. She knows it all—the routine, the answers. She's just teasing me, testing me, making me wait. "You need to put on the disguise, as if you're some butch girl, as if you're some boy-girl, and go scamming in the cafés for a bit of fluff. And when you're done, when you're satisfied, you call me up to wipe away the dirt and the sin. To put it all back together. That's okay, darling, that's what I do best."

Yes, it's the confessing.

The way I filled the young thing today, the way I gave her what she needed. That's what Jacqueline does for me. And still...

...I wish I had her power. Wish I could stand, as she does now, and undo the silver buckle from my jeans. Wish I could slide the black belt free from the loops, and use it. Use it. (Trembling. Slowly lifting off my halter at her request. Standing and dropping the skirt to the floor. Bending over the wood-railed sofa. Cringing as the belt finds my back once, hard, finds the tops of my thighs, the undercurve of my ass. Cringing as I see myself reflected in the mirror, the haunted look in my light eyes, the sin shining there, pure and simple.)

Wish I had the power, Jacqueline, to make it whole without you.

Her lips are tensed in a dark red line as she wields the belt. Her fingers grip the leather so tightly that her knuckles go white and bony. Her breath is ragged, but she never stops. Not until she's done—'til I'm done—not until it's over.

"Bedding those innocent little fucks, making them think YOU have the power."

Not crying. Not yet. She knows my limits, dances to the very edge and skirts away.

" 'Cause you like it, Alix. You need it."

In my jeans and leather jacket, I have a tiny spark of power. With that cock strapped to my body, growing warm from the slick heat of my body, I have a bit more flame. But nothing to compare to the bonfire that rages within the tight confines of Jacqueline. In her eyes, there is enough heat to burn me forever. In her heart, there is enough darkness to rule my world.

The belt finds my thighs over and over, finds the tender skin at the backs of my knees, the indents at the sides of my haunches. She is marking me well. It will be at least a month before I'll dare to go out again. Before I stand in front of my bedroom mirror, adjusting my cock, buttoning my fly, admiring the sheen, the gloss, of my hair against my skull.

How the girl liked to touch it, to stroke my hair as if it were animal fur, to pull on it while I worked her, while I fucked her. How she sighed and moaned and gave me up what I needed from her. Gave me all of her power. Power that Jacqueline happily takes away.

Crisscrossing welts of plum and dark burgundy stand out against my pale skin. Jacqueline stops to touch them, to pinch them, working now to get me to break. She wants to hear me moan, wants to hear me beg for mercy, but I will not give in. I grip the rail of the sofa tighter, drawing the muscles in my back into a taut line, offering myself to her.

"That's right," she says, reaching for the cane that stands in the umbrella rack by the door. "That's right, you need this. You'll take it."

She doesn't know. She thinks she does, but she doesn't. How lovingly I kissed that girl this afternoon. How I cradled her face in my hands as I made her come, how I licked and lapped at her mouth until it was bruised from my kisses. "Let me be yours," my new lover whispered, begged. What those words would do to Jacqueline—I do not know. I do not long to find out.

To be mine. The pale-faced woman could have no idea what it would mean. She possibly hoped for a spanking, a collar and leash set, a few rough moments followed by endless caresses. She did not have the filament burning inside her, the icy blue wire that lives inside me. She did not possess the need to submit, nor did she crave the pain. Pain, wondrous and consuming. At this point in my life, I have given up denying it. Given up wishing that I did not need it the way I do. Because I do need it. I do deserve it. And that is the biggest difference between me and the little girl I used for my pleasure...

She did not own the sin.

The cane lands on me and flames, like a living thing, against me. I stay still. "Count," Jacqueline says, somehow understanding how much I need this, how hard today was for me to bear. "Count the strokes for me," she says again, "Count them for me, Alix. Count them aloud."

"One," I say, as she makes me real.

"Two," a moan, my chin dropped low to my chest, my eyes closed tightly—that somehow makes it more bearable. Not seeing. Not staring at my feet, at the sofa, or (worse yet) at the mirror across the room. She'll force me to do that later, once I am fully marked, fully finished, she'll stand me and turn me and make me look back over my shoulder. Make me see myself.

"Three," harsh sob accompanies that number. Only three. Only three out of God knows how many. Jacqueline knows how many. She always knows how many strokes to take me there. It's never the same. There is no scale of equality—one encounter means ten strokes, another twenty. She'll use the belt only sometimes. Start with the cane others. It is never the same. For nothing is the same—no feeling, no need. Always changing, every shifting, like the colors of my eyes. The heat in hers.

"Four." Bitten off. My teeth digging into my bottom lip as I say it. I cannot recognize my voice. The rush of air behind it, the sound of power within it. Jacqueline hears it, too, and she knows (she knows) and I realize how long this beating will last. It will continue until that flicker of power is gone. She will break me. She always breaks me. It's as she said—what she does best.

"Five" is filled with impending tears. I have a high tolerance for pain, of course I do, but she is working the same area of flesh over and over.

Then a pause as she comes closer to inspect her work. It makes her proud, I can tell by the way she strokes the marks. It thrills her how closely she's lined them up, and I count them again as she touches each one. Her fingers, just that slight brush of the tips against my wounds, make me shudder. Oh, Jacqueline, take me there. Take me where I need to go.

A step back and "six" before I prepare myself. I stumble forward, losing my balance, but catch myself before I fall against the sofa. I will get two extra strokes for that, two more than infinity. I mean, she will tell me when she's reached my breaking point, and then she will take me two rungs beyond that. Can you imagine it? Your threshold...picture it...it's broken...you're a sobbing, crumpled heap on the carpet. You are nothing. But you're lifted, positioned, and forced to go beyond.

It's why I'm with her. It's why I'm hers. Because Jacqueline gives me what I need.

SEMIRAW

CORRINA KELLAM

I have a really bad habit of plucking out my pubic hairs. I don't pull them out of my labia, but off my lower belly away from my genitals where it is really painful. I wrap one or more around my index finger a couple of times and yank hard like I'm taking off a Band-Aid. It hurts like hell, especially when it takes a few tugs to get it to disengage. I want to do that to a woman with my teeth. In a perfect world, I'd find one with coarse hairs around her nipples and I could pull *them* out, too. The closest thing I can get to that now is to jerk my head when I'm going down on someone. The bridge of my nose bangs hard into her sensitive flesh leaving quarter-sized bruises all over her inner lips. The size and shape of the marks perfectly match my thumbs, so I can dig in again later and double the effect. I'm really good at pretending they are just accidents, that I was simply really turned on and couldn't control myself, that I didn't even realize what was happening. Eventually my lover will start getting edgy, progressively more nervous each time I go for her cunt. She'll get stiff like she's deep down afraid of what I'll do to her and she doesn't really want it enough to justify my consequences. That turns me on.

I didn't get far in my walk before I got distracted again. I keep watching a drugged-out tramp across the street. She hasn't moved voluntarily in the last half hour, but she's twitching like she needs a hit.

"Honey, you alright this afternoon?" Thank God for my low-pitched voice so I can pass long enough to get her attention. "You look like you could use a few grams of something wild. Why don't you come with me and I can fix you up."

She follows me in a skid row slink, a paranoid metered twisting of her body to keep an eye on what is going on behind her. She stays about

94

four feet behind me as I lead her down a few streets to an infested hourly-rented boarding house. I get a room in the back and promise to get out within three hours. The floor is sticky, littered with cigarette butts and shards from the smashed overhead light fixtures. The stairs creak and dip, and the handrail is busted, hanging defiantly from thick dull nails drooping obscenely out of wood. The door is secure. It leads to a small box of a room devoid of windows containing only a stained wet mattress.

I pull her in by the wrists and lock the door. The room is blank except for thin gray lines of light peeking in from the hallway. She doesn't say anything. I don't want to hurt her right off so I hesitate for a few seconds to keep my composure. I reach for her, pull her T-shirt up over her bulky black curls. She has small tight breasts. I massage her nipples while I guide her to the bed. She kicks her shoes off. Good woman.

At the edge of the mattress I take off her pants, tugging them down over her full thighs. She leans back to lie down. I grab her arm to keep her from collapsing, twist it around her back, her wrist flat below her shoulder blades. She groans but does not cry out. I drag my fingers up her thigh and push them violently into her cunt. I feel her flinch away from the small tears I'm making. I push her down on the bed and lean against her knees. I work my hand into her cunt, twisting my wrist to squeeze it in as fast as I can. She begins to protest. I punch her stomach hard with my other fist. She curls up, her muscles convulsing, and I finally get my hand inside her. I curl my fingers tight to make room and begin pumping, my wrist quickly drying up the little mucus she was producing, and then sliding more easily again as her body compresses with blood.

"Was that one pound or two?" I whisper.

I pull my hand out quick and put it against her face, her mouth, forcing her to taste her own cunt juice and blood. She squirms, clicking noises coming up out of her throat like she's going to throw up, then she bites me. I pull back, then lean against her throat straddling her. She coughs and thrashes while I push my thumb against her jugular, then she stops. I get up and check her pulse. She's fine, breathing softly. She'll just have one hell of a headache when they beat down the door in a couple of hours and wake her up. I drop the key on her chest and leave down the fire escape, dropping fifteen feet to the asphalt below.

My hands aren't too dirty. I knew there were chicks like that somewhere.

TOUCH MEMORY

MEG DALY

A few years after Alex's death, she started coming to me in the night. At first I thought they were dreams, then hallucinations. Mostly she would stand and smile at me. It was as if a warm breeze had filled the room. Then she'd disappear, slowly, like she was evaporating. One night, after I'd graduated college and moved to New York, Alex actually reached out and touched me, and that's when I knew it was her ghost, not my mind playing tricks. I'd started seeing a woman named Kirsten. I wasn't in love. Not really. But Alex didn't see it that way.

Alex grew relentless, appearing several times a week and always when Kirsten and I were having sex. That last night, Kirsten had just pushed me on my back, gripping my thigh with hers. I opened my eyes as Kirst was kissing my neck and there was Alex, naked and grinning. Alex reached and stroked my hair. Then she started to tease Kirsten from behind. Kirst rocked harder on my leg and I could feel her getting close to coming. She never acknowledged feeling anyone on top of her, but I noticed how her pace quickened as soon as Alex showed up. Kirsten cried out and Alex rose up to the ceiling. She stayed there, watching while Kirst nuzzled closer to me. My eyes pleaded with Alex—begging her to leave or bury herself inside me, I wasn't sure. The feeling of longing was the same. Then Alex blew a kiss and disappeared. I almost screamed after her. Kirsten must have felt my body straining because she reached between my legs. She just held her palm there at first. Desperately, I squeezed her hand.

"Oh so that's how you want it..." she said, and in one motion pinned my wrists over my head.

Kirsten shifted her hips, searching out my clit with hers. I sucked in my breath when she found it, and she began to rock side to side, until we were one motion. My body became a steady pulse, words like "please" or "no" welling up in my throat. I couldn't make a sound, though. I felt as if I was drowning. Parts of my body were breaking off and floating away. Kirsten was moving faster, pushing us both closer to climax. The solidity of her body pressing down on me left me nowhere to go but with her.

Then there was Alex again. Standing above me, blood covering her face and she was crying. She had her arms around herself, trying to hold in her insides. She'd come to me before like that, as if waiting by the side of a road. She would mouth my name and then slowly extend an arm to me. She was in so much pain, I could see it, and there would be nothing she could do to escape. Then I'm screaming and Kirsten is holding me. I break into a cold sweat and Alex starts screaming too. The whirling cloud comes and wraps around Alex like a sheet. She's spinning and all I see is blood. Then she's yanked away like a puppet and I've lost her. I lost her.

When I came to, Kirst had put a cold cloth on my face.

"Sweetheart," she said. Her eyes were a soft deep brown. "You're okay now. I'm here. It's safe." Then she said, "You can tell her not to come at moments like that."

And I wanted to say "I know." I wanted to say "You're right." But I couldn't form the words. Even if I could've made those sounds that translated into the absence of Alex, I didn't believe they could be true. That I could make her disappear just by wanting it.

I leaned into Kirsten and felt her soft breasts against me, and her thighs coming up under mine. I knew we would fall asleep like this, with her trying to shield me from my nightmares. But then that made me want to spit at her and shove her out of my bed. Couldn't she see what a skeleton of a human being I was? What was wrong with her that she'd choose to be with me?

I closed my eyes and slipped inside the river of myself. It was black and slick as oil. I shivered and Kirsten held me tighter. I was rushing to meet the ocean. Alex was there on her tiny boat with its splintering oars. She beckoned me and I'd spilled out into her ocean, like ink, I colored her waters, dissolving before she could reach me. *Alex give me your hand. I've turned as dark as night for you. I am spilling towards you. Do you see me? Do you see what I have become? It's all for you.*

I woke before Kirsten and slipped out of bed. I turned the shower on as hot as I could bear it. I let the water untangle my matted hair; as rivulets of scalding water snaked down the backs of my thighs. I rubbed extra conditioner into my scalp and methodically shaved my legs and armpits. I scrubbed the sweat and sex and night off of me, working the lather until I was practically chafing.

At breakfast, I downed two bowls of cereal, as we silently read the Sunday *Times*. After twenty minutes on the front page, Kirsten finally asked, "Beth. Aren't we going to talk about last night? Are you okay?"

"I'm fine."

Kirsten raised her eyebrows and made as if to protest. I jumped in, "I'm just like this. I get these nightmares and then they pass. I wake up the next morning, everything is still in its place, the world goes on as it always does. I feel fine. Really." I folded the Arts & Leisure section back into its original state, ironing it with my palms to make it look unopened.

"Beth! The way you talk about Alex—you sound like you can see her. Like she's in the room with us. I didn't bargain on a ménage à trois when we started seeing one another. Maybe if you talked to me about her, it would help. Help make her go away." Kirsten moved towards me, her robe opening at the breast.

"I don't want your fucking help!" I screamed and lunged at her. I felt the sting before I realized what happened—my hand on fire from slapping her. I felt like we were under water. I couldn't make myself move. Kirsten leaned against the door frame sobbing and gasping for air. I stood there, stunned, hating her, hating myself.

Kirsten stopped crying and glared at me. She kicked one of my old wood chairs out of her way, and bolted for the bedroom. The chair hit the linoleum with a crack. The echo settled around me the way a pond stills after a rainstorm. I heard her turning faucets angrily, then knocking things around the bedroom. She had to pass by the kitchen on her way out and I saw she was carrying her overnight bag and had a couple of sweatshirts I'd borrowed slung over her shoulder. She looked straight ahead, but I could feel her fury as if she'd shot me a final, nasty look. The door slammed and still I couldn't move. I stood there with my gaze fixed on the lime green paint peeling up near the heat pipe, listening to the catch and wheeze of my breath. All of a sudden I couldn't bear to look at anything. The stainless steel sink, the leaves outside, the blue pitcher full of peonies, the flyers stuck to the refrigerator—all of it shone with an unbearable intensity. My upstairs neighbor put on her Anita Baker album like she does every Sunday. I usually feel a sort of comfort in hearing her feet overhead and the muffled sweet voice from her stereo. But sounds of domesticity were excruciating in the wake of Kirsten's departure.

So I kept my eyes on the peeling paint. I started thinking about this game I played in junior high called Bloody Knuckles. A few of us, mostly girls, would sit on the crumbly sidewalk in back of the school. Someone would take a wide-toothed pink comb from her appliquéd back pocket and balance it carefully on top of her fist. Then somebody else would sit down opposite and put her fist against the first girl's knuckles, as if making a secret pact. That girl would try to grab the comb and whip its teeth across the other girl's knuckles before she had a chance to react. She'd shimmy her hand and give little false starts, but you couldn't pull your hand away until she really went after you. At the end of lunch period, we'd return to homeroom class grinning nervously, trickles of blood hardening between our fingers.

I looked down at my adult hands and noticed how like my mother's they are. The shape, the veins that pop out near the knuckles, the curve of the fingers, even the way they rest on a table. I pictured my hand cupping the back of Kirsten's head, her face pressed into my belly. I pictured my fingers undoing the buttons of her jeans. Then she was Alex and I was touching her for the first time, gingerly slipping my hand under her tank top, running my fingertips along the edge of her bra. Alex was sighing and I was moving my lips along her collarbone, searching out her nipple with my thumb. But these were my mother's hands. Was this my mother's touch? My mother who rarely touched me, not since I was small enough to lay on her lap for a backrub. I memorized the light breeze and strong grip of her fingers. I embedded those memories in my flesh.

What I had left of my mother's touch was stored in the hands she gave me, and was given in turn to my lovers. First Alex, then Kirsten, I smoothed their hair and stroked their arms like pressing the color from petals into one's palm. Touch was my mother's gift to me, yet what I wanted was something to give that was mine alone, not a memory of something missed, nor a continuation of someone else.

I didn't feel anything until it shattered. I must have found a wine glass, half-full of orange juice on the counter. I don't remember having been in the kitchen anymore—I was lost in the flakes of ceiling paint. My hand crushed the delicate glass, splinters gauged my skin and shattered at my feet. Blood welled up in my palm and ran down my wrist. The orange juice stung and made my whole arm even stickier.

I stumbled to the phone and dialed 911, barely managing to whisper the numbers of my address before I blacked out.

I'M SORRY

TRISH THOMAS

He's taller than you, twice your size. He's wearing tight blue jeans and thick black boots. His hands are big.

You know he's following you, but you don't speed up or cross the street. You don't try to get away.

He comes up beside you, wraps his arm around your shoulder, and lays the sharp point of a blade against your stomach. He whispers in your ear—*come with me* and steers you into an open garage. You smell old oil, gasoline, dust and the sweat under his arms.

He's rough with you. You knew he would be. You could tell by the way he walked down the street. It's what you wanted. It's why you're here, where you know you don't belong, where you think no one will see you. It's what made you drive past him, pull your truck over, and park. It's what made you get out, walk over to the pay phone, and pretend to make a call—so he could catch up to you.

He snatches a rag off a nail on the wall and ties it over your eyes. He shoves you all the way to the back and slams you, face down, onto the hood of an old Ford station wagon. He holds your hips and grinds into you from behind. Your nose picks up a familiar smell.

He reaches around you with both hands, rips open the buttons on your pants, and pulls them down to your ankles. No underwear. Your ass is bare. He spreads your legs with the toe of his boot and pulls a small leather harness off his belt loop. You feel him reach between your legs for your dick and balls. Ha. Fooled another one.

You love it when faggots think you're a boy, but he is not pleased. He grabs the back of your shirt with one hand and pulls you up to his face. Your feet don't touch the ground. He squeezes your crotch. It throbs

100

against his huge hand. You little fucking slut. You think it's funny that I didn't know. You don't move. You don't even breathe.

He drops you. You lose your balance and fall into him. The skin on his stomach feels warm against your face. You say, i'm sorry i'm sorry i'm sorry i'm sorry. He pushes you away. You fall backwards against the car. He yanks you upright by your hair and pulls out his knife again. Puts it up to your ear and pops it open. Drags it across your cheeks and over your lips. Your jaw drops. He runs the blade over your tongue. You jerk your head back. The tip of the blade nicks the roof of your mouth. You swallow your own blood.

He holds your head still and slowly pulls the blade out of your mouth. He scrapes it over your sternum, down past your belly. He grabs you between your legs and hacks off a fistful of wet hair. He rubs it between his fingers. He tosses it on the floor and spits on it.

He brings his blade up under the front of your shirt and makes a clean slice from the neck down to the hem. He turns you around and makes another slice down the back. Your shirt slips off your shoulders. Except for the pants around your ankles, you're naked. He leans forward and pins you down onto the hood of the car. One big hand on the back of your neck. Chips of rusty paint scratch your nipples. You know that smell from somewhere.

He unbuttons his jeans and lays his cock inside the crack of your ass. He backs off, pulls a rubber out of his pocket, and puts it on. Says it's for him, not for you. Says he doesn't want his dick to touch your slimy bitch insides. Says you make him sick. You love it that he hates you as much as you hate yourself. Cum drips down from your hole onto the crotch of your pants.

He spreads your cheeks and tries to push his dick into your asshole, but it's too tight and too dry. His dick won't go in, not even the tip. He gives up and jams it into your cunt, hard. You feel like you're ripping apart. You whimper. Smear sweaty fingerprints into the dust. He tells you to shut up. You say i'm sorry i'm sorry i'm sorry i'm sorry.

He slaps his hand over your mouth and pulls you up to his chest. Sweat drips off his forehead onto your face. You're what? You groan through his fingers. I'm sorry...daddy. He says, I told you to shut up bitch. You think I want anybody to know I'm fucking you?

Every time he pushes his cock into your cunt, your pelvis smashes into the side panel of the old wagon. Your legs are jelly. Your chest is scraped and raw. You feel bruises rising on your face. Your clit tingles. You wanna rub it with your hand, but you're afraid if you do, he'll stop. He doesn't want you to get off, he wants you to suffer.

He starts to groan like he's about to come, maybe he won't notice. You slide your hand across the hood of the car real slow and try to squeeze it between your legs. What the fuck do you think you're doing, bitch? He pulls both your hands behind your back and pins them between your shoulder blades. He takes off his belt and wraps it so tight around your wrists that your hand goes numb. He pulls your hips back into his groin and jams his cock into the bottom of your cunt. Your cervix aches. Your arms burn, half an inch more and they'll pop outta their sockets. Tears fill your eyes. You couldn't get away now if you wanted to. Do you want to? Maybe this time you've gone too far. What is that fucking smell? Is it...nah, it couldn't be. Oooh shit, you're really tripping now. You feel him pull out. Warm cum shoots onto the back of your neck and drips down over your shoulders. Ummm.

You hear his heavy boots thump across the concrete floor, away from you. Then...nothing. What, is he crazy? He can't just leave you here like this. What time is it? You gotta get back. You've probably got just enough time to get back home before...oh. Oh, good, here he comes, he's coming back.

That's what you think.

You think the front end of the car drops down from the weight of his body. You think you hear him flick open his lighter, inhale, exhale, snap the lighter closed. You think he grabs the knot on your blindfold and pulls your head up. You feel the lit end of his cigarette under your nose, almost touching his lips. You freeze. Your head drops with a thud.

You think he's behind you again, standing between your legs, flipping you over onto your back. Your elbows dig into the warm hard steel. You try to stand to take the weight off your arms, but he slings you back and pushes your legs up over your head. That's what you think. You think it's him holding your feet in the air, bracing himself, and slamming his dick into your asshole twenty, thirty, fifty, maybe a hundred times.

At first you screamed, begging him to please stop, please. Now your lips move, but no sound comes out. It feels like his dick is in your throat. Your asshole is on fire. Your intestines explode. Shit and blood everywhere. You're wasted. You can't see. You can't think. You can't move. You can't even feel your own body.

Hands. On you. Somewhere. You're falling. No. You're rolling. Now you're on your belly. The belt is off. You can feel your fingers. You can feel your arms. You're rolling. You're on your back again. The blindfold is gone. You see stars, shadows, something moving, the shape of a face right in front of yours. Focus. Two eyes drill holes through to the back of your skull. Oh, shit it can't be. It couldn't be. No. Yeah. Yeah, it is. Fuck. She's supposed to be at work.

You wonder how long she's been onto you. All these years and you never knew she could be so mean. You say, i'm sorry i'm sorry i'm sorry i'm sorry, maybe you even mean it, but it's too late, she's gone.

You pull yourself together as best you can. You stand, trembling. Pull your pants up and button them. Fumble in your pockets for a cigarette. A sharp pain shoots through your colon like a hot poker. You double over, gag, heave, nothing comes up.

You stumble out to the street. The morning sun stings your eyes. You open the door of your truck and climb up behind the wheel. You put your key in the ignition, start the engine, release the hand brake. You're sobbing, shaking, snot runs down your mouth. You look at yourself in the rear-view mirror. Your face is black and blue and smudged with soot. Your lips are cracked and crusted with blood. You swear this is the last time and wipe your nose on the back of your arm. Shift. Pull out. Drive slowly down the street.

Outta the corner of your eye you spot another one in the alley, leaning. One leg up, a bottle resting on his crotch. You pull over.

DYBBUK

ROBIN PODOLSKY

The first thing I knew was darkness.
I mean, I knew it was darkness and I was in it.
I had been elsewhere for a long time.

I could see perfectly,
her skin shining under the moon like stone.
It was her smell that drew me to her.
First I was seeing, then there was perfume that made me hungry, so I
had a mouth and a swollen tongue.
I was still the barest trace of flesh, rocking on the night breeze over her
bed. Then she moved; a shudder, a wriggle.
My body grew back, wanting.
When I remembered I had nipples they were already hard and my cunt
was hard on top and drooling below.
Just under the ceiling, I crouched in darkness. I grew heavy with flesh
and hunger for flesh until I began to descend, arms and fingers curved
to enfold, my legs open like a frog.
Nipples touched nipples and I felt her bush crackle as I crushed it with
mine.
I licked sweat on her temple and she sighed wet into my neck, drinking
my skin. She whispered my name and I knew who I was.

Na'amah.

The forest night breathed in her hair.
Creatures with shining eyes waited for me there and I dove in to meet them.

104

Her hands finished me, making my form as they found power in touching. I was her discovery, her creation, such delight she took in the long road of my torso, such a leisurely journey of lips and tongue and teeth. She gave me her kiss of fire, I whispered secret names into her mouths, with flaming tongues we wrote magic words between each other's thighs.

And now, they say she has a *dybbuk*, is possessed. Now she will never marry. She will never cut her hair. Every night she calls me, summons me with all the power of my forbidden name,

> *Na'amah,*

and I ride to her on the wind. No window can shut me out.
She eats no food.
Her body will die.
If she were someone else, perhaps she would climb out the window and meet me in the wood. Perhaps she would wear men's clothing, a peddler free and easy, roaming from village to town, making young girls dream and married women leave their own windows unlocked. Some of the girls I visit end up that way. Not her. A blessing in her father's house, her mother's pride and support. Such a nice girl. The best she can do is starve and stare, her eyes larger every day, gleaming black fire against skin white as the moon.

The rabbi litters the room with charms. He rocks for hours, bellowing prayers. He calls and calls for me. He wants to wrestle, but I'm not interested.

Every night she shudders pale against my skin. We have each other to eat and drink, she doesn't want her mother's cooking anymore.

She whispers my name. *Na'amah.*

I whisper stories of how it will be. We will be perfume on the wind, shadows under moonlight and no window will keep us out.

BIRD

MARIAN ROONEY

We had been travelling for what seemed like days. The sun hadn't moved in the sky overhead and the barren land had barely given way to a sparse covering of parched trees which clustered occasionally as if to promise the fringe of jungle towards which we were eternally headed, though perhaps never destined.

The heat and the hint of humidity made everything cling. I wondered when the dust would settle. I felt my clothes weighed down by it, the lines in my face etched deeper. The pristine linen in which I'd left Mexico City now hung in wilted creases about my arms and legs, furled like an old morning glory; I was afraid to remove my jacket. The bus churned on.

I rode with perhaps twenty women, every one of whom appeared to be in mourning. Their burned faces ranged from plump and shiny to startlingly mummified, yet each rose from a festoon of black which was suffocating to my eyes. An old woman behind me had placed an enormous bird's cage on my seat next to the window whilst she filled the seat adjacent to her own with an aromatic hamper of corn and ripe tomatoes, as well as some sprigs of green whose leaf I didn't recognize, but whose fresh scent offered a halo of relief from the heat.

The black wire cage contained a motionless, headless bird. Its swaying perch gave an illusion of animation, but after beginning the journey with a prolonged scrutiny of its dirty white torso and yellowed nails, which clasped the rail with the only hint of intense life, I was overcome by a mixture of nausea and foreboding, and had spent the intervening hours looking beyond the silent faces of the women, out into the monotony of the country slipping by me. Now I lowered my head into my hands and let my mind drift.

I had set out by train from New York five days before, only to arrive in Los Angeles to be told that Anne had never travelled north as her note suggested. It couldn't be described as a letter; even those had contracted into something just short of hieroglyphics by the time I'd decided to book passage from Southampton, and now I found that my deciphering too was unreliable, that any means of communication crumbled in my hands like old wiring in an abandoned home.

I had urged her to leave London while boats were still setting sail. My mother had made inquiries through the Orphanage of Our Lady of Perpetual Sorrow and had secured a certain welcome for Anne in a small town on the peninsula of Yucatan, where she would work in a sister orphanage until things improved at home, or until I came to fetch her.

She was beautiful that morning, wisps of escaped hair whipping at her face from beneath her brim as I handed her off to the ship's steward. Until a few days ago, I could easily conjure the smile she threw back to me from the deck, her lips a perfect, ripe curve in her bright face—but now I tried to shake a dizziness from my senses which obscured and distorted that mouth, peeled back from yellowing teeth, her eyes shining with too much light.

Only when dusk began to fall did the bus slow and turn from the endless dirt road toward the sounds of a small village. One stop was scheduled between the city and the town of Tulum, our destination, and I now saw without seeing that this would signal the end of savanna, and that the jungle would at last engulf us.

From the little depot, and through the dust kicked up by the halting bus, there emerged another black clad woman, this one about forty, trailed by four children, the eldest a girl, the three sleepy stragglers all boys. The mother stepped into the bus first and settled into the last remaining bank of seats. Two boys squeezed in beside her and she hoisted the third and smallest onto her dark lap; only then did she turn her attention to the stranded daughter swaying in the aisle of our idling bus. Gazing languidly from place to place her eyes fixed on me. "Mira," she said, jerking her chin in my direction. I glanced sideways and thought to place the birdcage on the floor, but as I reached for its handle my hand was clasped by the blotched claw of the old woman behind me. I turned, startled. Despite the rot of her teeth her smile was strangely sweet as she shook her head, and I relinquished the cage, staring into her odd, familiar eyes.

"Mira!" came a more insistent call from the mother to the girl. Gingerly she came forward, looking at me with both apprehension and embarrassment, then she gestured toward my lap and I realized that, as the lone man—and sole adult under forty—I was considered by the multitude of staring faces to be the only appropriate accommodation for this young woman's journey. To cover my own confusion I made a grand, sweeping glide of my hand across my lap, the attempted gallantry ending in an unintended thump to the cage, eliciting at last the missing, crested head of the squawking cockatiel—the women laughed. The girl turned and seated herself, and now the women smiled in approval and the driver, throwing the bus into gear, called out with worn cheer, "Vamanos."

The evening air was warm and the light from the sultry sky had turned a darkening gold, ebbing towards night. There was a scent of night blossom in the bus and I began to inhale deeply becoming intoxicated by the heady fragrance. I closed my eyes and it seemed my senses opened; gradually I began to distinguish the smells of the corn, the herb, the flowers and the flesh of the girl. Slowly lifting my lids, I gazed at the quarter profile turned to me. Her hair was dark silk, bluntly cut at her shoulders like a child's, but her cheek had a hollowing that bespoke the woman—I guessed she was fifteen or sixteen. I breathed in the warm sweetness of her skin as it rose from her neck and clavicle. Her arms were braced gently against the seat in front and I followed their upper curve, elbow to shoulder, in the last of the evening glow. And I didn't scruple, but naturally allowed my mind and eye to follow the luscious concave between her shoulder and chest before the swell of her new breasts, one of which was easily seen through the gaping armhole of her hand-me-down dress. As I watched, she turned her face slightly to me and laid her head down on her arms. I didn't move my eyes.

The boxy, cotton dress fell forward and I could see the weighty undercurve of her breast and the perfect red berry of her nipple. I felt alive in my body. I swallowed the last of the dust in my throat and my tongue ventured out to moisten my lips which parted in a new thirst. I wanted to lick that sweet berry, to circle it with the point of my tongue and then swathe the round of her breast with a wet, flattened stroke—even though the very bloom of her skin made mine feel like sandpaper, my tongue a cat's rough caress.

She shifted her weight slightly as the bus chuntered through a turn, and my hand rose up despite myself to steady her hip. The course straightened but my arm didn't fall back to my side. Without opening her eyes, she smiled. The road grew darker as the trees and foliage became more dense and a chill edge came to the air. The driver turned on dim overhead lights which flickered incessantly and were greeted by routine groans of protest. It was as familiar as a pantomime back home, and his exaggerated shrug as he flicked the lights back off was a staged black out.

In the cool darkness she moved sleepily closer, twisting at her slender waist so that her face lay against my chest. Her hair smelled of rain; I let my lips press against it. My hand still rested on her hip and now I allowed it to slide down over the curve of her bottom. She straightened her back and her breasts grazed my torso, her chin settled into the notch of my neck, her breath warmed my skin. Her drowsy arms reached up to circle my shoulders as if to secure a sleepy purchase. The bus was silent, there was an easing of old bones and then movement ceased; inhalations and exhalations grew heavy and regular. I let the air surround me.

I wanted to eat the soft brown lobe of her ear. I wanted to put my mouth over every part of her body. But I held still, breathing, letting the flesh that coincided with mine tell me what it could of her hard, dark nipples driving into my chest, of the two, almost sharp buttocks nestled against my groin. I imagined my thumb, wetted, running smoothly along her thigh and up under her loose dress, discovering her breast and crushing the cupped flesh, depressing the tip in a delicious inversion, and dragging down again, across her belly, dallying at the dip of her navel, catching at the top of her panties, dragging them too toward her softest self. She moved against my hardened penis. I felt her lips compress against my neck as one arm slipped from my shoulder to her lap. Reaching between her barely parted legs she touched me, her two fingers stroked the length of my shaft through the creased linen. The air burned in my nostrils. I felt her begin to tug at the buttons of my fly and, my hands about her waist, I raised her slightly so that she could free me. Her head never stirred from my shoulder, her body did not betray the least movement; only her hand, in small stealthy actions, delivered my erection to the cool, smooth antechamber of her closing thighs. They felt like marble, they felt like silk; I rocked my pelvis slowly, entwined by these inviting columns. She barely moved but I could feel her strong legs holding me. Her tongue drove into my neck, her mouth opened and closed again over my wet skin, her lower teeth scraped its surface. To remain still and silent seemed impossible; I raised her again and she curved her back, bringing her left leg over my lap; with her right thumb I felt her draw aside her gusset while her forefingers encircled my penis, placing the head inside her sweet, wet and swollen labia. With her knee on the seat beside the bird, she kept me there. I wanted to buck the length of me inside her. The muscles of our necks were rigid, our heads locked against each other in a brace of motionless tension. She lowered herself onto me; every pore prickled sweat, I crushed her buttocks in my hands as I came immediately inside her pulsing cunt. My empty throat was raw, my eyes rolled back.

The girl was gone, my fly was done and the bus had all but emptied when I opened my eyes. The old lady was reaching across my crumpled person to fetch her caged bird. I averted my gaze but she needed help to lift it around me; I stood and hauled it out from the window seat, handing it to her. Once again our hands met as she took the bird, her bright eyes turned up to mine and shone. I stepped first from the bus and handed her down to the steady ground of Tulum.

The morning air tasted sweet and I walked a dustless street, disheveled and content. When I saw a woman walking in the distance, I had almost forgotten that a journey has a purpose. Her fair hair fell down past her shoulders and she wore a huge and colorful dress, the skirt scattered with great red and orange blossoms.

"Anne!" I called. She didn't turn. I quickened my pace, "Anne!" A slight young man walking in the opposite direction touched her arm just as I was about to call again. "Anita," he said, and she smiled to face him, her skin burnished, her red lips shining. He pointed Anne toward me and her brows raised in amusement as she turned to the transformed and transported sight of me. I waved.

"Anita!" I called.

LUCKY GIRLS

NANCY STOCKWELL

Several years after the calumny, Barsi—Barcelona Celdoni, the musician, the violinist—worked very hard at writing fiction. She thought this might keep her from losing her creativity after she was unable to play the violin. God knows she tried so hard, every which way possible, to play the violin with three fingers, even going so far as to have a violin made and strung for the right hand. She asked me to help her with the fiction because we've been friends so long (and because I've had some success in getting my ideas published). Barsi wrote by using parts from her journals, but it was the same thing over and over. Her stories, if you could legitimately call them that, were always about stifled love, love in a narrow, confined world, love constricted by too many eyes, love in the spotlight, love always monitored, but love watched by less than blissful eyes.

Barsi intended to write fictional accounts of one thing or another but these stories always ended up as wild attempts to describe the sadness in her own innermost places. She always managed to look back upon a compelling joy attached to the same female singer and spoil the plot. Finally I realized her writing would never be anything more than love letter upon love letter to Cernya: Cernya Rossini, her lover, the singer who captivated us all, the one for whom the word *Diva* was coined.

You may know me. I am Muyhi. Al-Amin Muyhi, the philosopher and friend who loved Anna, the sister of the man whose violence changed all our lives. A dreadful crime. So dreadful, it was called a crime against the nation.

I remember a night in Florence just before Barsi and Ceryna went to the Mahgreb. They went to my place there, to my house. (It makes me poor to keep it now but I would rather die than give it up. So many of my friends have visited this house. It is a sacred place, I feel, because we have all been there.) That night Barsi and I had a buoyant conversation about love letters, a conversation much aided, I should point, out by a bottle of metaxa, the sweetly laden scent of frangipani, and the moon which leisurely lit up shadows in the courtyard as we talked. I remember Barsi saying, "When passion and need illuminate our little speck of dust, then we seem bigger to ourselves, almost out of place, oversized in the known universe and that is when the muse visits. You do not feel her until you grow big yourself!" We laughed at this.

The known universe! It was one of Barsi's favorite expressions. It made me think of her as an explorer, not just a musician or a person of the theatre or an ordinary like the rest of us, which she was. Cernya called down to us that she was coming to join us and not to utter another word until she could hear it all. She loved to hear us both play at being philosophers. We waited for Cernya, pouring a little more metaxa in each glass. When Cernya sat down, she kissed Barsi on the cheek and when she did the same to me, I could smell the soap and the musk lotion.

Barsi was going on about love letters: "We are compelled to explain this sense of importance, this over-size, this uncomfortable stellar position, as much to ourselves as to our lover. Perhaps all love letters are from someone who is in desperate need of explaining herself; love letters come from the woman in all of us whether the writer is technically male or female, but there is especially passion when the lovers are two women. Do you know why, Muyhi? No? Because being outside the bounds of expectation, we astonish ourselves. We feel so different, we must explain the difference; we feel so distant from others, we must explain light years. Since there is no conventional wisdom, we feel we're onto something incredibly profound. Am I being profound?" she laughed.

"It is easy to be profound on a night like this...when Mother Nature wears such a revealing dress," I remember saying, thinking how soothing the night was—and the metaxa and the frangipani!

"It is much simpler playing the violin," Barsi told us. She stretched her legs out before her. She had tall boots on that night, made of chocolate-colored leather. I wondered where she had got them. They looked expensive. She had on brown pants of a heavy cloth, which made her thin frame look more ample. "Violin playing is so simple: you keep an eye on the maestro, you wink seductively with all your heart at the singer and then you just play the notes bound to the completion. I thought at one time that it helped to look dramatic when I stood to play, but that's what got us into this dilemma, isn't it?" she said, turning more serious. She took Cernya's hand.

To understand the journal entry which follows, the one I have chosen to begin the biography of all of us, you must keep in mind that in the winter of 1894, Barsi and Cernya traveled to Africa in order to have some peace and quiet, to find a conducive atmosphere in which to make a decision about their lives, that being: whether to move from Turin to Florence and accept Maestro Prieto's deal. So it is an important place to begin. You will decide whether the change in residence made any real difference. I believe the thing could have happened wherever they went. I believe it was set in motion long ago.

Barsi and Cernya felt that they could not possibly make such an important decision with all the nonsense happening at the opera house; the Maestro's proposition was too disturbing. He wanted Barsi to wear a dress when she played! Good God! I could not even imagine it when Barsi first told me. Barsi was one of the finest looking women I had ever seen and when she wore men's evening clothes...well, how shall I say this? To be polite: it made one feel alive! Certainly they wanted to escape to think clearly. In truth, I know that deep down they wanted to make greater sense of their positions. Don't we all? They were living under a disguise; they might always have to live under a disguise. Both of them perhaps needed to touch the very quickness of their being in order to re-surface and face the disguise they would live if they took the new positions in Florence. But you decide. It is from Barsi's journal that we find the following entry describing their time in Africa. This is what she wrote in the winter of 1894. It is quite naked, I warn you.

The Mahgreb

We have been on the beach most of the morning. I am reading several chapters of Muyhi's manuscript which he has sent along with me. I also have my journal with me and have good intentions to keep a strict record of what Cernya and I do each day, (though I wrote nothing the first two days!)

It is easier to read Muhyi's fiction than it is to go through the simple process of listing facts, pro and con, in order to come to a decision. Why? Because a writer gives us hope of getting the total of life into perspective. A list is more like a silhouette. Making this decision gives me terrors! It gives me the feeling of being out of my body, and sometimes when I am alone, it has made me shake and curl up like a baby.

In the beginning, Muhyi's story is very compelling because it would seem that he has written a mystery. We believe only important things keep a mystery in them, do we not? Like life and death. And so I read on; I rush to put myself in the middle. Everything would be simpler if we did not strive for immortality. But then, of course, stories would be useless because seeing ourselves in them wouldn't matter at all!

I am so comfortable here in my nook on the beach, leaning against the soft, yellow dunes which are situated between the ocean and the plain where Muyhi grew up, his manuscript in my lap. He told me before Cernya and I left for this retreat, "Heaven knows if you'll have time to read this—sex can make nights so short! And hot days always fill themselves up with strange friends when you travel to Africa—but take this with you anyway. Please have a good time in my house." He kissed me on the cheek. Then he held me out from him and told me: "Stop worrying. You will come to a good decision. Love asks specific things of each of us—that is why I have given up trying to say what love is. Now I only write about scenery. See if I have described my birthplace well enough or how much I have lied for the sake of the story."

I must have looked distracted and somewhat downhearted because he said, true to his heritage, his birthplace, "Remember one thing: whatever the decision, Allah inspires it."

This last gave me little comfort as my problem with Allah is that Allah meddles only in what Allah fancies. That does not make life fair. Perhaps we are truly modeled on divinity. A divine being with the power of creation, creates what he needs in order to see his reflection (even women such as Cernya and myself, if we think highly of ourselves). So to live without mirrors is a curse from which even God rebels.

That is why Cernya and I have come on vacation. To figure out what it's worth to us to live without mirrors. That, and to experience the rather adolescent thrill of being alone and being free.

Cernya spent most of the morning at the table under the yellow and white shade cloth. Either she was there or she was back and forth, dangling her feet in the mosaic pool or pacing into the house for more oranges and that thin, crisp, peppered bread. She brought out a feta cheese with the bread and we had a truly gorgeous coffee with it for breakfast this morning. But too much cheese. It is bad for her voice. But she knows that. I don't need to tell her.

I must practice my part today. My part needs going over alone a few times. No, I'll put it off until tomorrow. Today is too beautiful for work. I can rarely act on a whim like this, putting off work. So I am completely on vacation!

Cernya is dragging a lounge chair through the sand. I guess you might call it a lounge chair. The seat is made of a blue-green canvas, the color of the water here. The canvas is looped between two wooden poles on a scissors-like folding frame. Very European in design. Modern Italian things give this feeling now, too. Simple lines. And the rounded edge is very much in style now. The rounded edge must be where East meets West because the oriental designers have always used it. Set designers who come to Florence make all the edges round no matter what piece we're doing. The Italians love it. Curved edges are sensual. It gives the set a gentle appearance and yet one always knows where the edge is, the last moment of solid ground, over which we could all slip so easily. That brings delicious fear. The thing drama depends on. We play with it every night in the opera house. In Spain they have bullfights. On an afternoon they put a man in the ring and face him with death. In Italy we are much more to the point. We put love on the stage every night and make it face a woman!

This act of condensing the conflict into music every night is Cernya's business—and mine too, after a fact. I always wonder if living this intensely will reverse on us? I always wonder if we'll pay for it. Live by the sword, die by the sword. Live by the drama, die by the drama? It bothers Cernya when this pessimistic side of me comes out. I don't know why I have it, except that my father constantly warned me about the reverse side of every coin, until all the fun was taken out of things. Isn't it strange to instill guilt in a child? Was I so unruly? Would I need such protection? What would it take to remove this feeling? Ah, well that's a topic for another day, perhaps.

For most of the day here on the Mahgreb, Cernya has stayed under the umbrella of the shade cloth and studied her libretto. She did not sing or hum, even briefly. She studied the pages, sometimes tapping a pencil on her thigh, sometimes on the pages. I know she is far away in her thoughts because she usually hums it out. When she tapped on the pages, it echoed to me like a tiny drum.

I have my things spread out on a dhurrie rug. I have a blue and white china water jug, a vial of oil, Muhyi's story, some playing cards, my score, and my journal. I brought everything I would need for a week but instead I watched Cernya. Though I tried to appear to be reading. One lover always knows when the other is watching, even when there are miles in between. So I was silly to pretend differently. This decision—it has caused a small chasm between us which appears and disappears. There is tension it in, for we do not know what lies ahead. Once she kissed me from where she sat, making a sullied gesture with her mouth and then she stared at me with an exaggerated look of need—to show me that she was aware that I was watching her. I didn't go over to her and throw her down in the sand because we're supposed to be working—and dwelling on our own thoughts. When her gesturing became too much for me, I looked over my shoulder to the house, letting the intense reflection of the sun glaring off the whitewash blind my eyes, in defense of that boundary in me which she is able to cross so easily. I was relieved when I looked back at her again and saw that she had gone back to her music.

When I looked back to the house, I saw Xenia, our maid. She was draping our new towels over the rounded, white edge of the little balcony on the second story. They are the new white towels we had used early this morning after we had bathed and made love. We made love outside in the small tiled pool on the east side of the house. Xenia found the towels in the sand near the sago palm. She must have just washed the towels, though they were not soiled.

The sun is so white today that I must try very hard to remember the exact pastel colors of this morning. This desert sun can wipe out memory by noon! As I caught Xenia spreading the towels to dry, I watched her shadow give them contrast and I watched as the towels became a dense, whitish pink in her shadow. It is eerie how just a shadow in the desert can change the color of a thing, or return color to it, like giving the blind sight again. No wonder these people are full of foreboding. No wonder that they thrive on change and suspense.

The new towels are of a fabric we discovered our first day here in the market. They call it Turkish toweling. It is rough and easily absorbs water and oils from the skin and hair. Cernya bought a long piece of the fabric from one of the sellers, for a price I thought was extravagant, but she is the Diva now and I know what she thinks: that by giving money away she can, just for the moment, touch the fleeting part of fame. She won't be romanced by spending for spending's sake for very long. I know Cernya. She is quite thrifty. When we came back to the house, she cut the long piece into three lengths. I told her I hoped we were not expecting company.

"Well Xenia deserves one, too," she said. I put my arms around her and kissed her cheek. I saw her sensitivity in a spot of color which had surfaced on her clear, soft, tan skin. I wanted never to live without her and I felt the energy in me begin.

Muyhi says that a good lover is transformed into a great lover only by attachment to a wise and generous heart—even if it is only for one night! I remember him smiling like a fox after he made this observation.

Cernya rubbed me hard with the new towel and I felt new sensations on the outermost surface of my skin. How can the most superficial level of existence remind you of the depth of your feelings? I don't understand this part of life. Perhaps the truth of the matter is that I am not as deep as I hold myself out to be! I must remember to ask Muyhi what he comprehends on this subject. He is much smarter than I. He is a better philosopher. But he also puts much practice into the craft of it. Well, I am smart enough to memorize a treble clef and sensitive enough to know how best to play the notes for the most provocative singer in Italy. So I, too, practice my aesthetic! Much of it in private! Unlike Muyhi, I get paid for doing it. It is my job to illuminate the singer and the composer. And to embellish their talents.

Cernya has gotten completely enthusiastic about discovering this new fabric. We don't have these kinds of towels in Turin yet. Cernya says she believes the Greeks have fabric like this but that for some reason the Italians have missed it. I tell her that we are too busy singing about ourselves, and too busy coloring the story this way and that. We are the wastrels of romance. But what else is there? It is the life we were given, to do with as we please.

The first day we were lying in the cool room beside the updraft tower because we had not adjusted to the heat when we first arrived. We talked and tried kissing but it was much too disagreeable for that. In a way, the kissing felt like a distraction from confronting our decision. I thought the conversation which took place instead was rather ridiculous. I don't remember how we got to this point but...

"The Italian idea of a compliment is to possess a thing," Cernya said.

"You think I am so weak?" I replied. I felt abruptly patriotic, as if she were referring to my heritage.

"No, not you. I feel safe with you. Perhaps because we have discovered that we are equals. Though that took some time; you thought you could out play anyone," she reminded me. "The fact is that you, my dearest wild, maddened heart, possess the wild side of power. You understand what is between the lines. I find that irresistible."

I tremble when she says things like that. I've never known a woman who could do this to me.

"I am only an embellisher," I tell her.

"You have saved me from a frugal, hard life, a life where all the emotions soon become misers. But never mind all that now," she said and kissed me hard on the mouth. I kissed her even harder but she stopped abruptly.

"Did you know my mother was Turkish?" She looked at me with a very serious expression. "I never told you that? Ah, then possibly I never told you that she had an affair with Shubert."

I have known Cernya six years, well six years and two months—we met in the fall of 1888 in Turin, not far from where we live right now. It seems odd not to know everything about her by now. I thought both her parents were Italian. I thought that explained what the papers now call her "Mediterranean fire." Her hair is dark and curly. Her nose is thin. So I suppose it could be true.

"Is that right," I say. "And I suppose you are a little quarter note in one of his sonatas?"

"Don't be ridiculous, Barsi. Everyone knows that Shubert was a woman."

I stopped dead still for a moment—until I realized that she had taken me. Finally I said, "And how does one know that?"

"They listen, my darling. They listen!" She laughed, enjoying her joke.

"So I wonder how your mother ended up in her arms then? Was your mother also deaf or was she as queer as you? Perhaps it's in your blood."

"My mother," Cernya began, "before she had to jump into the sea and swim from Turkey to save her neck, met Shubert who happened to be on vacation. Shubert was in her usual disguise—as a man. My mother was attracted to him and she was very surprised, of course, to learn the truth. My mother wrote me only one letter in her whole life and in it she advised me to at least make sure of the sex of an attraction before proceeding with anything else."

"Oh I cannot believe anything you say, Cernya. When your mother left Turkey, when she jumped into the sea, to where did she swim?"

"To Lesbos."

"Puuh, what a story. Ridiculous," I laugh.

"You think so? Go look on a map. It is the closest shore."

"Perhaps that is where we will end up, too. In the sea. Trying to save our necks. Cernya, we must decide if we will go to Florence or not."

"Have some feeling, love. We have just gotten here."

I have learned so much from Cernya, more than I think most women are ever lucky enough to learn from a lover. From men you learn nothing. At least not about yourself. I know I have an unusual relationship. Unusual sexually and, consequently, unusual in so many other ways—which seems to be a confusing circle to me at times. With Cernya, my experience has been to have questions and then to realize from her that I have always known the answers. Perhaps I already know the answer to the dilemma.

I do not discuss our sexual relationship with my friends: Carlos, Bette, Nadia, and only very generally with Muyhi who seems compelled to tell me nearly everything about his circumstances. I find I am proud and embarrassed by certain things all at the same time. A certain shy-ness washes over me when I think of the way Cernya and I express our physical needs. I am proud that it gives each of us so much pleasure and that I have had the courage to explore it. We know each other inside out: that is the armor I wear in the world. The secret familiarity between us protects me. What we do, we do because it makes us happy. It is our fate, I believe, to be women who can love one another.

Perhaps it is a lover's allegiance which protects the other. Cernya might fault other people, and sometimes does, but if you are in with Cernya, you are in. She has a fierce sense of allegiance. I believe I have it, too. Cernya says that liking to talk to each other is itself unusual. She says it is the ultimate intimacy to be fearless to say what you feel—and you can only be fearless when you know that your lover relishes your thoughts. She says none of her friends can ever talk to their lovers in this way, that they have too much hubris in their own mystique and that underneath they are ashamed of one thing or another. We often talk about why two women can be lovers but we have no answers yet. She says that we are lucky because we have no one we must answer to.

I look back to the house again to see the changing colors. It is like a watercolor being painted in a dense gouache right before my eyes. The towels are pink, even violet, in Xenia's shadow. Cernya is still reading. I can feel her wanting my company, without even searching for a look on her face. It is true. I hear her put down her pages. And now I hear her voice. It is as smooth as fine, white sand.

"Ahhhhhh." The note she sings seems to begin involuntarily. (It is a thing any great singer can do!) "Aaahh, Barsi," she continues, "please. Please come. You know that I am a slave." She reaches a G with this word. Then she thinks a little. She continues, "You make me a vegetable. A stew of sex. My only world. My garden." She sings it with much acting and clowning, imitating the twanging, whining Moroccan music of a tzi-gane and then she turns it supremely operatic at the end. She holds out her arms, stretching into the air toward me, spreading her fingers wide, palms open. I get to my feet and walk toward her. We look at each other and I begin to laugh. I am thinking of Xenia having to hear all this. Per-haps she is even watching. Perhaps she watched us earlier this morning!

This morning at sunrise, after our bath, I did not have to reach very far inside myself to find my feelings for Cernya. She was there pressing against me, rubbing me with the new towel and playing with her tongue in my ear, whispering that we should make love again. She said I should come back into the water again, back into the water made green by the tiny tiles lining the pool, and lie with her at the shallow end. The water here at Muyhi's is smooth and heavy, nearly viscous like guava juice, and it contains limestone which makes it look very light and turquoise on the surface. Deeper down the water is green because of the darker tiles in the bottom. And in true Moroccan delicacy, the grouted lines between the tiles in this pool are painted with a thin gold line. The pool shines, especially in the early morning light. The morning light here pretends to know nothing of the busy heat of the day, sneaking around corners, filling pools like a handmaiden with a jug of ancient oil, until suddenly it is noon.

As we lay in the pool this morning, Cernya took my arm at the wrist and guided my hand. She spread out my hand and stroked the length of my fingers. Then she folded my fingers slowly, one by one, into my hand and then ran her hand over the surface of my skin, smoothing my knuckles with oil which she had floated on the water in a shallow dish. She pulled my hand underwater and put it between her legs. Then she pressed the ball of my fist against her. I kept it there, moving slowly in the water until finally I lengthened my fingers and moved inside her. We kept on like this, floating with each other, ebbing gently and then rushing shortly forward until my entire hand was inside her and my leg was between her legs. I held my hand inside her to my wrist until she pushed me backwards just a little. I complied, but only just a little because I was now the embellisher and I would stop only when no more was possible, only when all the fantasies of our plot against the world were woven into numbness.

The water is shallow to the shoulder as we lie on our sides but I seem to swim in deep water, and do not drown. She slides down on my hand and begs me to hold her just above the water line, just above the point of no return, with one arm around the small of her back while she moves, and with the other arm I move the water over us, as if we are swimming in this turquoise sea. I make the water reach and recede and reach again against her nipples before I touch them. Her broad hand pushes hard against the waves of muscles in my stomach. She puts her weight against me. I am caught needing to feel her against me. We kiss and we stay close to each other, as close as two people ever get, I think, as we each find that extraordinary place where there are diamonds on the ocean floor and mountain tops with great, green hills. Sometimes I have no fantasies as I am reaching the height of my sexual being, only the weight of her against me, what I think of her, the sensual parts I see, the beauty I am so privileged to share. And it is enough to put me over the edge. Afterwards when her full weight is against me, I believe I know how much the soul weighs.

A small part of the sky began to lighten while the other part of the world was still Moroccan blue, deep and bright. This time of early morning has a brilliant color that is hard to describe. You see it only near an ocean and only on mornings when the moon survives. Stars are dragged back to earth and it seems as if I can feel them here with us in the pool like heat on my back, as if they are her fingertips lightly touching me everywhere before she arches and holds me fast. And when I come up from underwater, breathing hard, exchanging the last possible taste of her for pure air, I look up to see that the world here on the desert has changed color and now rests so easily bruised in brightness, brightness everywhere.

But back to the present. (I am prone to remember sex with Cernya. I re-live it in my mind because it is the truest mirror we have. I feel it is important to write it down here, in case there is a time when my life is cut short and our lives in their truest sense go unnoticed.)

"Put your hand under here," Cernya instructs, having left her lounge chair and come to stand above me. She wants to play but she looks very serious! She pulls her Moroccan robe up over her thighs. "See what the Moroccan pancakes are doing to me? What devils are those pancakes? The rghaif? Do you like them? And those sfenj?" She asks me these questions as she moves my hand in and out and around her thighs. "I will show you how to make sfenj someday," she tells me, lowering her voice to give the word for pancake a sensual meaning. I look at her. Yes, it is true what they say about her: She has Mediterranean fire. She draws out her words. It makes me think how lucky I am in this world. "You must first squeeze dough through your fist, like this," she continues. She curls my hand into a fist, caressing each finger one by one. "Make an opening in your fist just the size of an egg and let the dough squeeze through," she instructs, playing a French chef, speaking French. She squeezes my fist. "You must let the dough fight to get out, and when it does you must then slide these three fingers into it," she says, taking up my other hand. "But only for a minute...." She looks at me, slowly pulling my one hand away from the other. Then she laughs. "Sfenj will make me fat. Will my voice become larger or will it be stifled from the fat around my neck? Perhaps a little fat around the neck will make me famous. If I eat myself into a grotesque shape in this life will you love me in the next life, Barsi?"

"I think in the next life you will be a green parrot," I say kissing her all over and burning. "You talk so much, you'll come back as a green parrot. Perhaps even a fat green parrot!"

"And you?" she asks.

"Well, for me then, I pray to return as a sailor." I close my eyes. I touch her beautiful neck and throat wherein lies all the joy. I am thinking of joy and of something called ecstasy as I stare at Cernya with my eyes closed.

I believe sometimes we must be crazy to feel as if we are two stars exchanging light in a purple sea. It is impossible to deny our need of each other. But I would think us even crazier yet if we deprived ourselves of such a profound indulgence. Still, I believe that we are completely insane to be lovers in a world where our truest identities can last only as long as the oblivion of making love. Do we make love over and over again just to re-live, for one brief moment, the reality which we always seem to bargain away?

* * *

I loved Barsi and Cernya. I loved them so deeply because they were all of us. They were the heart of us all.

THE SNOW QUEEN

DOROTHY ALLISON

I like my fairy tales hard-edged.

It wasn't the boy. It was the season.

I never go south if I can help it. Never take my wolves past the third tree line. I know the rumors, the stories the goodwives tell when their babies cough their lungs out and the husbands huddle by the fire, bitter herbs pressed against their throats. They blame me and my wolves, me and my winds, me and my ice-bright jewels tempting human and beast farther from fire than they can stand.

Contemptible. Do they blame my sisters when summer scorches the wheat and pulls down the corn? Ah, maybe they do. Maybe they curse my sister, Blaze, when fevers take their children, curse Westward, when the spring is too bitter and the nights give too much frost or not enough. The seasons are not ours to rule. We ride the currents, only make them on occasion. But not so often as the humans imagine or we would like.

That season was strange. I cannot explain what happened otherwise. I was bored. Neither wolves nor bears could distract me, though I hunted both. I took my bitches against the great-legged grizzlies and rode the shoulders of my great bear to terrorize the wolf packs.

But it was not the boy. Not as they imagine. Not his peach satin cheeks or his sturdy brown thighs. Not his childish laughter, nor crowing shouts. Not the way he ran and hunted up near the tree line. Not even his stubborn disregard of my wind. It was his eyes. I saw them reflected in my shuttle blades—pearly blue and stone gray, with small glints of gold when the winter sun flared. He looked at me when no one else had dared. He lifted his head and dared my glance. Boy without

123

fear. Boy without sense. I would gnaw his bones and tease my animals with his fat.

That was what I intended. His body as prize. His life as penance. But when I pulled him into my carriage he wept on my hand and his tears were cold. Cold. That is so rare. Humans bleed hot. The cold was not human. That I felt it at all was a shock. That he did not scream when I dragged him up to my breast. That he looked up at me still. Fearless boy. Fool. My toy for the winter or the year.

I never saw the girl. Not then. And if I had seen her, had taken her, might not everything have been different? Perhaps. But the day I took the boy I think she was not what she became. For when she came that time, she could not be missed. Eyes bright as a pride's whelp, teeth set like a great bear, and frost and defiance all over her—a mantle without fear. Fear is quick and hot.

Defiance long and cold.

Since her, I only take girls.

YAGUARA

NICOLA GRIFFITH

Jane Holford comes to the jungles of Belize on assignment: to photograph epigrapher Cleis Fernandez and her project at Kuchil Balum, the Place of the Jaguar, a partially excavated Mayan site. She expects to take her photos and leave, as she has always done, untouched by her subjects, using her camera to distance herself from the world around her. But in the jungle, Jane finds herself drawn to Cleis, intrigued by Cleis' obsession with Kuchil Balum's ancient glyphs—images of jaguars, women, and ritual. One day Cleis is wounded at the site and tended by a local villager. She heals too quickly, and she begins to disappear into the jungle at night. Cleis is changing, and Jane is afraid.

Cleis' fever lasted three days. She was up and about before then. "Don't tell me I should rest. I'm fine. Never better. I don't need two good arms to study the glyphs. And the rains won't wait."

The first couple of days at the site, Jane kept a surreptitious eye on Cleis, but gave up when Cleis caught her at it and glared. They worked in silence, Jane moving crabwise with camera and tripods along the walls, changing filters, checking light levels; Cleis making notes, taking measurements, staring blankly at the trees and muttering to herself.

On the fourth day, Jane got back to the shack to find Cleis sitting on the bed with her notes, and the remains of the splint piled in a heap on the table. "I took it off," Cleis said. "My arm feels fine. It was probably just a sprain."

There was nothing Jane could say. She cleared away the mess.

Something had changed since Cleis' accident: children now ran past

125

their shack, playing games, and more than once Jane had seen villagers walking through the trees to their milpas, mattocks on their shoulders. They had greeted her with a smile and a wave.

Sometimes, too, she would look up from her camera to see Cleis and Ixbalum together, out of earshot, talking. Jane wondered why Ixbalum was now willing to speak to Cleis; wondered what she was saying, what craziness she was spilling into Cleis' eager ears. But she did not ask. Instead, she tried to push Cleis from her mind by working from first light until last. At night she would lie down, exhausted, and fall into a troubled sleep. Her dreams were vivid and fractured. More than once she woke to find Cleis gone from her bed. *Where did you go?* Jane wanted to ask, *And how?* But she never did. She imagined Cleis and Ixbalum gliding through the jungle, looking into the dark with their golden eyes...

One night her dreams were jumbled images: time running backward while she watched the ruins reform into a city; vast storms overhead; Cleis talking to her earnestly, explaining, "Ixbalum doesn't care what I know anymore. It doesn't matter what the children tell me. I'm hers now." Jane woke drenched in sweat. She looked over at Cleis' bed: she was sleeping like a baby.

Am I going mad?

She needed to get away. She got out of bed, pulled on her clothes.

She waited until just after dawn to wake Cleis. "The photography is ahead of schedule, and we need supplies. I'm driving to Benque Viejo. I'll be gone two or three days."

Jane had expected to reach Benque Viejo, walk through its streets, loud with traffic and thick with the stink of leaded gasoline, and come slowly out of her nightmare. All the time she was pulling Belize dollars from her wallet for bottled gas and beer and canned food she wondered when it would stop feeling strange and dangerous to be back in the world.

She booked herself into a hotel and took a bath, but the water was only lukewarm and she found herself longing for the lake with its water cabbage and kingfisher.

After weeks of eating fish and fruit and corn, the steak dinner was alien and almost inedible. She left a tip on the table and walked from the restaurant into the street. The sky was dusky pink, streaked with pearl gray clouds. She wished Cleis could be there to see it. And then she knew she did not want to spend three days here in Benque Viejo when she could be at Kuchil Balum. The rains would be coming soon. There was no time. Because when the rains came, Cleis would go back to New Mexico, and she....

What is happening to me? She did not know. All she knew was that she had to get back.

* * *

It was mid-afternoon of the next day when she parked in front of their shack. Cleis was not there. *Probably at the site. No matter.* Jane took her time unloading the supplies, nervous about seeing Cleis again.

Then there was nothing left to do; she had even washed the enamel plates that had been lying on the table—the same plates she and Cleis had eaten from the night before she had left for Benque Viejo. She tried not to worry. Cleis had probably been eating straight from a can, too busy to take the time to prepare anything. She checked the shack one last time, then set off for the ruins.

The waterfall fell peacefully, a flock of black and orange orioles wheeled about the crown of a tree at the edge of the clearing, but there was no Cleis.

"Cleis!" The call echoed back, and Jane remembered the last time she had called to Cleis here. Had something else happened, something worse?

She ran through the ruins, calling, ducking in and out of half-excavated buildings. Nothing. Maybe she was at the village, talking to Ixbalum.

Two women stood at the well, a man plucked a chicken on his doorstep. They looked up when Jane ran into the clearing. "Cleis?" she asked. They frowned. "Cleis?" she asked again, pantomiming curls falling from her head. "Ah," they said, and shook their heads.

Jane ran to Ixbalum's hut. The door was closed. She banged on it with her fist. No reply. She banged again, then pushed her way in.

Without the candles, the hut was cool and dark. There was no one there. Jane brushed aside bunches of herbs on her way back to the door, then turned around again and plucked a leaf from each bundle. She could look at them later, see if any matched the ritual leaf on the glyphs.

She was just putting them in her pocket when Ixbalum came in.

The Mayan woman stood there with her arms folded, looking at Jane, looking at the floor where one leaf lay in the dirt. Jane picked it up and put it in her pocket with the others. This woman had already seen her naked and drunk; Jane was too concerned for Cleis to feel any shame at being found in Ixbalum's hut. "I want to know where Cleis is."

Ixbalum said nothing. Jane could feel herself being studied. This time she did not cringe.

"If you know where she is, I want to know. She's pregnant, and I think that fall was more of a shock than she knows. I want to take her away from here." *Do I?* "I'm asking for your help."

Ixbalum moved so suddenly that Jane thought she was going to strike her, but Ixbalum reached up past Jane's left ear and drew a leaf from one of the bunches. She held it out to Jane.

"I don't understand." But she did.

Ixbalum shook the leaf in front of Jane's face. The message was unmistakable: Take it. Jane did. Ixbalum nodded, very slightly, then made a *Go now* gesture and turned her back.

Not knowing what else to do, knowing only that it was pointless shouting when neither understood the other, Jane went back out into the sunshine. The leaf was a big one, dull gray-green now, but it would have been bright when fresh, the color of the paste Ixbalum had smeared on Cleis' shoulder. It had six points, and a tracery of veins like a spider's web.

* * *

Night came as a rising cloud of living sound. The creaky chorus of a thousand insects rubbing together chitinous legs and wing combs echoed and reverberated through the trees. Fireflies streaked the dark with yellow.

Jane lay on her back on her bunk. Her arms were grazed and scratched from pushing aside branches, being caught by unexpected thorns. She had cut her palm on a frond of razor grass. Her throat was sore from calling. For the first time she was unclothed and not covered with a sheet. She lay naked to the world, as an offering. *Please come back. Just come back safe.*

* * *

Cleis returned at dusk the next day. She pushed the door open and walked in slowly. Her hair was filthy, her face drawn. She stopped when she saw Jane. "You're back early." Her voice was flat with exhaustion.

Jane wanted to touch her face, hold her, make sure she was all right. "I got back yesterday. I've been waiting, and worrying. I went out look-ing—" Cleis swayed a little. "It's dangerous to get too tired out there."

Cleis sat down on her bunk, sighed and closed her eyes as she leaned back against the wall. "I didn't know you'd be here to worry."

"I just..." Jane did not know how to explain why she had come back early. "I just wanted to know where you've been."

Cleis' eyes flicked open. Underneath, her skin was dark with fatigue, but the eyes themselves were bright, intense. "Do you? Do you really?"

Jane took a deep breath; she felt very vulnerable. "Yes."

* * *

"The simple answer," Cleis said, over a cup of hot tea, "is that I don't know where I've been." They were sitting at the table, a Coleman lamp drawing moths that fluttered against the screen. Jane had insisted that Cleis eat something, rest a little, before talking. "The complex answer.... What do you know about dreaming?"

Jane was momentarily thrown off balance. "Not much."

"Dreams are something I researched in my twenties, a long time before becoming interested in Mayan civilization. Simply stated, the human brain exists in three parts, one cobbled onto the other, communicating uneasily, each with different...behaviors. There's the first evolutionary stage, the reptile or R-complex, the crocodile brain whose realm is sexual, aggressive, and ritual behavior. Then when mammals evolved from reptiles, they developed the limbic system, which meant they perceived the world differently—in terms of signs, and vivid sensory and emotional images. To do this, they had to bypass the crocodile brain, suppress it. They couldn't ignore it altogether, though, because it controlled a lot of the body's physical functions: the urge to fuck and fight and eat."

"What does all this have to do with where you were last night?"

"I'm getting there. Anyway, mammals found a way to turn the R-complex, the crocodile brain back on, harmlessly, during sleep. Which means, of course, that our dreams are the crocodile's dreams: sex and food and fighting." Her eyes were bright. "Haven't you ever wondered why we get clitoral erections during dreams?"

"No."

"Then some mammals developed the neocortex. We became self-conscious. Ever wondered why you can't read or do math in your dreams?"

Jane opened her mouth to say she had never noticed whether or not she could, then remembered countless dreams of opening books only to be frustrated by meaningless squiggles.

Cleis noticed and nodded. "The neocortex handles analytic recollections. It's usually turned off when we dream. That's why dreams are so hard to remember. When I change, I become a mammal with no neocortex. My waking state is like a dream state. When I change back, when I wake, I remember very little. So, in answer to your question: I don't know where I've been."

There was a bubble of unreality around Jane's head, around the whole room. Change? She concentrated on her hands, neatly folded together before her on the table. *My hands are real.* "What are you trying to tell me?"

Cleis reached out and touched those neatly folded hands. "I think you already know."

Jane felt very calm. She pulled the six-fronded leaf from her pocket. "You believe in this."

Cleis said nothing.

"You think...you think that those glyphs of scarification on the purdah wall are...that the ritual wounding has purpose." She remembered Ixbalum shaking the leaf in her face. "You think your accident wasn't an accident. That the paste Ixbalum put on your wound infected you with some kind of, I don't know, changing agent, a catalyst. That you can become...that you change into a jaguar."

Now laugh. Tell me it isn't true.

But Cleis just nodded. "Yes."

"Do you know how that sounds?" Her voice was very even, but her heart felt as though it was swelling: so big it was pushing at her stomach, making her feel ill.

"You've seen the evidence with your own eyes—"

"I've seen nothing! A wall, some pictures, some leaves. You got drunk, pulled the wall on top of you, broke your arm and probably took a bang on the head. Ixbalum fixed you up. You disappear at night and come back looking like hell, with a pseudo scientific explanation that basically boils down to this: you can't remember and you're not responsible. All the evidence points, not to that fact that you've discovered some mystical Mayan rite, but that something is wrong in your head, and getting worse." She put the leaf down carefully on the table. "Look at it. Look at it hard. It's just a leaf."

"I've read the dates on the stelae, Jane. Kuchil Balum, Place of the Jaguar, was occupied up until the sixteenth century."

"What has that got to do with—"

"Think!" Cleis' voice was thin and bright as wire. "The lowland Mayan culture began to die more than a millennium ago: population pressure, some say, and crop failures, but I'm fairly sure it was more to do with a loss of faith. But not here. Here the power of the gods was tangible. Young girls from every family were sent to the purdah house at puberty. They were ritually wounded, infected. Some changed, most did not." She searched Jane's face. "Every family had the opportunity, the chance to join the elite. That welded the community together in ways we can't even begin to comprehend."

A moth fluttered frantically against the window screen.

"But even jaguar gods can't stand against guns and missionaries," Cleis continued. "So they pulled down their beautiful stone buildings and built themselves a village that appears unremarkable. They hid, but they've kept their culture, the only Mayans who have, because they have people like Ixbalum."

They sat for a moment in silence. Jane stood up. "I'll make some more tea."

She busied herself with the kettle and teapot. There had to be a way to get Cleis to see past this delusion; some way she could persuade Cleis to pack her bags and leave with her and have her head X-rayed. She did not know what to say, but she knew it was important to keep the dialogue open, to keep Cleis anchored as much as possible in the real world.

The kettle boiled. Jane brought the pot to the table. "It's not the same without milk," she said.

Cleis smiled faintly. "Being an ignorant American, I don't think it's the same without ice."

She seemed so normal.... Jane asked sharply, "When you change, how do you think it affects your child?"

Cleis looked thoughtful. "I don't know." She leaned forward. Jane could feel Cleis' breath on her face. She wanted to strain across the table, feel that breath hot on her throat, her neck. "You haven't asked me how it feels to change. Don't you want to know?"

Jane did. She wanted to know everything about Cleis. She nodded.

"It's like walking through a dream, but you're never scared, never being chased, because you're the one who's dangerous. I'm not me, I'm...other."

"Other?"

"Here, now, I have a sense of self, I know who I am. I can use symbols. It's...." She frowned. "It's hard to describe. Look at it this way." She patted the table. "I know this table is made of wood, that wood comes from trees, and that this wood is pine. Underlying all that knowledge is the ability to work in symbols—tree, furniture, wood—the ability to see beyond specifics. When I'm changed, symbols, words...they become meaningless. Everything is specific. A barba jalote is a barba jalote, and a chechem is a chechem. They're distinct and different things. There's no way to group them together as 'tree.' The world becomes a place of mystery: unknowable, unclassifiable, and understanding is intuitive, not rational."

She toyed absently with the leaf.

"I'm guided by signs: the feel of running water, the smell of brocket deer. The world is unpredictable." She paused, sighed, laid her hands on the table. "I just am," she said simply.

* * *

The rainy season was not far off. The days were hotter, more humid, and Jane worked harder than before, because when she was busy she did not have to deal with Cleis, did not have to look at her, think about how her skin might feel, and her hair. She did not have to worry about getting Cleis to a hospital.

The nights were different.

They would sit outside under the silky violet sky, sipping rum, talking about the jungle.

"The jungle is a siren," Cleis said. "It sings to me." Sweat trickled down the underside of her arm. Jane could smell the rich, complex woman smells. "Especially at night. I've started to wonder how it would be during the rains. To pad through the undergrowth and nose at dripping fronds, to smell the muddy fur of a paca running for home and know its little heart is beat beat beating, to almost hear the trees pushing their roots further into the rich mud. And above, the monkey troops will swing from branch to branch, and maybe the fingers of a youngster, not strong enough or quick enough, will slip, and it'll come crashing down, snapping twigs, clutching at leaves, landing on outflung roots, breaking its back. And it'll be frightened. It'll lie there eyes round, nose wet, fur spattered with dirt and moss, maybe bleeding a little, knowing a killer is coming through the forest." Cleis' nostrils flared.

Jane sipped her rum. She could imagine the jaguar snuffing at the night air, great golden eyes half closed, panting slightly; could taste the thin scent molecules of blood and fear spreading over her own tongue, the anticipation of the crunch of bone and the sucking of sweet flesh. She shivered and sipped more rum, always more rum. When the sun was up and she looked at the world through a viewfinder she did not need the numbing no-think of rum, but when there was just her and Cleis and the forest's nightbreath, there was nowhere to hide.

And so every night she staggered inside and fell across her bed in a daze; she tried not to smell the salty sunshiny musk of Cleis' skin, the sharp scents of unwashed hair, tried not to lean towards the soft suck and sigh of rum fumes across the room. Tried, oh tried so hard, to fall asleep, to hear nothing, see nothing, feel nothing.

But there would be nights when she heard Cleis sit up, when she could almost feel the weight of Cleis' gaze heavy on the sheet Jane kept carefully pulled up to her chin, no matter how hot she was. On those nights she kept her eyes shut and her mind closed, and if she woke in the middle of the night and felt the lack of heat, the missing cellular hum of another human being, she did not look at Cleis' bed, in case it was empty.

But one night, Jane woke sitting up in bed with her eyes open after a dream of sliding oh so gently over another woman, sliding in their mutual sweat, and she saw that Cleis was gone. *I'm alone*, she thought, and was suddenly aware of every muscle in her body, plump and hot, of her thighs sliding together, wet and slippery, of her skin wanting to be bare. *There are no cameras here.* She lay her hand on her stomach, felt tendons tighten from instep to groin. And before she could really wake up and realize what she was doing—tell herself that this was not the same as being alone in her own room, one she could lock—she was standing naked before Cleis' empty bed, before the wooden corner post. It came to mid-thigh, a four-by-four rounded off at the top and polished. She stroked it with one hand, her belly with the other. Her pubic hair was a foot away from the post; a foot, then eight inches, six. She sank to her knees, rubbed her face on the post, held one breast, then the other. One thick drop of milky juice ran down the inside of her thigh. She pressed her belly to the wood, stood up slowly, feeling the top of the post run down between her breasts, down her stomach, her abdomen, then moved away very slightly, oh so very slowly, so the post skipped a beat then skimmed the tops of her thighs.

"Oh yes," she said, imagining Cleis lying face down in front of her, moonlight on her buttocks. "Oh yes."

She crouched down, crooning, leaning over the post, palms resting on the bunk, feet braced on the cool dirt floor. She began to lower herself.

The door creaked open. Jane froze. Something behind her coughed the tight throaty cough of a jaguar; another drop of milky juice ran down her thigh. The animal behind her rumbled deep in its chest. Jane did not dare turn around. It rumbled again: *Don't stop.* Her vulva was hot and slick and her heart thundered. The cough behind her was closer, tighter, threatening: *Do it now.*

Jane licked her lips, felt the golden eyes travelling up her Achilles', her calves, the back of her knees, the tendons in her thighs, the cheeks of her bottom. She dare not turn, and she dare not disobey, nor did she want to.

"Ah," she said softly and laid her cheek on the sheet. *Between Cleis' shoulder blades.* Touched the rumpled blanket above her head. *Cleis' rough curls.* And lowered herself onto the beautifully smooth oh so lovely rounded and rich wood. *The swell and heat of Cleis.* She moved gently.

"Oh, I love you." And she felt breath on her own clenching bottom, the close attention of whatever was behind her, and suddenly she knew who, what, was behind her and loved her, it. "Yes, I love you," she said, but it was a gasp as she felt the wood round and slick between her legs slide up and down and her breath caught and "Ah," she said, "ah," and she was grunting, and then she felt a sharp cool pressure against her shoulder where claws unsheathed and rested, possessive, dimpling the skin, and she was pulling herself up and over that wooden corner, *Cleis' soft plump slippery-now cheek*, her face tight with effort, and her breasts flattened on the bed as she thrust and her chin strained forward and the muscles under her skin pumped and relaxed and sweat ran down her legs and the room was full of a rumbling purr. Fur brushed her back and she was pressed into the bed by an enormous weight, a weight with careful claws, and the heat between her and the wood was bubbling up in her bones and "Ah!" she shouted, "ah!" hardly able to breathe, and could not stop, not now not now, and she humped and rocked and grunted until she shuddered and screamed and opened and pushed and came, curling around the bunk *around Cleis* like a fist. Sweat ran from her in rivers; a pulse in her temple thumped.

Claws slid back into their sheaths, the heat and weight withdrew. A throaty rumble: *Don't move.* And then it was gone.

Jane buried her face in the damp sheets that smelled of Cleis, that smelled of her and Cleis, and cried. *I don't know where I've been,* Cleis had said, *when I change back, I remember very little.*

* * *

When Jane woke up, Cleis was fast asleep in her bunk.

THE LITTLE MACHO GIRL

KATE BORNSTEIN

It was terribly cold and nearly dark on the last evening of the old year, and the snow was falling fast. In the bitter cold and encroaching gloom, the wind whipped through the clothing of any poor souls stranded outside, to freeze them in their very tracks.

She clicks the remote once.

"Fuck The Weather Channel," she says to herself. "Goddamn depressing, that's what I say."

The American Bandstand guy has replaced the images of the storm on her forty-eight-inch screen. Dick somebody, right? What the fuck is he laughing about?

Safe and warm tonight inside her office on the thirty-fifth floor, she draws her bare feet up beneath her in the large leather chair behind her executive-sized desk. Both pairs of her shoes are ruined or gone. A young man lifted her not-yet-out-of-the-bag Reeboks on the subway. He'd been part of a gang of performance artists, who'd laughed as they'd danced off with her running-shoes, saying they could use them as cradles for the twin births in their nativity program. She had to wear the fucking Gucci's to the office—ruined those suckers in the slush, damn it. And she'd had to carry those goddamn sample cases the whole way, as though she were no more than a common salesperson. She shudders and draws her feet further up beneath herself. Leave it to the Chinese Army to want to do business on New Year's fucking Eve. Well, she wasn't going to lose this account—no way. Sheffield and Buck had bids in, but her own company's blades were going to be the official knives of the Chinese Red Army, and it didn't matter to her whether she had to miss New Year's Eve to cinch the deal.

135

But the phone does not ring.

The fax machine is silent.

Damn it!

Click. The large-screen television in her office offers up the evening's news: family shots, parties.

Click. Couples going out for dinner and drinks. Fuck 'em all.

Click. A diamond is forever.

Click. The television winks out.

She glares balefully at the phone. General Ping is over an hour late. Bastard better call—she isn't about to go through this day without closing that deal. If she doesn't sell this lot of blades, the CEO is going to hang her ass out to dry. She snorts once. That asshole is most certainly at the company party right now, smiling that ice cold smile of his, the one he'd taught her when she'd first joined the company, the smile she scares herself with in the mirror nowadays. She's vice-president in charge of overseas marketing, and she can play hardball with the toughest of the guys. But tonight is going to make or break all of that.

She shudders involuntarily and hugs herself—a gesture she hasn't done for years. Her fingers trace the toned muscles of her forearms. No sign of the scars anymore—Doc did a good job. Ha! She'd paid him enough!

Click. More parties, more people laughing, dancing, singing, laughing, kissing...laughing.

Click. Silence.

She doesn't dare leave the office without this deal. Her eyes drift to the sample cases, and before she can stop herself, she opens each one. Revealing row upon row of gleaming, razor-sharp cold-forged steel blades.

One more glance at her arms, scar-free now for...what was it? Four years, ever since she joined the company. Four years since she'd become as hard as she had, as cold as any of the assholes working here. No...colder. Four long years since she'd made herself bleed. She looks longingly down at the blades.

"Yeah...yeah...what the fuck," she says softly to herself. It'll take the edge off waiting for General Whatsis-Ping to call. She barks a short laugh.

"Or put the edge on," she whispers.

Slowly she draws a long, curved blade from the sample case—she cannot stop the small animal cry that escapes her lips. Holding the blade between the thumb and forefinger of her left hand, she lightly scrapes it across the fine down on the back of her forearm. Oh, yes: as sharp as she might hope. Hell, she used to do this with her father's razor blades!

She takes a deep breath and, eager and sure, cuts the warrior mark into her upper right arm.

Ohhhhh, yes.

The warmth of the pain spreads swiftly through the rest of her body.

Yes, yes, yes. It really is a wonderful cut: blood dancing out behind the blade and trickling down her bicep. But more truly wondrous, it now seems to her that she is kneeling beside a small burning brazier with polished brass feet and intricate brass ornamentation. She can see the irons heating up to white hot. With a small whimper, she lifts her thighs to present herself for the brand when, lo! The blood from her mark stops flowing, the brazier and irons vanish, and she has only the red-stained blade pressed between her fingers to remind her of this vision.

Breathing heavily, she shakes her head. Omigod, she thinks, I can't go back into that space. No no no—I've got too much going for myself in this job, can't give it up for that. Yet, even as she thinks no, she takes a second blade from the case and slashes more deeply across the first mark on her arm. She cries out in joy and pain, the blood pours willingly down her arm. And where one or two drops fly from her blade onto the wall, it becomes transparent as a veil, and she can see into the room beyond: a dungeon! Beneath bright lights, a young slave lies on a table, eyes closed, a ceremonial dagger piercing the upper thigh.

Who's that laughing with such pure delight? The creature on the table? Or herself?

What is still more wonderful, the slave jumps down from the table, and hobbles across the floor, knife in thigh and all, right up her. But the bleeding in her arm ceases, and once again she is left alone in her darkened office.

"Gotta stop this shit," she says aloud, but she's already grabbed the third blade and, crooning softly to herself, she cuts a deep circle into the top of the vertical slash on her arm. Blood seeps from her wounds, suffusing her with a warmth she's not felt in years. A moan escapes her lips as she lifts her eyes to the next vision: herself, pierced with hundreds and hundreds of needles, each sparkling and dancing in the light of the now blazing brazier. Taller and taller she grows, this pierced apparition, till the needles themselves seem to her like stars in the sky.

Stars indeed. The bleeding has stopped, and she's looking out through the office window into the New Year's Eve night. A star falls, leaving behind it a bright streak of fire. "Someone is dying," she thinks to herself, for the woman who first collared her, the only person who had ever loved her, and who was now dead, had told her that when a star falls, a soul was leaving the physical plane.

She drags a fourth blade through her arm. Blinking, dizzy, she lifts her head to see...her first owner, the woman who had first put a collar round her throat and called her "mine."

"Ma'am," she calls out to this vision, her voice hoarse with tears uncried for four long years, "Please, take me with you. I know you'll disappear when my arm stops bleeding. You'll vanish, like the branding irons, the slave with knife in thigh, and the girl who was pierced like the night sky itself."

She quickly takes blade after blade from the case, and cuts here and there, everywhere all over her body, for she wishes so deeply to keep her lover with her. Her blood flows with a heat that is more intense than the summer sun itself, and her lover, who has never appeared so large or so beautiful, takes the still-bleeding one into her arms, and makes a final cut: deep across her throat.

"You knew I always wanted to do that, didn't you love?"

She can no longer speak to answer, only shake with ecstasy. And they both fly upwards in brightness and joy far above the earth, where there is neither coldness of heart nor hunger of soul, for they are together and they are in love.

In the dawn of morning, there lies the young woman, with pale cheeks and smiling mouth, curled up in her over-large leather chair; she bled to death on the last evening of the year; and the New Year's sun has risen and shines down through the window upon a slashed and bloodless corpse. The woman still sits, in the stiffness of death, holding the blades in her hand, many of which are yet stained with her dark blood.

"It's because the China deal fell through," said some, "She couldn't take the pressure," said others. And in the very highest offices, they agreed, "It's a man's job after all." No one ever imagined what beautiful things she had seen, nor into what glory she had entered with her lover, on New Year's Day.

ADDICT GIRL #1: DRUG-FREE AFTERNOON

KAREN GREEN

It was five o'clock and a tough day for Addict Girl. Though she had been cruising since nine AM seeking that special orange bag of Gleam, she found squat.

Addict Girl started using Gleam in early 1989. One shot of the shiny stuff and she was hooked. Gleam was special though, not like any of those placid downers or frightening whirlwind uppers Addict Girl had tried in the past. Gleam was subtle, in a manner. And it had style. Most importantly, though, Gleam didn't make Addict Girl puke.

Addict Girl started shooting Gleam for the first time this year. In the past, Gleam was good smoked or tossed in Coffee. But Addict Girl was bored with an easy lulling ride. Times had changed and the demand on her super drug powers were increasing as the city became more violent and obsessive.

Addict Girl walked complacently this Saturday. Her arm ties and cape drooped and she felt a little conspicuous in this outfit with nothing to make her arms puff and her eyes widen. She didn't feel strong like a super hero. To deal with this sense of fragility, Addict Girl slipped into a phone booth and donned her finest X-Girl tee and brand new old corduroy shorts. It was a stiff ninety degrees today and the lack of Gleam was paling Addict Girl's normal charm.

The only residue left from her super hero outfit was the permanent utility belt Addict Girl had sewn into her flesh a year ago. When she started shooting Gleam, it frustrated her that she had to carry a purse or have pockets. And then, of course, she could never keep anything for more than ten minutes without forgetting it. The utility belt settled that issue and offered room for a permanent transportable musical system. It was specially designed, however, so she could choose to play music directly into her brain or let it run through speakers that she had inserted in her cheeks. Addict Girl loved to freak people out by opening her mouth and singing entire rock songs. Most times, people ran from her, and she laughed.

Addict Girl, now disguised as Princess Pure, plopped *Live Through This* into her utility belt and headed towards the Karma Factory, a club well-known to Gleamers; it offered the only potion to soothe, albeit moderately, the constant numbingness lack of Gleam manifested.

The Princess sat down at the bar. The increasing number of young Gleamers running around made her sick. They respected her. It was an annoying kind of respect though, like the kind given to a dying king from his energetic sons.

"These girls are just shit, anyway. i mean, they'll never have the guts or the power to get past me, not even in fifty years."

i twisted my bar stool inward, facing the television screen. i didn't want to be social today. If any of these girls were carrying, they wouldn't be in here. No use wasting my energy.

i pulled the blue and orange shake up to my lips. It's got a sharp taste, some sort of choline and peach juice base with a jumble of mind-glueing chemicals. Thank god, 'cause my mind was in so many pieces at the moment. i swung my stool around just in time to catch Flabberjaw's eye when she walked in. She smiled what could only mean a great score. i jumped off my stool, ditched my toxic totaller and followed her out the door.

"Here," she said, looking around us suspiciously. "Put this in your coat, i don't want to have it on me right now. i don't want to jinx this."

"Fucker," i said under my breath. She'd done it again, broken the silence. She'd done good fetching me in the bar without a word. Flabberjaw was known for her bad luck with the cops. She'd come to me for training in some of the more self-protective addict arts. i didn't really want to take her on as a student (sometimes you just know), but i always give people at least one chance to learn. i gave her a few key ethics to remember. Like, don't think about having the drugs on you, clear your mind of it all and just think about that slice of pizza you're gonna go buy. She wasn't turning out to be such a good student. She always forgot the very basic rule of not drawing attention to yourself by looking all around in paranoia. i huffed.

"You broke another one. Let's go down this alley for a minute."

Flabberjaw's eyes dropped. She hated this part, and so did i. But lessons must be learned and it's a given fact that pain and knowledge run hand in hand. It was sad 'cause Flabberjaw was smart; there was something keeping her from being in control all the time. i told her to put her hands up on the wall. She did. i unbuckled her belt and pulled it out of the loops of her shorts.

i reached back with the belt and slapped it against her ass thirteen times. i didn't look at her or anything after, i just walked out of the alley carrying her drugs.

When i got to the end of the alley, i saw a flashing red light. Instantly i put up my super-ego shield. Since my powers were dull, i wasn't very good at masking myself. The cops saw me and ran into the alley. There was no escape; they grabbed me, yelling, "Where's your friend? We saw you two coming down here! Fucking lesbian freaks." One cop cuffed me while the other one dragged a haggard Flabberjaw from further down the alley. They plopped us in the car and took us to the station.

Greita stood by and watched Addict Girl and Flabberjaw disappear into the cop car. She smiled. After the car was out of sight, she slid down the alley. Greita scoured the weeds and trash for a while, finally coming up with a little plastic treasure. She knew Addict Girl wouldn't let those cops haul her ass while she had any drugs on her. Greita dipped her straw into the powder and sniffed.

It wasn't long before Flabberjaw and i were set up in a nice little cell. We'd been strip searched, but luckily the cops found nothing. They kept us holed up for a while to scare us, but they couldn't keep us here very long. i turned to Flabberjaw.

She looked up at me meekly, "i'm sorry, A—"

i cut her off. "Look, you're not sorry. You want to get caught. Don't you even see it? What's the use in being a bad girl if you don't get caught? You must be catholic."

i paced quietly around the cell for about twenty minutes. Flabberjaw curled up on the corner of her cot, waiting for the punishment i would no longer deliver. i sat down next to her, put my arms around her.

"You're gonna be better off on your own for a while, baby. Trust me. When you learn control...."

Flabberjaw started bawling.

"Hey baby, c'mon," i pulled her head to my chest, "Lighten up. This is life, you die in the end."

i heard the lock down the hall opening. A cop came in and released us. He looked at me fearfully. During the strip search he tried to get me to take off my utility belt and he had to leave the room when he realized it was sewn into the flesh. It wasn't a bad job or anything, but sometimes the weight of the belt tears the flesh apart so it gets scabby pretty easily.

i took the bus from the police station to the stop a few blocks from my apartment. i was approaching home when i saw Greita sitting on my steps. She looked very self-satisfied.

"Hey Greita," i said, trying to pass by without a big conversation. i was exhausted.

She grabbed my calf, wanting to throw me off guard. She stood up, hovering her fist near my face. She was laughing.

i dodged the fist coming at my head, but the other one impaled my gut. i bent over, trying not to leave myself open. Greita kicked my side. i grabbed her foot right before it hit again and pushed her backwards down the stairs. She lay dazed on the sidewalk. She started to get up. i fiddled with my keys and ran into the building, slamming the door behind me.

"Fuck, fuck, fuck."

i ran into my apartment and headed for the bathroom. i puked twice in the toilet and once in the sink. The phone rang once and was picked up by the answering machine.

"You filthy cunt." Click.

i was pretty sure it was Greita calling. i ran to the window and saw her fat ass hobbling down the street. "Cunt." i was worried, though. i didn't understand why the dyke mafia would send one of their "initiates" after me. i mean, i didn't owe 'em money, and we'd been on pretty good terms since i took one of the dons for a nice flight around town a few weeks ago. The phone rang again.

"Hey, baby, it's me. There's a revolution going on out here, where the fuck are ya?"

i dashed to the phone. "Cindy Brady, what the fuck is up? i just got attacked by Greita. Come over here; i gotta take a bath. i can't go out into dangerous territory feeling like this."

"Alright Supergirl, i'll come by. Maybe i can pick you up something on the way."

"REALLY!"

"Anything for you, baby."

i plopped the receiver onto the cradle, pranced over to the stove and put on some water for tea. The summer tended to get rough in what i fondly refer to as Girly World. Lots of steamy hot girls with raging hormones. A wet dream or a nightmare depending on your state of mind.

Addict Girl fantasized fondly about the seething young girls while she showered. Her long hair was flipped up in a towel and her skinny naked frame lay peacefully on the bed when she heard Cindy's keys in the door. Cindy walked into Addict Girl's kitchen, turned left and entered a spotlessly clean bedroom.

"Wow, what happened?"

"Punishment."

"Students. But they don't deliver, eh?"

She tossed an orange packet on the bed. i wanted to look cool so i didn't jump on it. i sat up, picked up the bag and put it on the night stand. Cindy bent over and started kissing me. She grabbed the bag off the night stand and went into the kitchen.

"Let's get on the road, little girl."

"Hey."

i jumped off the bed and followed her. She already had the works out. Finally.

THE ANGEL AT THE TOP OF MY TREE

BY PAT CALIFIA

Caught up in the Christmas spirit, Adolpha decided to go shopping. How nice it was of all the merchants to remain open well after dark. In downtown San Francisco, the antique steel-blue lights along Market Street were decorated with enormous candy canes and reindeer. Shop windows were lushly lit, golden boxes full of expensive and precious things. Well-dressed and well-fed men and women hurried along the street, loaded down with shopping bags and parcels, eager to pick up one last present or head for home with the bundles they had already amassed. Between them lurked figures who had not partaken of the season's bounty; dirty, thin people who begged change from their betters or begged their personal tormentors to leave them alone.

Adolpha had shaved her cornsilk blond hair at sundown. By now it had grown out to an inch of stubble. The cold was all the artifice she needed to put a cruel blush of color on her Teutonic cheekbones, and her mouth had always been blood-red. Tonight she wore a very brief leather miniskirt and a matching black leather jacket, lined with scarlet silk, of course. The tailoring was Italian, very chic, very naughty. She thought the clothes would have been expensive if she'd had to buy them, but Adolpha never carried cash or American Express. Her big green eyes were her line of credit. Underneath her leathers she wore nothing at all, being immune to the chill. Her black stockings were held up by lacy elastic tops, and she maneuvered on seven-inch stilettos as if the brick sidewalk was just another Paris runway.

Before allowing the warm air, silver tinsel, and discreet carols of Nordstrom's to suck her in through its thick glass doors, Adolpha paused and took a deep whiff of the street. Really, she could not see that cities

144

had changed much since 1887. Victorian London had its clouds of coal smoke; San Francisco in 1997 had carbon monoxide. The gutters still smelled of sewage and rotten food. Horse-drawn carriages and electric trolleys seemed equally indifferent to the welfare of pedestrians, and the street people were, if anything, even more desperate, despite the absence of snow. She took in the crowds with the delighted smile of a vegetarian gourmand contemplating the glossy rows of organic produce at the Berkeley Bowl, and swept into Nordstrom's, eager to enjoy her portion of greed, the joy that comes from avid consumption.

Riding the escalator was a treat, although she had to resist the temptation to rise an inch or so above the steps and alarm the shoppers thronged behind her. She had artfully positioned herself in line so she would be ahead of a matronly woman who was taking a young boy shopping for a suit. It was delightful to hear their twin reactions to the view, like an operatic dialogue in her head, the older woman's fear and dismay paired with adolescent disbelief and delight. It was sweet to be adored, and equally savory to scare someone. She resisted the temptation to introduce them to a whole new set of family values. There was time, still, she was fresh from her nap and wanted to look around a bit.

Of course, she headed straight for the shoe department. The buyers at Nordstrom's had to be perverts. Just look at all the thigh-high boots, platform heels, leopard prints, Lucite pumps, sharp metal spikes, little-girl shoes with padlocks on the straps. These shoes were positively pornographic, erotic verses in latex, patent leather, kid, and steel. She found a row of seats, made everyone who was seated there leave, and positioned herself in the middle of the row. The chairs were not upholstered with leather, and she frowned at the sensation of plastic against her half-bare bottom. It was annoying to be reminded of the store's faux elegance, its pretentiousness. Americans craved only the illusion of exclusivity.

Now, that salesgirl over there, perhaps she was the one to drag under the mistletoe for a nice, long kiss. Adolpha stared at the back of her head until she abandoned her customer, turned, and came to inquire submissively if there was anything that Madam would like to see. She was a cute little thing, with her dark brown hair cut in a Dutch-boy's bob. Adolpha liked girls who wore ties with boy's shirts. She was a little thin in her dark slacks and fashionable loafers, but there was no time to fatten her up. Her name was Jamie, this was not what she had in mind when she graduated from high school, she was from Santa Monica, San Francisco was so cliquey and drinks were too expensive, she was thinking about moving back to Southern California and staying with her parents for a while, and Adolpha did not care to pay attention to the rest of it.

"I think you should measure my foot first," Adolpha purred, and crossed her long, long legs. Jamie sank to her knees and removed one of Adolpha's viciously high heels. The foot arched in her hand like a cat imperiously ordering you to pet it right there. So Jamie stroked it, and for some reason the rasp of the black silk stocking against the palm of her hand made her feel hot and sweaty inside the buttoned-down Oxford shirt that concealed her small breasts. She wanted to loosen her tie.

Instead, she ran her hands up Adolpha's legs, confirming with her fingertips that the stockings were perfectly taut and the seams aligned as if they'd been painted on with a laser. The muscles in the calves bunched beneath her hands, and she kneaded them, and continued kneading up, shifting her hands to palm the inside of a pair of perfect slender thighs. The silk stockings were like sandpaper on the sensitive inner surfaces of her hands, and she wanted so much to soothe them against this woman's skin.

Somehow she had forgotten to put the scale beneath her customer's feet, and was kneeling instead between her legs. She could see Adolpha's sex, the pink lips clearly visible because the pale pubic hair had been severely clipped. Jamie's breath caught in her chest. She ran her hands off the tops of the silk stockings, toward skin. But she barely got to experience the downy texture of Adolpha's thighs before her head was rudely shoved down, into the gray Berber carpet.

"Measure me with your mouth," Adolpha said, and the words were like a sonorous hymn in Jamie's head, a Gregorian chant that heralded and sanctioned the forbidden. She was afraid, afraid, but then there was a warm feeling like a touch behind her eyes, and she knew only desire. She took Adolpha's stockinged toes into her mouth, and adored them with her tongue. She was vaguely aware that customers were standing around in shock, watching a tall blond woman with a crewcut spread her legs and feed a salesgirl her feet. The manager of the department was heading toward them, and Jamie did not understand why he had not already shouted at her to stop, stop! But then it seemed to her that everyone was frozen in place, because Jesus told us to love one another, and here she was loving someone perfectly. It was like a nativity scene, she thought as she licked up toward Adolpha's knee caps. People would stand in front of them with their hats in their hands and admire them and think deep and beautiful thoughts, they would be inspired and awe-struck because it was holy, holy to press her mouth against the elastic roses and hunger for Adolpha's symmetrical Art Deco labia and the pink topaz of her clitoris.

Then her mouth was on rose petals, skin at last, and Adolpha's long fingers were in her hair, guiding her. Jamie had vague memories of a drunken party long ago, falling backwards onto a friend's bed, an awkward pleasure provided with pearl-tipped cheerleader fingers and lips that tasted of peach, passing out more because she was not sure she wanted to reciprocate than because of her blood alcohol level...but this was not like that. There was no intoxication except the sweet smell of Adolpha's body, no awkwardness at all because she was firmly held, directed, and there was no possibility of failure. She would give anything, anything to do this perfectly, to hear just one small sigh of delight from the woman who had gathered her up and given her a purpose.

So she used her puppy tongue and dizzy lips to give Adolpha pleasure for as long as she would graciously suffer it. And Adolpha was happy to take from her, to muss her hair and smear her face, and brand her soul with a deep hunger for cunt. It was delicious to allow a human being to feed on her, Adolpha found. It felt so wicked, and it was also endearing, to see them parody the act that sustained her own life. Caught up in fantasies about Jamie's fragile neck and strong young heart, Adolpha came, and quickly came again, mercifully blinding Jamie to light and sound by enclosing her in the grip of her strong pale legs. Jamie thought she would weep, she was so delirious and glad.

Then she was tossed back on the floor, out of breath, confused and bereft. The carpet burned her hands, and she had a bump on her head, she had landed that hard. Adolpha had spotted her prey. As she got to her feet, ready for the hunt, she did Jamie the favor of making everyone forget what they had just seen. Everyone except Jamie, that is. Let her sort it out, Adolpha thought, amused by the many possibilities that presented themselves. There was room for one more sweet young submissive in this wicked world. Let her find her proper place. Adolpha grinned, and mentally whistled for her quarry.

This was Monica Bradshaw, who had honey-brown hair with artificially-enhanced blond highlights, freckles on her shoulders, and a mouth that was too tight to be beautiful. Monica Bradshaw was terrified of turning thirty. She had an MBA from Harvard, and she was working as a manager for a company that was not a bank and not a stockbroker, but it did something with money, Adolpha was too impatient to figure out exactly what. Monica Bradshaw was pissed off because she kept hitting the glass ceiling. She wanted out of her current job, which was supervising secretarial services, so she could get her smart-yet-sensible shoes on the fast track to real money and prestige.

Just one week ago, the higher echelons of her company had okayed her proposal to down-size her department. Monica had promised them the same level of service with a much smaller investment in employees' salaries and benefits. One-fourth of her staff was going to get their layoff notices tomorrow, a week before Christmas. If this didn't catch the eye of the old-boys' network and put her in line for a promotion, Monica Bradshaw had a backup plan, which was to fire everybody and obtain "administrative support" from independent contractors.

Adolpha was more than happy to give Monica Bradshaw the recognition that her talents deserved. Almost lovingly, she petted her way through the obsessions, phobias, traumas, irritations, and fetishes hidden in the cortices of Monica Bradshaw's maniacal little mind. Adolpha did this as she stalked behind her intended, who was whisking through the lingerie department. Her first act of possession was to take hold of Monica's frantic wolverine personality, tear up her list of rush-rush-rush things to do, and send it away on a tropical puff of indolent air. Slowing down, looking a little confused and concerned, Monica began to actually look at all the lovely silky things around her. And she dutifully picked up the items that Adolpha selected for her. Looking a little distracted, she shed, one by one, her navy blue blazer, her blouse, a white satin Bali bra, a gold chain, a skirt that matched the blazer, white flats, pantyhose, and a scrungy pair of old Jockeys for Her which had been the only clean underwear in Monica's drawer when she got dressed for work that morning.

"What, no ankle chain?" Adolpha laughed, and pivoted the puppet to make it face her for the first time.

Monica Bradshaw was not happy with what she saw. Adolpha reminded her of the white-trash punk girls who occasionally intruded on her much more middle-class circle in high school, girls with wild colors in their hair and switchblades in their Hello Kitty pocketbooks. No one could have mistaken Adolpha for anything other than a woman, but her affect was far from womanly. The ultrashort hair combined with the micromini, deep cleavage, and nasty shoes sent strong conflicting signals. "Come here, if you want to be killed" was the slogan that came to Monica Bradshaw's mind.

"Aren't you the clever one?" Adolpha said aloud, and erased the insight. She made her chosen one pirouette in the aisle, and as she turned, she donned, one by one, the pieces of the costume that Adolpha had made her glean from the pastel rows of slinky merchandise.

First she rolled stockings up her shapely, aerobicized legs. They were a dark brown color, and had no seams, but they were silk, thirty dollars a pair if anyone was counting anything other than Monica Bradshaw's perky, ruddy nipples. Adolpha abhorred nylons. Monica then stepped into a pale pink G-string, and a matching push-up bra. Over that went a champagne-colored, mid-thigh length slip in moiré silk. It was slit up the back far enough to provide a glimpse of the top of Monica's stockings, and cut so exquisitely that lace would have been superfluous.

"You don't really need shoes, because you're not going to be walking much," Adolpha said. She allowed Monica to come to a halt. She was a bit out of breath. But she had performed the difficult maneuvers with an unusual amount of grace. Could it be that there was another side to this petty bully of a middle-manager, something in her soul besides a pocket calculator and the day's NASDAQ quotes? She looked lovely, dressed this way. The colors Adolpha had picked made her skin look translucent. Adolpha bit her lower lip and made Monica perform a series of ballet exercises, using a rack of garter belts as a barre. Not half bad. "Perhaps you do need shoes. Dancing shoes," Adolpha said, and with that thought a star was born.

On their way out of Nordstrom's, Adolpha snagged a pair of pink satin slingbacks and personally slipped them onto Monica's somewhat oversized feet. "Let's find a more appreciative audience," she told the shivering woman, and took her down the escalator toward the street. "The women in this place look as if they've never had an orgasm, and the men look as if they dribble rather than spurt." They headed for the Tenderloin, protected from unwanted attention by Adolpha's fierce powers. It was dark and cold. The wind had picked up, and sped between the tall buildings with a vengeance. Adolpha disliked the taste that exhaustion lends to the blood, so she picked Monica up and carried her along. She did not bother to dispense forgetfulness as they traveled. What were these weaklings going to do, stop her and take Monica away from her? That would be amusing.

Besides, she was busy working on Monica, fondling her breasts and her consciousness. The tits were nice, but the rest of it was such a mess. It would have taken hours for Adolpha to change the root directory of Monica's mind. The fundamental assumptions ("I will never have enough," "No one cares for me," "I am not safe," "I need to ignore other people to get what I want," etc.) were hard as bedrock. Adolpha tried dislodging Monica's obsession with money, and met with surprisingly stiff resistance. So she planted a little seed in the granite of Monica's heart, a little spark of erotic hunger. The red vine of sex need grew quickly, twining itself about the green vine of cash hunger, and Adolpha laughed to think where she was taking this rare plant to flower.

Finding the red-light district is the same in every city, she thought. As drunks and shit get thicker on the street, so do hookers and drug dealers. Soon she was in the middle of a neighborhood that offered wares every bit as expensive as the big department stores on the main thoroughfare. But this sort of business could not put its merchandise in bright windows. The darker and dingier an establishment was, the more piquant its commodities. Adolpha stopped outside a place she knew quite well, a dance emporium called Sugar and Spice. Its signs declared "And everything naughty, that's what our girls are made of!"

Adolpha sent Monica through the door ahead of her. She wanted to see the reactions of the patrons to her new acquisition. Feeling cruel, she did not soften Monica's perceptions of the place. She just kept her walking forward, making her stalk like a panther in heat toward the stage. But inside, it was the soul of a prim, bright young woman who looked down on sluts and strumpets, an ambitious professional who would never dream of sleeping with her boss to get ahead, who heard men hoot their lust at her and smelled the freshly-spilt semen in the private video booths.

The main attraction at Sugar and Spice was a large, glass-enclosed stage surrounded by booths, where patrons kept a blind from coming down and closing off their view of the dancers by constantly feeding quarters into a slot. This created a distance between the strippers and their admirers that Adolpha found completely appropriate. Let men hang their dripping tongues and dicks out, panting like the dogs they were for a favor they would never receive. She sent Monica among them like a clipper ship, majestically overturning dinghies with its wake. Like the noble wolf she was named for, Adolpha followed her, declaring the boundaries of her territory. A lucky few of the customers managed to touch the tips of their fingers to Monica's silk slip, creamy breast, or dusky thigh, but when they saw Adolpha's snarling mouth and prominent, pointed teeth, they suddenly felt rather the opposite of being blessed by fortune.

Adolpha had been here before. It was one of her favorite places to hunt. In a small city like San Francisco, it was necessary to become familiar with the few places where prey could be snatched that would not be missed. One of her favorite dancers was performing, a tough little Asian punk who wore combat boots with a ballerina's tutu. Since she had already removed her top, there was no telling what blasphemy she had done to fashion and femininity to cover her breasts long enough to get up on stage. She had a platinum-blond stripe in her long, thick black hair, and she wore kabuki makeup. Her name was Poison, and her dance was full of martial arts moves that made the more traditional shimmying she did seem ironic to any observer who was not a halfwit.

Adolpha thought Poison was delightful, as touchy about her independence as a Shinto priestess, thoughtless about displaying her sexuality, as if the world had already been made a safe place where women ruled, inviolable as Amaterasu.

Adolpha ejected one of the spectators from his tiny enclosure and sent him away with a strong suggestion that he find a video viewing booth with a glory hole and suck cock until his throat was pummeled raw. She directed Monica to take his place, and stood behind her to prevent her from being violated by anything other than the spectacle of female flesh, pride, and hostility. She also sorted out some of the male reactions that were going on all around them and funneled a few of them into Monica's mind, so she could feel her own body charged with the adoration and raw need the audience brought into the dark plywood stalls along with their heavy rolls of quarters.

"I am going to make you do that," she told Monica Bradshaw, who was breathlessly observing Poison's hands, cupping tits and crotch, and tits again. "Then you will be the one who makes them feel that way."

There was enough left of Monica's original consciousness for her to feel a great deal of panic and denial at this threat.

"But I thought you were a heterosexual," Adolpha said, teeth gleaming. "This is what it means to have traffic with men, my oh-so-ornamental one. Now go like the little lamb you are, and do me proud."

She took Monica out of the booth and sent her back stage, past a sleepy-looking, dirty-blond butch whose neck was ringed with hickeys. Adolpha's mouth tingled at the smell of blood so close to the surface, but she made herself wait. This was Bo. As the houseboy of Poison and two other bitch goddess strippers, her life was almost as hard as Adolpha would have made it. Best not to tamper with another she-wolf's province, Adolpha thought, chuckling at Bo's memory of her weekend, which seemed to have been spent in front of the fireplace, fisting two of her mistresses while the third whipped her shoulders. Having been in Bo's mind before, it was child's play for Adolpha to suppress the bodyguard's complaint about Monica's trespassing, and whisk the new toy up on stage.

Poison was not pleased to have another woman join her. She was collecting a decent amount of tips, and she did not want to share. For some reason, Adolpha disliked the idea of toying with Poison's perceptions. Perhaps it was the kinship of their sadism which made her feel as if this would be poaching. So she put Monica on her knees and stretched out her lovely hands in the universal gesture of submission. "You're so beautiful," Monica said. "Please let me serve you."

She began with adoring Poison's combat boots, petting them with her hands and then with her mouth. Adolpha enjoyed applying just enough pressure to Monica to force her to commit these strange and humiliating acts. It took a high level of skill and concentration to get the behavior she desired out of her quarry without actually changing her personality enough to make her enjoy it and begin to submit voluntarily.

Of course, there was a natural feedback process which Adolpha could not control, which was bound to change Monica into another woman altogether, even without the vampire's mental manipulation. She knew that men were watching her and becoming terribly aroused. She also knew she was safe from their intrusive touch, and so their arousal became contagious. The fact that money was being shoved through peepholes toward her satin-encased pussy was also a powerful aphrodisiac. As Poison rubbed her clit with the tip of her boot, she got wet, and the wetness was a most effective reinforcer, miles ahead of M&Ms. Adolpha found herself becoming a little annoyed when Monica unlaced Poison's boots and removed them without prompting, so she could lick her feet and ankles. The sudden absence of resistance made her feel as if she were going to tip over.

"If you try to go higher than that, I'm going to slap you," Poison warned Monica, taking off her skirt and revealing her trademark gold lamé G-string.

Adolpha bet herself it would take a dozen slaps for Monica to persuade Poison to let her put her tongue on the metallic strip of fabric. She relished, vicariously, the oiled and polished sensation of Poison's thighs beneath Monica's hands. The dancer's old-ivory skin was incredibly smooth and soft, and the muscles underneath it were like liquid steel. Bullets would bounce off her hard little ass. She smelled, Adolpha thought, like the most wonderful incense in the world, and wasn't it exciting to participate like this in someone else's first experience of approaching a woman's cunt? Shouldn't every woman have a lesbian experience at least once before she dies? Yes, Adolpha thought, oh yes. However, she declined to stay in Monica's place while the promised slaps were administered. Those she was content to watch from the outside, dipping briefly into Poison's riled-up mood as one dips nigiri into soy sauce that has been made explosive with wasabe.

Things were getting very hot on stage. Poison was about to break management's strange regulations which prohibited certain sex acts on stage, in the vain hope that this would prevent the theater from being busted. Adolpha was not sure that she wanted to share all of Monica's cherries, and so she strolled on stage, pleased to hear the gasp of surprise and recognition that burst from Poison, who just now remembered having seen her before in all kinds of strange situations. "Go," Adolpha advised her, not unkindly. "Take all this money and go home, and forget."

The assembled crowd could not believe their good fortune. Adolpha strolled the perimeter of her Plexiglas arena, letting them get a good look at her light-year-long legs and melon-round ass cheeks. She unbuttoned her jacket enough to give them all a peek at her cleavage, but as the dominant member of this duo, she was not about to shuck everything and shake it for them. Oh, no. That was someone else's job.

"Now that you have begun your instruction, you may proceed to a more advanced level of service," she said gravely to Monica Bradshaw, who was groveling on the floor, all purpose evaporated from her scrambled and cornered mind. "Put your succulent mouth to my shoe, little girl, and make it pretty. That's it. Yes, you are right to be cautious. I am hard to please. Ass higher in the air, my dear, let everyone see you in this state of need. Now peel them down, my babeling, softly, slowly, an eighth of an inch at a time. Oh, yes, let us all see how wet the shiny curls of your little parts have become. What is it that the sweet one needs? Come follow me, now, my darling little slut, and we will make sure all the gentlemen are equally educated about your base and bottomless need."

Adolpha pivoted, forcing Monica to come after her, shambling awkwardly on hands and knees, legs spread in a hapless invitation, heart aching for something, but no image to answer her mind's question about what it was she wanted with such fervor.

"Why, this, of course," Adolpha answered, overflowing with charity. She bent and touched Monica there, in the place that was sore and chafed from being wet for so long, and as Monica came so did many other people. Adolpha's slender finger was like a claw upon her clit, and she gave herself up to pleasure as the fallen deer gives itself up to the arrow in its heart. There was so much money on the stage that Adolpha kicked up a bit of a breeze to blow it toward the exit, where Bo could collect it. She was still standing guard for Poison, who was changing into street clothes backstage and getting one hell of a headache.

" 'Tis the season to be jolly," Adolpha announced. She waited a bit, then added, "It is better to give than to receive." She bent to Monica, kissed her tear-stained cheeks (much saltier than blood, those tears), and stage-whispered, "What have you gotten me for Christmas, my angel?"

Monica stared about herself in shock and disarray. The spaghetti straps of her slip had slunk down her arms, and her body was half-bare, looking hauntingly lovely even in the nasty greenish fluorescent light of the theater. Her voice was rusty from lack of use, but a pressure between her ears told her she must answer this unfair and ridiculous question. "I-I'm afraid I haven't got anything for you," she quavered.

"Oh, but you're wrong. So very wrong," Adolpha said, shaking her head. "You have so much to give me. All that you are, all that you could have been, that is the fruit that I am about to pluck."

Adolpha picked her up with one hand. Monica gasped to feel her feet leave the floor. "Put your soles on my shoulders," Adolpha advised, and so she did, not having any choice. "Pretend I am a tree that you are going to climb," Adolpha said, twisting her other hand between Monica's thighs. "A Christmas tree, I think, ablaze with glorious tapers, decked with every bonbon and gimcrack a child's greedy fancy could hope to see. And you are about to become the angel at the top of my tree."

Monica screamed as Adolpha's hand took possession of her channel, and cried out again in fear and triumph when Adolpha, glaring at the mental effort it took, levitated her until she stood without support upon the air. It looked as if the only thing that held her up was Adolpha's upraised arm and fist. It was a pretty sight, but it apparently had blown the audience's fuses, because the tips had faltered and a deadly silence had fallen over them all. Even those who had run out of quarters half an hour ago were compelled to remain and witness what was about to occur. For once in their lives, they wished an obscuring curtain would fall to protect what was left of their innocence, but they were not going to be granted the mercy of blindness.

Adolpha began to turn Monica's body, still holding her up in the air. Slowly, slowly, she made her rotate, gradually picking up speed until she was swimming in a circle upon the impaling fist of her captor. Despite the sobs of orgasm and terror that came from her victim, Adolpha insisted that she hold a graceful pose straight out of Swan Lake. This was supposed to be a dance club, after all.

And then the ballerina came to earth, soaked with sweat and other juices, wrung out and exhausted by passion fulfilled, fucked beyond her wildest dreams of sexual excess. (Which, in Monica Bradshaw's case, had actually been domesticated dreams of passion defeated.)

Adolpha slowly and deliberately tore the clothing from her body, discarding each tiny rag as if it were putrid. She bared her fangs and approached the cringing woman. Once, twice, three times she slowly chased her widdershins about the stage, and now some of the men in their booths were screaming and pissing themselves with fear, beating on the walls to try to smash their way out.

Really, it was a pity, Adolpha thought, by all rights it should be the men whose lives she took. They were the ones she hated. And she didn't mind killing them on general principle, especially if she happened upon one in the act of assaulting or abusing a woman. But she didn't like the way they smelled. Their blood had an offensive taste, as if it was slightly spoiled. And then there were those prickly necks, ugh, it was like trying to eat a salad of stinging nettles.

Adolpha loved other women. Their bodies stirred her the same way that works of fine art or great vistas stirred other people. Women were her passion, firmly at the center of her life. She had always felt that way, even before the world had a word for gay girls or bulldaggers or lesbians or dykes. This obsession had made her peculiar even in a culture that had no strictures against same-sex intimacy. And now, because this was where her lust had taken her, she would not even need to harden her heart before she received what she needed to live.

And so she took Monica in her arms, caressed her back and shoulders, and granted her the favor of one last climax, one that was so intense it brought tears to both of their eyes. Monica hardly noticed the fangs in her neck or the fading of her own vital signs as her blood passed obediently into Adolpha's painfully hungry mouth. As Adolpha's arms tightened about her, Monica's loosened until they fell back limply. There was barely enough blood left in her body to leave a faint trail down Monica's shoulder and breast. Adolpha dropped the body before she could see the pitiful red drops kiss the chilly, lifeless nipple. She felt no gratitude, just repletion.

She was warm now, heated to boiling, full of light and life, happy and sleepy and not a little high. She licked her teeth and contemplated the little crowd that was motionless and mute, still in thrall to her terrible will. She was tempted to simply leave the body and go, and let them all deal with the consequences, as expiation for their crimes against women. While she thought about it, she made all of them wail for Monica's death and scratch their own cheeks and chests. She tweaked each one of them, pinching out the bits of them that were mean or thoughtless toward women, twisting their narrow little souls in a more matriarchal direction. By the time they left this place, they would not remember what they had seen, and none of them would ever again fondle his secretary's bottom, slap his wife, pay a housekeeper minimum wage, or slight his daughter's ambition. And all of them would sleep with their hands clasped tightly around their own necks, curled up in the fetal position, as if they dreaded the sharp teeth of some night-flying succubus.

Adolpha forced herself to pick up Monica's remains. Her skin cringed instinctively from contact with the corpse. Humans were so distasteful when they were empty, as unsightly as used-up tins of soup. Her brother Ulrich was fond of mortals, wasn't he? Then he ought to pay his last respects to this one! His insufferable mortal companion could help Ulrich to fill in her grave.

There was just time to leave them both this little token of her affection, before dawn crowded night from the sky, and the crawl space of the Neptune Society's crematorium became Adolpha's shroud. She sought the wild dark wind, thinking how very glad she was that she had not left all of her Christmas shopping till the very last minute this year.

CONFESSIONS OF A BLOOD EATER

VANESSIAN SAMOIS

The life of the flesh is in the blood.
—Leviticus 17:11

And another truth is that you suspect you want to be condemned so that you can sin more freely.
—Cixous

"You've cut yourself!" I exclaimed, as you turned the hand towards your eyes.

"Yes," you murmured as a bright red trickle slowly wound its way down your arm, "the knife slipped."

"Let me see," I said, compulsively grabbing your hand so that the soft, blood-streaked palm was but inches from my mouth. Overcome by the sensation that buzzed in my body like a mild electric shock, I averted my eyes from the carmine stain, whose beauty heralded the arrival of damaged flesh, whose color fascinated me by virtue of its incipient orientation. The blood inside your body had escaped—just a little, but with an insistence that more of it lay, contained within, aching to be let out. The cut ran across the lower side of your right hand, dipping beneath the knuckle of your pinkie finger. It was perhaps an inch and a half long. Blood dribbled out in ominous droplets. I had to swallow to keep from getting excited. "It's not very deep," I said unconvincingly, as you pulled your hand away. And then you did a terrible thing: you turned your hand towards your lips and made a loud slurping sound as you sucked up the resinous fluid. My gaze fixated on your mouth; it parted, letting a pink tongue dart against the red wetness that streamed over translucent skin.

It was a thoughtless gesture, instinctual, embellishing your movements with a subtle eroticism, which had until then failed to attract me.

I tried to go back to my work, but you stayed within the vicinity, placing the wound to your mouth at repeated intervals, as the blood continued to seep out. I wanted to place my tongue in your mouth, to join with you in tasting the sweet nectar that you imbibed; the slurping sounds of your lips meeting liquid upset me terribly. Until then, I'd never seen you from this perspective.

You were dying a little. While the miniature wound bled, you were losing life. It was a silent dissipation, a loving transmission that exuded drop by drop as the red elixir sprang from your veins. You would die if the blood continued to flow, like a hemophiliac whose scratch has doomed him. This fact greatly excited me; my senses rippled beneath its implication. The idea rested in my mind like baby spiders hatching, overcome by the avalanche of life struggling to get out. Fleeing, crawling, dangling, it dripped and each drop was your life springing out, rolling onto the hardwood floors of the execrable; a world that drank your blood as quickly as you spilled it. Your skin, the organism of life, pulsated; a thin wall of tissue, a transparent state of temporary stasis, keeping this dwindling life within you, screened from the world, screened from my desires, which careened down darkened corridors towards you.

I wanted a share in this spillage of life, to take upon my tongue the sacred substance—but I was afraid that once I put my mouth upon the beautiful gap, nothing would stop me from tearing your flesh savagely, from ripping with my teeth the skin covering your veins, from letting my tongue fester in your throat to suck away the life there. A senseless battering emerged from inside me, warping all inward convolution of thought. The minor occurrence of a miniature wound hinted at imminent catastrophe.

Yet you didn't suspect my thoughts and feelings on this matter. My composed face, though covered in beads of sweat, did not convey the tumult that your bloodletting caused. I had never revealed to you my fascination with the death which we all carry within. "Why don't you get a Band-Aid?" I suggested. You ignored me, placing the wound to your mouth, while your eyes darted off to the side and your left arm wrapped itself around your waist as you hunched forward slightly, in meditation over the taste of your body, perhaps. If anyone glimpsed you from afar, they might assume that you were worrying a fingernail.

"For God's sake, the blood!" I tried to control myself, but the concept of consuming you proved too great. "Give it to me!" I whispered finally, keeping my eyes averted so that my glassy stare would not transmit to you its unnatural luminosity.

It gaped, with red lips spread wide, while a rivulet of hot liquid seeped from its middle; I joined my tongue in ecstatic union with the sapphire flow, each time sucking up the resinous fluid that refilled the narrow crevice.

You drew back, horrified.

"You shouldn't have shown it to me!" I hissed, as my tongue fully engaged itself, sliding in and out of the wound like a snake impregnating an uncommon orifice. When I closed my mouth upon the cut, your eyes jumped open in surprise, as something inside you recoiled, but they sprang back, like a mechanical toy in a box, allowing some unnamed desire to briefly show its face. Moments later I became acutely aware of your half-closed eyes and the ecstatic look that overcame your features; you seemed to lose the ground beneath your feet....

"It hurts," she says, head bent back, body thrown across the sheets, while I, the incubus, greedily suck away. The delicate sips which I imbibe from her throat are the only portions that sustain my existence. Her hands clutch in ecstatic display of temporary loss of sense; her eyes no longer see; all ten of her fingers grapple with my frame as my tongue makes its curious way into her parting flesh. Lolling in our incestuous bed, I am the larva living inside her neck.

There was an insanity to the blood eating; my desire had catapulted itself into a feeding frenzy of the mind, where I was, now, swimming inside your body, dissipated in purple corridors reeking of millenia-old excrescences. Blood sacrifice, love as the ultimate absorption, union through cannibalization, sex through decapitation, orgies beneath blood infested moons, obscure forms coming out of repressed regions of the soul, incantation, witches' oaths, the horror vacua of the present moment spread across my mind like a black stain of ink.

Then blackness, total blackness. There was no way out. I equated ecstasy with a raw urge to dissolve into nothingness, to drown in a bloodbath that debased you, relegating me to the category of the subhuman. This bloodletting, like hooks attached to my mind, baiting my sensibility, pulling apart my brain with subtle tugs.

You're squirming. You're writhing beneath me. Pain arches across your raised brows, your mouth—vermilion, like the blood that seeps through the incision.

I took it, the little knife. As I probed your neck with my tongue, seeking the appropriate vein, I jabbed it quickly, just a scratch actually. And then as it sprang forth, as its beauty crept out to meet me, as you drew your head back, I couldn't help but make a meal of you. Perhaps in horror, perhaps in apathy, I couldn't repress malign urges...

It was too late. I was consuming your flesh in glorious mouthfuls; a consumption that broke the internal grip of inhibitions within you. Who knew how long they'd been lying in wait? You who could do nothing but gasp and stare in disbelief at what I was doing. You didn't want me to know that you were enjoying it.

You thought you could escape didn't you? While armies of demons lined up outside your door, all with evil in their eyes. They were waiting to take you apart. I had not escaped even though I too find those I can take advantage of. In my wake, one can clearly see the havoc that an unrestrained passion can wreak. Whether it's vengeance, hatred, an excess of something too long ignored, a mind too finely tuned for the insults of existence, I don't know. I craved things I knew I could never have—the long swaying rhythms of the unreachable juxtaposed against the constraints of a dull consciousness.... I had to hide in order to live, my true nature rising up in me like a Trojan horse, to defeat the enemy, a subtle takeover in the disguise of the unnamable. I could have chosen to do nothing, to refuse to pay heed to the dragons smashing themselves to bits within. I could have, but every choice has its consequence. I could have died pure by not having lived, my soul heavy with lack of release.

Raven locks adrift on milk-white skin. The perforation mark on the area of the left side of your neck, only an inch above your clavicle, affecting me with aphrodisiacal intensity, unnerving me to the point of despair. The craze that gripped me, an ecstatic delusion that transported my mind into a divine hell, as sensual corruption rampaged through the nerve centers of my body.

Toys and shorn locks and love ripped open on its side. As you lay there ravaged all I could see was the beauty in your imminent death.

It was bleeding, while beating within: your heart. A persistent nakedness that throbbed its way from moment to moment, squeezing out fistfuls of blood at every gasp. Blood, the beautiful amalgam of liquid life that comprised your physical existence. How many times had my heart bled within, without spilling drops, letting the poison of pain sicken my body until I needed a transfusion from the body of another—yours. And what is it like to suck from another, the source of life which is precious to her? My tongue is the humming bird that hovers delicately in mid-air while imbibing the nectar of the tender stalk, a wholly natural absorption. The blade, pencil-thin, piercing the skin, running through it again and again, punctuated by silence and a certain languor amidst pain and droplets of blood that ooze out of the delicate wound. Ruinous droplets, all following one another along a path of uncertainty, until they puddle in a mercury-crimson pool at the feet of the despondent; the flowerhead drunkenly reeling, arms akimbo, legs splayed apart while somewhere music can be heard.

Quivering and shaking, I decided to incense your lack of inhibition by asking that you "take" from me.

"The blood...?"

"Would you like...?" I asked.

"?"

"Here," and with a simple slice of the self-same dagger, I laid bare the vein on the right side of my neck. Then it was your turn to taste in your mouth the salty fluid. You evinced, just for a moment, slight hesitation, perhaps disdain, but your tongue unconsciously licked your lips as you approached the moist tear. A beautiful feeling it is, to feel someone sucking your life from you. At first, as usual, my mind leaped in instinctive fear—it was too soon to die—but when your lips formed their adulterous union with my ruptured flesh, I was all for a throat slashing, lost within the grip of destructive passion as I was, nailed by a despotic hunger that equated pain with pleasure.

Was it so bad? And that sweet sickly scent rolling between us. Your animal consumption got the better of you, moments earlier you would have been disgusted...but now? Let it flow, cake yourself in the mire (the blood) of another's constraint, an oasis in the desert of emptiness. My fingers depleted your moral awareness, you wanted to open me up and jump inside, crawl inside my heart and never come out. But I am human after all. I bleed and die. You had to keep your lolling to a minimum. There would be more next time. I promised. Lollipops for everyone. You see, it wasn't so bad. I wasn't about to kill you. Your scream was unlikely to be extinguished in the quagmire of fate.

Covering my mouth with a luxurious kiss, you rubbed your breasts against me saying, "Oh, I could kill you...."

My body was an insect stuck through with a silver pin as you grappled with the satiny life that exuded from my skin. You made a mess of yourself over my blood, reveling in the way that sycophants do, incapable of doing anything but rut beneath hollow-eyed moons. You had a funny way of slipping in, like you'd always known my insides, as if a meal of blood was as normal as drinking a glass of water. "This is good. It's like wine," you murmured. I was at a loss for words. Covered in blood, my grasp on consensual reality had all but dissipated. We talked about it afterward.

You: "You've corrupted me. What have you done?"

Just laughter (mine). "I've corrupted you. Yes, you were too pure for all of that."

"That? You mean this reveling in the physical mire of another's insides?"

"Insides? It's only blood. It's not as if you'd consumed excrement."

"No, worse."

"How so?"

"You're making me into one of those sick people who do evil things in darkened rooms..."

"I'm making you? I'm not inviting you to become a serial murderer."

"No, worse."

"Oh come, what's this about right and wrong? You've got to learn to get beyond all that."

"But it's wrong! Can't you see—?"

"Drinking your blood? It just takes oral sex a step further."

"Yes, and that's why it's sick."

"You really need to lighten up," I say. "Look, after the way you acted—(you can't lament...) don't deny who you are."

"Who I am? Did it ever occur to you that I was happy with myself the way I was?"

"There's always room for improvement."

"And this is a step up?"

"In a manner of speaking."

A heavy sigh is released (hers). "You know deep down that it's sick."

"How do you know how I feel? It's a preliminary phase one goes through before growing accustomed—"

"—to becoming a physical parasite? Shit, I've become a deviant. The worst kind."

"You truly amaze me. First you enjoy yourself, then you rationalize."

"I'll never forgive you."

"Someday you'll thank me for it."

"For doing what? Making me want to hide in a bathroom every time I cut myself?"

"Stop it. You're getting carried away."

"Yeah." And then you walked away, perturbed and unconvinced, as a monster eased its way out from within.

You: "And the implications?"

Me: "It's just a kind of existence, that's all. You'll leave behind parts that never served you and become something you'd never imagined."

"A vampire? Please."

"Don't analyze it so much. What's more important are your feelings."

"I feel like shit."

"It'll pass."

"This is beginning to sound, oddly, like a psychiatric session."

"I'm beyond all that."

"You're going to hell."

"I am in hell." Then: "I give with what I take."

"What kind of cryptic crap is that?"

"It evens out," I say adamantly. "Perhaps I'll go to hell, but I've learned to accept it. You will too...."

"Go to hell?"

"You really have a lot of growing up to do. If you really feel bad about it, go to church and atone for it...but watch out for the bodies of the children standing nearby—they might start to get to you...."

"Damn it! You've sent me to hell!" you screamed.

"Stop it!"

My morbidity frightened you, an elegant striptease that left your soul bare, your mind defenseless.

"No, not that again. No more talk of death. The purpose of life is to...."

You were insulted by all that senseless melancholy, that dragging of the soul through the mud, the tragedy of the soul that couldn't find it in itself to act (properly).

"Jump finally!" or "Find someone to stone you!" Isn't that what you said? "Who needs to talk about it, after all God put us on this earth to...."

Yet I too was horrified when I initially realized that I was turning into a vampire. Especially since I was a vegetarian. But like an itch that only makes you scratch harder, the more I took, the more I needed to take. I'd been taken over by the mysterious power found in blood. The phenomenon had been documented recently in psychiatric literature. Small boys had been observed, behaving like vampire bats, raiding livestock pens at night, armed with razors. They'd suffered from a rare blood disease called Poryphyria, an erythropoietic deficiency of the blood that caused sensitivity to light and a bizarre craving for live blood....

There were others.

I obsess about blood, even among strangers. It's all I think about, and it frightens me. Standing in their midst, I can only think of the red-stained insides their bodies contain. My amorous pursuits are hence mere ploys at skin and neck games, contacts made among twisting veins standing out against pale backdrops of skin, giving me the ulterior motive to embrace others in order to breathe in the rose scent of their skin, beneath whose surface ebbs and flows the rosy river, driving me crazy with its insistent presence. The quivering insides, my incessant orgasmic relationship to a world of passion, making certain others resemble flowers. Beautiful, soft creatures, possessing scents whose perfume exudes manically from prepossessing stems. Smiles, concealing whole truths. Who can deny that they have a kind of life in them? A naked life shorn of petty cares, a vibrant juissance which has a mind of its own, whose arms seek to embrace another in silent passion in the heinous act of the unspeakable. Your hand in my hand, my head bent over your neck, absorbing the spilled life. Others cannot understand. I mustn't let anyone know. It is why I've learned to hide so well. I can feel their hatred from afar. When they peek into my mind it horrifies them, what they see. Their fear or surprise easily withers into seeds of hatred— dry and ugly, which they water with the urine of their incontinency, their wilted mortal consciousnesses, which cannot see the strength in evil. They want to kill me with their mediocrity, with their insistence on a life lived in a certain way.

And so I keep away from them, though certain aspects of them appeal to me greatly.

It's like when I am about to fuck someone, the feeling that comes over me when I am bent over the pale neck of my victim-lover. It is a penetration that transcends penetration, a taboo beyond all conceivable taboos. My tongue laps something far more substantial than the secretions that are meant to flow out of the body—tasting something so forbidden, so personal, that without it, I would die.

Blood—I could see clearly—came to signify for me something symbolic, a thing that only certain physical beings contained. And it was this something that their lives could be equated with. A separate, inert substance, as distinct as the element of gold—it became the (unconsciously) coveted material possessed by others that I could knowingly steal with my tongue. And it is minor bloodletting that sustains me most, for I do not harbor within my dark brain visions of violence and massacre; nor do I envision debacles of a daunting nature where body parts are hacked to pieces with malignant thrusts of vicious hatchets.... Rather, I seem to enjoy the letting of negligible amounts of the dark liquid, which gives me the impression of controlling on tap the vast resource of another's life, which I let leak out in artful spurts, filling, with my tongue, the crack in the wall of a great dam, staying the impending flood that threatens to inundate me at any moment, portending the release of the spirit, the death of the body. What free flowing love could be found in the veins of another, your veins!

Blood and fear. Fear of death. Spillage. Contamination. Impurity and violence. I brought you to the point where you wanted to stick knives in me. I always said that...but you had to make the first move. The first dagger thrust, then a twist. Why not? My heart was on a silver platter anyway.

Brick-red sunset. Eyes turned up to the ceiling. Blood oozing from the walls in my nightmare and black water engulfing me....

I took the red ribbon of liquid from you as a sign of fidelity. With a few malignant thrusts, my tongue had entered a sacred ground, profaned an ancient temple. Through you I could unburden myself of my desire and my guilt, both which sprang from the other. As night fell, a thousand silent hands clapped. I'd stay awake throughout, incapable of sleeping in a space that transcends space, my head thrusting its way through the sheets, your silent body resting beside me. Like the sun, its presence followed me everywhere. How can anyone understand what it's like to ride beneath the light of infinity and have the power of life burned into one's brain? Such was this passion. My haunted mind, from memories past, caress the truths that time squeezes from my bloodied heart.

I would have to have more soon. It was increasing. I needed it more often now. And I was not prepared to live without it. I walked, I spied, I listened.

At the party that night we saw them: the innocent couple. There was something spiritual about them, I could tell right away. A beautiful bond existed between them, which I wanted to rend, because I knew and they didn't, how sweet they were, how childlike. Remember? A man and a woman, not very young, not newlyweds. She'd been divorced, with a nine-year-old boy. But they emanated a purity that was in fact a little stifling. It was this purity that excited you. At first you stood off at a distance, watching them. When you came closer, you couldn't believe how they didn't know, how they hadn't detected its presence in you: the presence of evil, knowledge of the forbidden.

He, with his guileless blue eyes and snub nose. An accountant. She worked for an advertising firm. Virgo and Aries. But you wanted to sully their stainless sensibility, to bring them down to the level of the unrevealed which you knew lurked inside them somewhere.... How, you reasoned, could a love be so pure? How could they share in such beautiful innocence, it incensed you. After all....

When you walked up to them you said: "You two make a wonderful couple. I just wanted to tell you that." And then they sensed your interest and it made them slightly uncomfortable. But it was too late, you had spied their secret from afar: they were uninitiated and this lack desperately wanted you to insert yourself between them. Somehow you could imagine them doing things they'd never imagined. Yes, it would be good for them, liberating. Their innocence made them the most appetizing specimens. And they were ripe for it. You'd have to get them interested somehow. After a few words of exchange (you were discussing dreams), you realized that they were adults after all, not dreamy children. Though from afar they had appeared so blissful. You had to focus on their innocence, you had to catch the scent and drink of their cleansed souls because you felt you owed it to them. After all, they were not children—how had they managed to retain their innocence for so long? It was abnormal.... She was dark, dressed in black, with large doe eyes that seemed in constant fear or awe. He was blond, of heavy build, short hair. No nonsense, secretive. You saw between them a love you once knew, long ago...and couldn't help staring. But they knew nothing, so absorbed in themselves they were. You almost expected her to lift her fork and start feeding him from her plate as they huddled together, absorbed in gustatory diversions.

And how like you to become enamored of willful debauchery, to wriggle with contentment when you saw me fixate on them while fingering the knotted thong that hung from my neck. "Let's get it over with," you'd said, proceeding to laugh and talk your way into their innocent hearts.

You couldn't resist, after I'd taught you how to open veins. It was a sport. You wanted more and needed more. How many times did you drag me, face down to that lower region of yours, beseeching me, with spread (open) thighs, supple fingers kneading their way over heated organs, palpating veins and natural orifices, telling me: Suck! Suck!

You wanted to divide them up into little dishes, but I said, "That's enough." How could you do that to a pair of people who had nothing in common with us, whom we'd just met? You see, it was all very simple. We were to spare them their lives in order that we could go on living. But you got carried away and a little discipline was in order. "Did I tell you or didn't I that we were to treat them to a little disaster?" We were to bring them down to our level so to speak. You were to open her legs if you wanted to, but please her first. Then in the throes of orgasm.... Kinky love-joy. Why not just come upon them in their sacred gloom? Don't let their puerility nauseate you. Why not spread the flower of shame far and wide, let them eat from the forbidden apple? Yes, that's it. The allegory of evil acted before their eyes. Did you ever... and if yes, then...here—an apple. Take a bite. What does it signify? Oh no. Of course we're going to separate you. You come with me. She goes with her. We meet later at a designated place as agreed, after a certain rite has been enacted. It's actually quite painless. "Rite?" Do I hear a hint of suspicion in your question? Creeping laughter. Ritual. Like ritual slaughter. Eyes roll in their sockets. This is not going to be a pig slaughter. This is a seduction. Here, lie down beside me. Now let me...unloosen your pants and let me take a look. The skin. The veins. I'm in for the kill. Insides heaving. Flanks drenched in sweat. Party leaves, the Chinese lantern lurching in the breeze. Bolts issued forth, the emboldened leave-taking, the stripping from the body, nakedness. Red-gold and blue skin. Thigh neck vein, the hothouse in full, suffocating cycle of debacle and debauch.

Ripe voluptuosity preening inside another, I can almost feel the hot nakedness of the corridors, canal to the absolute. An unbelieving evaporation, the genius of the flesh. The only room in my heart is that vacant repository where certain torture devices lay waiting. Come in, make yourself at home. I experienced the pain like laughter. It heartened me, filled me to no end, rooted out my innermost contempt.

It took you over, slowly, inch by inch, the way diseases do. Your new identity, a formidable creature consisting in the things you thought you never could be. It is a fever of the mind, this vice, whose fury dismantles proper thoughts, yet leaving the scaffold of proper actions intact, making me (and now you) undetectable specimens of lust.

Though imperceptible to the discerning eye, my vulgar identity, which causes disruptions in the cobwebbed brains of the falsely righteous, in truth dissipates me too. It creeps out of me at night in an attempt to escape the closed spaces that bind my blackened soul.

Throughout, I have remained hidden from the retributive justice that civilized societies are resplendent with. My secrecy increases my hold on the little weapon that hangs suspended from my neck, hidden beneath the folds of my clothes.

And yet—what is this thing inside me? What creature lives and breathes in the dangerous confines of my love-lanced soul? A tormented creature, it has broken down doors and trampled lesser selves, yet I never gave it precedence, dominion. It was like a vine creeping in surreptitious fashion, emitting wraith like signatures (tendrils) which spiraled endlessly into empty space. I thought I knew what I contained within, but it never dawned on me. I became a snake in order to live through its skin, descended to the lower realms, squirming my way through the rotted flesh of the unfortunates, slithering through the pie-eyed night, hungry for the pureness of decadence, intent upon betraying the best intentions, those best intentions that live, all alone, in the hothouse of the heart. It's not so bad—once you've embraced damnation, it is a peculiar state of being.

And as you might guess, my favorite color is red. It is said that eating from red plates stimulates the appetite....

PUMPKIN PIE

SANDRA LEE GOLVIN

The only consolation is the pumpkin pie.

God knows Harry doesn't give a damn. Even if pumpkin is his favorite. And I don't give a damn either. So that makes us two people who don't give a damn in a trailer park in the middle of the fucking desert. When you get to that point even doing the laundry loses its meaning. I mean, no satisfaction left even in small things like clean sheets or the smell of T-shirts dried on the line.

Hotter than hell in the San Joaquin valley and the air's been still for days. Harry's gone with his Flick My Bic attitude and ask me if I care.

Everything was in its place, the housework done and the dead day stretched ahead of me like the power lines down Highway 5 when I got the idea to bake the pie.

Fight fire with fire, I thought. Actually, the pumpkin part came later, after I'd made that perfect white shell and had to find something to put in it. Pumpkin pie is always best because everything you need can be found in the pantry. Not a single fresh ingredient except the egg and that I could get from the Rhode Island Red that lives under the storage shed out back.

Every morning before dawn I strap it on. Sleep with it under the pillow. She don't believe in leaving nothing to the imagination. Wants her own space. That's how it has to be she says. She's got a great idea. Get me my own bed. There's no room for a regular bed she says, she's got a great idea. Get me a dog bed. Not those little foo foo jobs but a nice big wicker one like for a Rotweiller or a Great Dane. Before her I didn't strap it on like that, every day come rain or come shine. But how can you be ready for the inevitable she asks. She don't believe in wasting time. Hunting down things unnecessarily that you could just as easily have attached to your person. Don't let me see you without it she says. It's refreshing I can tell you. Most girls they don't want to know what's going in down there, don't want to see nothing. Just close their eyes in the dark and wait for home delivery. Not her. She wants to inspect. You gotta be prepared to stand at attention under a two-hundred watt bulb so she can see what she's getting.

The Crisco in the big blue can reminded me of Harry's dick and the time he'd greased it good and put it up my rear. Harry still had some good ideas back then.

The remains of a sack of Pillsbury bleached white flour with the three X's on the label drifted into the sifter, a fine clean powder like the stuff we'd snorted New Year's Eve that made me want to leave my skin on the card table like a snake. That stuff was long gone, but the desert holds other potent medicines that'll do the job. Harry likes his medicines.

I added sixteen tablespoons of Crisco, white on white, and cut the mixture with two mismatched silver butter knives. The cutting rhythm cheered me up. I began to enjoy the feel of those knives slicing through that white pulp over and over like the way the oil well next door keeps slashing at the same place in the earth year after year. I'd mark those X's like they were brands on old Harry's sweet white ass. I liked the idea of roping him down and marking him good, letting the blood trickle down his cheeks and into the crack between his legs. If the pie doesn't work, maybe he'll go for it. I'll tell him it's for old times' sake. Harry can be sentimental if you get him after a couple shots of rye. I checked the cupboard for Old Overholt and helped myself to a hit of Harry's private stash.

She had me standing like that the very first night. Strapped it on me herself. You know how those guys must feel when the Queen taps that sword on their shoulder and makes them royalty, just an ordinary guy does something right, all of a sudden everyone's gotta call him *Sir.* That's how it was with her. Yeah, she was on her knees in front of me but it didn't matter, she was still the Queen. It didn't seem right to have my head up higher than hers but there she was with my saber down her throat nursing like it was mother's milk. Just when I thought I could reconcile myself to it she rises up to her full majesty and shoves me back down where I belong.

I remembered the time Harry took one of these butter knives to my waist-length hair, blood red in those days courtesy of Lady Clairol, sawing away like a logger I'd seen one time on a trip up Highway 5 past Mt. Shasta into Oregon. Nothing came of it of course, Harry too loaded to make good on his threat. I cut it off myself a couple days later while Harry was cleaning one of his guns, tied it up in a pink ribbon and left it for him on his red plaid pillow with a note that said *To Harry, Love always, Mother.*

When she lifts up that skirt, I get hit with a smell that could drive my truck. Then she pushes her holiness into my face and tells me to lick, pointing her knife at my butt just for emphasis. Well, I didn't need no orders but I was happy to get them just the same. It was the ordering that made me know I'd come home. When she told me loud and clear what she wanted, it was like hearing the word of God for the first time. Down there on all fours in the hot sand is where I had my epiphanal moment, when it came all over me like summer hives exactly what it meant to be a man. No one had ever treated me so good.

I lit up a Parliament and took a good hard drag. I was getting hot. I took off my orange flower print apron, removed my cotton nightgown and put the apron back on. I lit the oven.

I put the ball of dough, just enough for a single crust, onto a big piece of wax paper and whacked it hard with the old wooden rolling pin. I took another drag of my cigarette and began to push the rolling pin back and forth across the white pulp until it flattened into a near perfect circle. I unloaded the dough onto the metal pie tin I had located miraculously in the far corner of the cupboard under the sink and used my thumb and forefinger to make a pretty-as-a-picture Betty Crocker crust. I even remembered to poke holes in the bottom with a fork so it wouldn't puff up like it did that Thanksgiving when Harry jerked off into the turkey before I stuffed it.

Sometimes when I'm laying in my bed all cozy with the smell of straw and dirt I think real fondly of my quivering meat. It's the meat that's the ticket to ride, that makes her love me like I was Richard Burton. She's crazy but it's okay with me. Sometimes crazy is a relief when you're working on the line day after day. You just want someone to come home to who will put your slippers in the oven and maybe threaten you with scissors. You don't get much of that kind of passion out on the line unless Old Man Martin's having one of his constipation days.

I dumped the cans of Libby's brand pureed pumpkin and Borden's sweetened condensed milk into the bowl where I'd mixed the dough. Out the screen door I lit another Parliament and stood on the back porch while the hot desert wind blew electric on my naked flesh, making my skin vibrate all over to its touch. I rubbed my bush lightly up against the wiry euphorbia plant next to the steps, pocketing the hand-like branch that snapped off before it hit the ground. I let the heat carry me to the metal storage shed Harry had won from old man Martin in a crap game. The steamy air continued licking me as I bent to search for an egg from the prize chicken that had come with the shed.

I get by dreaming of Pismo and the Queen. I'd hunk up on my Harley and pop wheelies in the sand when she said it was okay. Once I missed and it really pissed her off. She whipped out her knife and cut the tires to shreds. We had to throw the chassis into the back of the pickup and never come back. A woman like that can teach you things about being a man that you never could've conjured in your wildest mind.

Back in the house, I cracked the shell sharp against the porcelain and dropped the still warm insides into the bowl. Legs spread, I inserted the handle of the rolling pin up my cunt and worked it as far up as it would go. Then I fucked myself, letting my cum drip from between my legs into the bowl of filling. I stirred the mixture with my fingers, dumped it into the crust and shoved the pie in the oven.

The heat was nearly unbearable. But I like it that way. I lit another Parliament and turned the oven up.

It's about how they do it to you with their smell, how something sweet like lilac mixes in with the dead fish odor and makes all your parts go to water like you're saying hello to the sea. It's that big.

I went back outside where there was nothing. I scanned the sky for turkey vultures but those old buzzards had gone to find death elsewhere. I could imagine the sequoias across the barren space past the trailer at the edge of the world. Pumpkins wouldn't grow here, they need too much love. Harry had bought the seed packet for the color of orange on the backside, said he could picture that color painted in targets around my nipples. I read somewhere orange was the color of insanity. My mother wore orange every day of her life.

After the sacrifice, everyone seemed to be wearing orange. Harry came around the day it happened, just in time to clean the knife. I had seen him all the way down the beach, Pismo it was, a scrawny figure vomiting on the sand, and I said to my father, "Daddy, see that guy. That's the man I'm going to marry." I had an instinct for these things.

The ocean smelled especially fishy that day in a beautiful way that hurts to remember. It was red tide, or the grunion were running silver, or the seaweed floated black on the waves. Everything combined in a way I didn't understand so that the perfect thing to do was take that blade to Daddy's long pink body as he lay naked there, eyes closed kissing the wind. I needed to see the blood, the color of life, on the sand, and to feel that life run out in pretty little red rivers down to the sea. The ocean was Daddy's favorite place so it was fitting that he should die there.

It was that smell that made me bring home those pumpkins. It came wafting off those big orange squashes and the coincidence killed me. I never knew squash could smell in a way that'd make you hard. The farmer at the roadside stand treated me right too, talking about "Yes sir" and "Can I help you sir?" and "You sure got a fine looking truck there sir." I could see his little wife eyeing the bulge between my legs just under the silver buttons of my Levi's and sweat on her upper lip like she had an itch only a real man could scratch. I drove that truck around the dirt road into the pumpkin patch and I waited for the little woman to come tippy-toeing out the back of that shed and sure enough I had judged the situation right. She come running to me low down and creepy like the mouse she was, scurrying her little body up into my flatbed in amongst the pumpkins I purchased from her old man a dollar a bushel pick your own and I did.

I forgot all about Harry until he showed up beside me painted blue wielding a knife. Except I realized it was my knife. I recognized it as the one I'd used to carve Daddy's flank like I'd carved the roast pig each year at Lent. Daddy lay face down in the fire pit I'd clawed in the sand with my nails, a MacIntosh apple in his mouth. I had looked for a Red Delicious but all I could find was the MacIntosh. It barely fit in his mouth especially since rigor mortis had already set in and his jaw was clamped shut. That's where Harry found me, trying to jam that apple in where it didn't want to go. I asked him for lighter fluid and banana fronds.

Harry always did have great timing and with Daddy dead now, I needed a man. Of course Harry wasn't a man but he did such a damn good imitation of one, he was a better man than most of the men I knew. Harry knew when to keep his mouth shut and that's something I respect in a man. He knew better than to ask questions about women's business.

I whipped out my manhood and the mouse didn't bat an eyelash, just went to sucking and gnawing like she hadn't eaten in weeks. She was on there like a rabid dog on a bone and no amount of shaking could get her off. Well, I knew how my Queen would react if I was to come home with half her tool disappeared and the thought gave me the willies. But it was too late. The mouse had done it, bitten off damn near the whole thing and was laying on those pumpkins with the stub in her mouth twitching and grinding in the noonday sun for all the world to see.

Daddy tasted good that night, after I cooked up the marinade according to his favorite recipe—ketchup, honey, dry mustard and a shot of tabasco. I ate the dick and balls just like Daddy would've wanted me to. Harry kept the fire burning and ate only the toes. I didn't tell Harry Daddy had athlete's foot. By the time I found Harry sucking on those knuckles, it was too late for warnings and besides Harry looked so happy blue in the moonlight with his tits on end.

Harry slept on a wicker bed by the back door of the trailer. I picked that bed up at Polly's Poodle Parlor on Halcyon Street that first night after we finished eating Daddy. I liked the one with the red plaid cushion. Harry promised not to pee on it so I bought it with the tenspot I'd found in Daddy's old chinos before I burned them. It was an extravagance, I know, but I had an expansive feeling that night about Harry and about destiny so I sprung for it. Even spent the change on a pint of Old Overholt that I used to wash Harry down by the side of the road behind the Coulterville 7-Eleven.

I applied Daddy's old razor blade to make my mark on Harry's left tit then poured that whiskey on until Harry screamed at the moon. That's when I knew I'd been right about Harry and about destiny. We hunted through the dumpster for Three Musketeers and Parliaments and Harry licked my pussy clean better even than the Caldwell's old Rotweiller that used to visit me in the night with his tongue hanging out and spit on his chops. Fuck, the world looked great that night under that green and red light of the 7-Eleven.

In the morning, Harry called me "pumpkin" and I kicked him in the face. I'd already started seeing orange and I didn't like him rubbing it in. He couldn't help it though. I was so good to him he kept on calling "pumpkin, pumpkin" until I broke his nose and the taste of blood made him happy and quiet at last.

I couldn't explain the pumpkin lady to my Queen. How Her Majesty was the one who made it all possible. My manhood I mean. It's what I learned from her that makes the pumpkin ladies of the world come on after me, scent me out from a distance like dogs in heat. Before my Queen taught me about strapping it on and being at the ready, I couldn't get the time of day from a sweet little mouse but now, well it's kind of like she's created a monster. I can't tell 'em no when I can see they need it so bad, and they can tell ain't nothing makes me happier than making them happy. They just call on Sir Harry and there I be.

Fortunately dicks are a dime a dozen, except where we live in the boonies you can only get 'em by a catalog. We're on the mailing list of everyone who ever gave two minutes of thought to what new fangled contraption can put a woman over the top this week.

On trash day we headed east into the desert. I needed the sand but the ocean made me weep. I kept my back to it and let the dry places, the Mojave and the San Joaquin, be my sea. Harry turned out to be a good provider. He managed to eke food and shelter out of the driest, dustiest places in the state. Harry played it for what it was worth, just like he used to play the slots every weekend up at the gas station on Lone Pine Road. He'd set himself up first thing in the AM with his Milwaukee brew and Camels at his favorite machine, and I could find him there working most every Saturday and Sunday.

It's just sneaking back home and the time lag between now and when special delivery brings the meat that's damn near impossible to navigate. You think the Queen won't notice I've only got a little stump and a couple of sorry little balls left where her honeysteak used to be? I'll be a dead man for sure.

Lately though things have changed. He's gone for long periods of time saying he has to take care of his mother.

I had in mind to distract her with those pumpkins, with their orange color it'd be like waving a red flag in front of a bull. She gets real hot and bothered when she sees those golden squashes all round and sweet cut fresh from the earth.

Last week I caught sight of his old Dodge pickup filled with the prettiest pumpkins I'd ever seen and it not the season. I waited at home for him to bring them to me but they never showed. Not the pumpkins, not Harry. I found him the next morning curled up in his wicker bed out in old man Martin's shed, the truck's flatbed empty as the place in my chest where my heart had been.

But I couldn't take the chance my Queen would smell the juices Miss Mouse drizzled over every one of those prize pumpkins when she climbed up on them, her lips spread and what was left of my dick in her mouth. Boy, was she a sight to behold, bouncing around in the back of my truck as I went whipping through her old man's fields at top speed after he showed up at the back door of the shed with a shotgun in his hands and a genuinely scary look in his eye.

See I knew something that guy didn't. Until I met my Queen, I'd been trying to figure women out for years. I knew from my mother that they were the opposite sex, but opposite of what? Mother wasn't telling. You want to know what the Queen did for me? I'll tell you easy as pie. She made me feel like a man. You think that's simple? You think feeling like a man's a thing most men feel? No sir. Most men spend their whole lives trying to feel like a man without ever once finding a toehold on that slippery mountain of masculinity. She taught me this secret and I'll be forever grateful: It's more important to feel like a man than to actually be one. As soon as you feel like one, before you know it everyone acts like you are one, like you got that certain heft between your legs that means you got a ticket to ride.

There's that euphorbia, in bloom by the back door, with its milky insides that could kill a person if ingested improperly. The plant looks like a million green fingers giving the bird to the dead seething air. I feel a kinship with the euphorbia that I've never known with pumpkins. Pumpkins always leave me feeling insulted by their plump orange heartiness that lies about life in the desert. The euphorbia. There's a plant I could love, all wild and deadly like the rattlers that greet me in the dusk of summers too long to measure in human time.

With all her wisdom and what she done for me, it killed me to lie to my Queen. All those pumpkins gone to rot with her name on them, all those seeds that would never grow to the vine. In a way, though, it wasn't really a lie. In a way each of those pumpkin ladies is my mother. I see her in their hunger, the years I watched that woman who said she birthed me as she ate herself alive, pulled out her insides and devoured them, the entrails of pumpkins wrapped in old newsprint and destined for garbage like so much bad luck. I watched, I was helpless to stop her until every sign of life had been scooped out, hollowed to bone, and then I carried her in a squash leaf down that empty road that runs the long way from there to here and I cast her into the sea. Her seeds, her seeds I spread across the sand where they baked to flint in that impossible Pismo sun.

Harry never liked the euphorbia. Not that he ever said anything, that's not his style. One time I heard him taking a whiz outside the back door on his way in from one of his drunks, and in the morning, I smelled that acid piss scent on the lower branches. I know what Harry's piss tastes like and I sucked gently on a green finger just to confirm what I already knew. Later I vomited blood and remembered about the other properties of euphorbia. Harry's piss had never affected me that way even in large quantities straight up.

It happened as I gathered them into myself at the early blue time of day: that's when my Queen appeared before me—suddenly—like Cinderella with her rodent horsemen at the ball. I fed her my mother's seeds, just the way I feed them to all the would-be queens, into the cunt where I pray for something orange to grow big enough inside to burst the bindings that hold the dreams.

Maybe that was when it started, some kind of wet declaration of war, a back-door emancipation proclamation, sneaky like Harry can be.

I think I'm going home to my Queen now. I'll go down to her in the kitchen where she lives and I'll plant those seeds in that hallowed place of her own sharp majesty. I'll remind her about the magic carriage you can make from squash. Maybe she'll even bake me her specialty, the famous pumpkin pie. I'll take her in my arms right there at the table where she rolls the dough, and when she punches me in the face, we'll remember the sweet taste, the orange taste, the forgiving taste of pumpkin when it's fed to you, hand to mouth, by someone you love. .

And now here he is gone again, doing that mealy-mouthed mama's boy routine with some woman he says is his mother. As if I care. I'm glad I baked that pumpkin euphorbia pie. No regrets. I just hope Harry comes home soon or I'll eat that goddamn pie myself.

AND SALOME DANCED

KELLEY ESKRIDGE

They're the best part, auditions: the last chance to hold in my mind the play as it should be. The uncast actors are easiest to direct; empty stages offer no barriers. Everything is clear, uncomplicated by living people and their inability to be what is needed.

"What I need," I say to my stage manager, "is a woman who can work on her feet."

"Hmmm," says Lucky helpfully. She won't waste words on anything so obvious. Our play is *Salome*, subtitled *Identity and Desire*. Salome has to dance worth killing for.

The sense I have, in those best, sweet moments, is that I do not so much envision the play as experience it in some sort of multidimensional gestalt. I feel Salome's pride and the terrible control of her body's rhythms; Herod's twitchy groin and his guilt and his unspoken love for John; John's relentless patience, and his fear. The words of the script sometimes seize me as if bypassing vision, burrowing from page into skin, pushing blood and nerve to the bursting limit on the journey to my brain. The best theatre lives inside. I'll spend weeks trying to feed the sensation and the bloodsurge into the actors, but...but I can't do their job. But they can't read my mind. And people wonder why we drink.

Lucky snorts at me when I tell her these things: if it isn't a tech cue or a blocking note, it has nothing to do with the real play as far as she's concerned. She doesn't understand that for me the play is best before it is real, when it is still only mine.

"Nine sharp," she says now. "Time to start. Some of them have already been out there long enough to turn green." She smiles; her private joke.

"Let's go," I say, my part of the ritual; and then I have to do it, have to let go. I sit forward over the script in my usual eighth row seat; Lucky takes her clipboard and her favorite red pen, the one she's had since *Cloud Nine,* up the aisle. She pushes open the lobby door and the sound of voices rolls through, cuts off. All of them out there, wanting in. I feel in my gut their tense waiting silence as Lucky calls the first actor's name.

* * *

They're hard on everyone, auditions. Actors bare their throats. Directors make instinctive leaps of faith about what an actor could or might or must do in this or that role, with this or that partner. It's kaleidoscopic, religious, it's violent and subjective. It's like soldiers fighting each other just to see who gets to go to war. Everyone gets bloody, right from the start.

* * *

Forty minutes before a late lunch break, when my blood sugar is at its lowest point, Lucky comes back with the next resumé and headshot and the first raised eyebrow of the day. The eyebrow, the snort, the flared nostril, the slight nod, are Lucky's only comments on actors. They are minimal and emphatic.

Behind her walks John the Baptist. He calls himself Joe Something-or-other, but he's John straight out of my head. Dark red hair. The kind of body that muscles up long and compact, strong and lean. He moves well, confident but controlled. When he's on stage, he even stands like a goddamn prophet. And his eyes are John's eyes: deep blue like deep sea. He wears baggy khaki trousers, a loose, untucked white shirt, high-top sneakers, a Greek fisherman's cap. His voice is clear, a half-tone lighter than many people expect in a man: perfect.

The monologue is good, too. Lucky shifts in her seat next to me. We exchange a look, and I see that her pupils are wide.

"Is he worth dancing for, then?"

She squirms, all the answer I really need. I look at the resumé again. Joe Sand. He stands calmly on stage. Then he moves very slightly, a shifting of weight, a leaning in toward Lucky. While he does it, he looks right at her, watching her eyes for that uncontrollable pupil response. He smiles. Then he tries it with me. Aha, I think, surprise, little actor.

"Callbacks are Tuesday and Wednesday nights," I say neutrally. "We'll let you know."

He steps off the stage. He is half in shadow when he asks, "Do you have Salome yet?"

"No precasting," Lucky says.

"I know someone you'd like," he says, and even though I can't quite see him I know he is talking to me. Without the visual cue of his face, the voice has become transgendered, the body shape ambiguous.

"Any more at home like you, Joe?" I must really need my lunch.

"Whatever you need," he says, and moves past me, past Lucky, up the aisle. Suddenly, I'm ravenously hungry. Four more actors between me and the break, and I know already that I won't remember any of them longer than it takes for Lucky to close the doors behind them.

* * *

The next day is better. By late afternoon I have seen quite a few good actors, men and women, and Lucky has started a callback list.

"How many left?" I ask, coming back from the bathroom, rubbing the back of my neck with one hand and my waist with the other. I need a good stretch, some sweaty muscle-heating exercise, a hot bath. I need Salome.

Lucky is frowning at a paper in her hand. "Why is Joe Sand on this list?"

"God, Lucky, I want him for callbacks, that's why."

"No, this sheet is today's auditions."

I read over her shoulder. Jo Sand. "Dunno. Let's go on to the next one, maybe we can actually get back on schedule."

When I next hear Lucky's voice, after she has been up to the lobby to bring in the next actor, I know that something is terribly wrong.

"Mars...Mars...."

By this time I have stood and turned and I can see for myself what she is not able to tell me.

"Jo Sand," I say.

"Hello again," she says. The voice is the same; she is the same, and utterly different. She wears the white shirt tucked into the khaki pants this time, pulled softly across her breasts. Soft black shoes, like slippers, that make no noise when she moves. No cap today, that red hair thick, brilliant above the planes of her face. Her eyes are Salome's eyes: deep blue like deep desire. She is as I imagined her. When she leans slightly toward me, she watches my eyes and then smiles. Her smell goes straight up my nose and punches into some ancient place deep in my brain.

We stand like that for a long moment, the three of us. I don't know what to say. I don't have the right words for conversation with the surreal except when it's inside my head. I don't know what to do when it walks down my aisle and shows me its teeth.

"I want you to see that I can be versatile," Jo says.

The air in our small circle has become warm and sticky. My eyes feel slightly crossed, my mind is slipping gears. I won't ask, I will not ask.... It's as if I were trying to bring her into focus through 3-D glasses; trying to make two separate images overlay. It makes me seasick. I wonder if Lucky is having the same trouble, and then I see that she has simply removed herself in some internal way. She doesn't see Jo look at me with those primary eyes.

But I see: and suddenly I feel wild, electric, that direct-brain connection that makes my nerves stand straight under my skin. Be careful what you ask for, Mars. "I don't guess you really need to do another monologue," I tell her. Lucky is still slack-jawed with shock.

Jo smiles again.

Someone else is talking with my voice. "Lucky will schedule you for callbacks." Beside me, Lucky jerks at the sound of her name. Jo turns to her. Her focus is complete. Her whole body says, I am waiting. I want her on stage. I want to see her like that, waiting for John's head on a platter.

"Mars, what...?" Lucky swallows, tries again. She speaks without looking at the woman standing next to her. "Do you want...oh, shit. What part are you reading this person for in callbacks, goddamnit anyway." I haven't seen her this confused since her mother's boyfriend made a pass at her years ago, one Thanksgiving, his hand hidden behind the turkey platter at the buffet. Confusion makes Lucky fragile and brings her close to tears.

Jo looks at me, still waiting. Yesterday I saw John the Baptist: I remember how he made Lucky's eyebrow quirk and I can imagine the rehearsals; how he might sit close to her, bring her coffee, volunteer to help her set props. She'd be a wreck in one week and useless in two. And today how easy it is to see Salome, who waits so well and moves with such purpose. I should send this Jo away, but I won't: I need a predator for Salome; I can't do a play about desire without someone who knows about the taste of blood.

"Wear a skirt," I say to Jo. "I'll need to see you dance." Lucky closes her eyes.

* * *

Somehow we manage the rest of the auditions, make the first cut, organize the callback list. There are very few actors I want to see again. When we meet for callbacks, I bring them all in and sit them in a clump at the rear of the house, where I can see them when I want to and ignore them otherwise. But always I am conscious of Jo. I read her with the actors that I think will work best in other roles. She is flexible, adapting herself to their different styles, giving them what they need to make the scene work. She's responsive to direction. She listens well. I can't find anything wrong with her.

Then it is time for the dance. There are three women that I want to see, and I put them all on stage together. "Salome's dance is the most important scene in the play. It's a crisis point for every character. Everyone has something essential invested in it. It has to carry a lot of weight."

"What are you looking for?" one of the women asks. She has long dark hair and good arms.

"Power," I answer, and beside her Jo's head comes up like a pointing dog's, her nostrils flared with some rich scent. I pretend not to see. "Her dance is about power over feelings and lives. There's more, but power's the foundation, and that's what I need to see."

The woman who asked nods her head and looks down, chewing the skin off her upper lip. I turn away to give them a moment for this new information to sink in; looking out into the house, I see the other actors sitting forward in their seats, and I know they are wondering who it will be, and whether they could work with her, and what they would do in her place.

I turn back. "I want you all to dance together up here. Use the space any way you like. Take a minute to warm up and start whenever you're ready."

I can see the moment that they realize, ohmigod no music, how can we dance without, goddamn all directors anyway. But I want to see their interpretation of power, not music. If they don't have it in them to dance silent in front of strangers, if they can't compete, if they can't pull all my attention and keep it, then they can't give me what I need. Salome wouldn't hesitate.

The dark-haired woman shrugs, stretches her arms out and down toward her toes. The third woman slowly begins to rock her hips; her arms rise swaying in the cliché of eastern emerald-in-the-navel belly-dance. She moves as if embarrassed, and I don't blame her. The dark-haired woman stalls for another moment and then launches into a jerky jazz step with a strangely syncopated beat. I can almost hear her humming her favorite song under her breath; her head tilts up and to the right and she moves in her own world, to her own sound. That's not right, either. I realize that I'm hoping one of them will be what I need, so that I do not have to see Jo dance.

And where is Jo? There, at stage right, watching the other two women, comfortable in her stillness. Then she slides gradually into motion, steps slowly across the stage and stops three feet from the belly-dancer, whose stumbling rhythm slows and then breaks as Jo stands, still, watching. Jo looks her straight in the eye, and just as the other woman begins to drop her gaze, Jo suddenly whirls, throwing herself around so quickly that for an instant it's as if her head is facing the opposite direction from her body. It is a nauseating moment, and it's followed by a total body shrug, a shaking off, that is both contemptuous and intently erotic. Now she is facing the house, facing the other actors, facing Lucky, facing me: now she shows us what she can do. Her dance says this is what I am, that you can never be; see my body move as it will never move with yours. She stoops for an imaginary platter, and from the triumph in her step I begin to see the bloody prize. The curve of her arm shows me the filmed eye and the lolling tongue; the movement of her breast and belly describe for me the wreckage of the neck, its trailing cords; her feet draw pictures in the splashed gore as she swirls and turns and snaps her arm out like a discus thrower, tossing the invisible trophy straight at me. When I realize that I have raised a hand to catch it, I know that I have to have her, no matter what she is. Have to have her for the play. Have to have her.

When the actors are gone, Lucky and I go over the list. We do not discuss Salome. Lucky has already set the other two women's resumés aside.

Before we leave: "God, she was amazing. She'll be great, Mars. I'm really glad it turned out this way, you know, that she decided to drop that crossdressing stuff."

"Mmm."

"It really gave me a start, seeing her that day. She was so convincing as a man. I thought...well, nothing. It was stupid."

"It wasn't stupid."

"You didn't seem surprised—did you know that first time when he...when she came in that she wasn't...? Why didn't you say?"

"If I'm looking at someone who can play John, I don't really care how they pee or whether they shave under their chins. Gender's not important."

"It is if you think you might want to go to bed with it."

"Mmm," I say again. What I cannot tell Lucky is that all along I have been in some kind of shock; like walking through swamp mud, where the world is warm silkywet but you are afraid to look down for fear of what might be swimming with you in the murk. I know that this is not a game: Joe was a man when he came in and a woman when she came back. I look at our cast list and I know that something impossible and dangerous is trying to happen; but all I really see is that suddenly my play—the one inside me—is possible. She'll blow a hole through every seat in the house. She'll burst their brains.

* * *

Three weeks into rehearsal, Lucky has unremembered enough to start sharing coffee and head-together conferences with Jo during breaks. The other actors accept Jo as someone they can't believe they never heard of before, a comrade in the art wars. We are such a happy group; we give great ensemble.

Lance, who plays Herod, regards Jo as some kind of wood sprite, brilliant and fey. He is myopic about her to the point that if she turned into an anaconda, he would stroke her head while she wrapped herself around him. Lance takes a lot of kidding about his name, especially from his boyfriends. During our early rehearsals, he discovered a very effective combination of obsession and revulsion in Herod: as if he would like to eat Salome alive and then throw her up again, a sort of sexual bulimia.

Susan plays Herodias; Salome's mother, Herod's second wife, his brother's widow. She makes complicated seem simple. She works well with Lance, giving him a strong partner who nevertheless dims in comparison to her flaming daughter, a constant reminder to Herod of the destruction that lurks just on the other side of a single yes to this step-daughter/niece/demonchild who dances in his fantasies. Susan watches Jo so disinterestedly that it has taken me most of this time to see how she has imitated and matured the arrogance that Jo brings to the stage. She is a tall black woman, soft muscle where Jo is hard: nothing like Jo, but she has become Salome's mother.

And John the Baptist, whose real name is Frank and who is nothing like Joe: I'm not sure I could have cast him if he had come to the audition with red hair, but his is black this season, Irish black for the O'Neill repertory production that he just finished. Lucky says he has "Jesus feet." Frankie's a method actor, disappointed that he doesn't have any sense memory references for decapitation. "I know it happens offstage," he says earnestly, at least once a week. "But it needs to be there right from the start, I want them to think about it every scene with her." *Them* is always the audience. *Her* is always Jo. Offstage, he looks at her the way a child looks at a harvest moon.

Three weeks is long enough for us all to become comfortable with the process but not with the results: the discoveries the actors made in the first two weeks refuse to gel, refuse to reinvent themselves. It's a frustrating phase. We're all tense but trying not to show it, trying not to undermine anyone else's efforts. It's hard for the actors, who genuinely want to support each other, but don't really want to see someone else break through first. Too scary: no one wants to be left behind.

There's a pseudosexual energy between actors and directors: there's so much deliberate vulnerability, control, desire to please; so much of the stuff that sex is made of. Working with my actors is like handling bolts of cloth: they each have a texture, a tension. Lance is brocade and plush; Susan is smooth velvet, subtle to the touch; Frankie is spun wool, warm and indefinably tough. And Jo: Jo is raw silk and razor blades, so fine that you don't feel the cut.

So we're all tense; except for Jo. Oh, she talks, but she's not worried; she's waiting for something, and I am beginning to turn those audition days over in my memory, sucking the taste from the bones of those encounters and wondering what it was that danced with me in those early rounds, what I have invited in.

And a peculiar thing begins: as I grow more disturbed, Jo's work becomes better and better. In those moments when I suddenly see myself as the trainer with my head in the mouth of the beast, when I slip and show that my hand is sweaty on the leash—in those moments her work is so pungent, so ripe that Jo the world-shaker disappears, and the living Salome looks up from the cut-off t-shirt, flexes her thigh muscles under the carelessly torn jeans. We have more and more of Salome every rehearsal.

On Friday nights, I bring a cooler of Corona and a bag of limes for whoever wants to share them. This Friday everyone stays. We sit silent for the first cold green-gold swallows. Lance settles back into Herod's large throne. I straddle a folding chair and rest my arms along the back, bottle loose in one hand. Lucky and the other actors settle on the platforms that break the stage into playing areas.

It starts with the actors talking, as they always do, about work. Lance has played another Herod, years ago, in *Jesus Christ Superstar,* and he wants to tell us how different that was.

"I'd like to do *Superstar,*" Jo says. It sounds like an idle remark. She is leaning back with her elbows propped against the rise of a platform, her breasts pushing gently against the fabric of her shirt as she raises her bottle to her mouth. I look away because I do not want to watch her drink, don't want to see her throat work as the liquid goes down.

Lance considers a moment. "I think you'd be great, sweetheart," he says, "But Salome to Mary Magdalene is a pretty big stretch. Acid to apple juice. Wouldn't you at least like to play a semi-normal character in between, work up to it a little?"

Jo snorts. "I'm not interested in Magdalene. I'll play Judas."

Lance whoops, Frankie grins, and even the imperturbable Susan smiles. "Well, why not?" Lance says. "Why shouldn't she play Judas if she wants to?"

"Little question of gender," Frankie says, and shrugs.

Susan sits up. "Why shouldn't she have the part if she can do the work?"

Frankie gulps his beer and wipes his mouth. "Why should any director hire a woman to play a man when they can get a real man to do it?"

"What do you think, Mars?" The voice is Jo's. It startles me. I have been enjoying the conversation so much that I have forgotten the danger in relaxing around Jo or anything that interests her. I look at her now, still sprawled back against the platform with an inch of golden beer in the bottle beside her. She has been enjoying herself, too. I'm not sure where this is going, what the safe answer is. I remember saying to Lucky, Gender's not important.

"Gender's not important, isn't that right, Mars?"

Lucky told her about it. But I know Lucky didn't. She didn't have to.

"That's right," I say, and I know from Jo's smile that my voice is not as controlled as it should be. Even so, I'm not prepared for what happens next: a jumble of pictures in my head, images of dancing in a place so dark that I cannot tell if I am moving with men or women, images of streets filled with androgynous people and people whose gender-blurring surpasses androgyny and leaps into the realm of performance. Women dressed as men making love to men; men dressed as women hesitating in front of public bathroom doors; women in high heels and pearls with biceps so large that they split the expensive silk shirts. And the central image, the real point: Jo, naked, obviously female, slick with sweat, moving under me and over me, Jo making love to me until I gasp and then she begins to change, to change, until it is Joe with me, Joe on me—and I open my mouth to shout my absolute, instinctive refusal— and I remember Lucky saying It is if you think you might want to sleep with it—and the movie breaks in my head and I am back with the others. No one has noticed that I've been assaulted, turned inside out. They're still talking about it: "Just imagine the difference in all the relationships if Judas were a woman," Susan says earnestly to Frankie. "It would change everything!" Jo smiles at me and swallows the last of her beer.

* * *

The next rehearsal I feel fragile, as if I must walk carefully to keep from breaking myself. I have to rest often. I am running a scene with Frankie and Lance when I notice Lucky offstage, talking earnestly to Jo. Jo puts one hand up, interrupts her, smiles, speaks, and they both turn to look at me. Lucky suddenly blushes. She walks quickly away from Jo, swerves to avoid me. Jo's smile is bigger. Her work in the next scene is particularly fine and full.

"What did she say to you, Luck?" I ask her as we are closing the house for the evening.

"Nothing," Lucky mumbles.

"Come on."

"Okay, fine. She wanted to know if you ever slept with your actors, okay?"

I know somehow that it's not entirely true: I can hear Jo's voice very clearly, saying to Lucky, So does Mars ever fuck the leading lady? while she smiles that catlick smile. Jo has the gift of putting pictures into people's heads, and I believe Lucky got a mindful. That's what really sickens me, the idea that Lucky now has an image behind her eyes of what I'm like...no, of what Jo wants her to think I'm like. God knows. I don't want to look at her.

* * *

"Did you get my message?" Jo says to me the next evening, when she finally catches me alone in the wings during a break from rehearsal. She has been watching me all night. Lucky won't talk to her.

"I'm not in the script."

"Everybody's in the script."

"Look, I don't get involved with actors. It's too complicated, it's messy. I don't do it."

"Make an exception."

Lucky comes up behind Jo. Whatever the look is on my face, it gets a scowl from her. "Break's over," she says succinctly, turning away from us even before the words are completely out, halfway across the stage before I think to try to keep her with me.

"Let's get back to work, Jo."

"Make a fucking exception."

I don't like being pushed by actors, and there's something else, too, but I don't want to think about it now, I just want Jo off my back, so I give her the director voice, the vocal whip. "Save it for the stage, princess. You want to impress me, get out there and do your fucking job."

She doesn't answer; her silence makes a cold, high-altitude circle around us. When she moves, it's like a snake uncoiling, and then her hand is around my wrist. She's strong. When I look down, I see that her hand is changing: the bones thicken under the flesh, the muscles rearrange themselves subtly, and it's Joe's hand on Jo's arm, Joe's hand on mine. "Don't make me angry, Mars," and the voice is genderless and buzzes like a snake. There is no one here to help me, I can't see Lucky, I'm all alone with this hindbrain thing that wants to come out and play with me. Jo's smile is by now almost too big for her face. Just another actor, I think crazily, they're all monsters anyway.

"What are you?" I am shaking.

"Whatever you need, Mars. Whatever you need. Every director's dream. At the moment, I'm Salome, right down to the bone. I'm what you asked for."

"I didn't ask for this. I don't want this."

"You wanted Salome, and now you've got her. The power, the sex, the hunger, the need, the wanting, it's all here."

"It's a play. It's just...it's a play, for chrissake."

"It's real for you." That hand is still locked around my wrist; the other hand, the soft small hand, reaches up to the center of my chest where my heart tries to skitter away from her touch. "I saw it, that first audition. I came to play John the Baptist, I saw the way Lucky looked at me, and I was going to give her something to remember...but your wanting was so strong, so complex. It's delicious, Mars. It tastes like spice and wine and sweat. The play in your head is more real to you than anything, isn't it, more real than your days of bright sun, your friends, your office transactions. I'm going to bring it right to you, into your world, into your life. I'll give you Salome. On stage, off stage, there doesn't have to be any difference. Isn't that what making love is, giving someone what they really want?"

She's still smiling that awful smile and I can't tell whether she is talking about love because she really means it or because she knows it makes my stomach turn over. Or maybe both.

"Get out of here. Out of here, right now." I am shaking.

"You don't mean that, sweet. If you did, I'd already be gone."

"I'll cancel the show."

She doesn't answer: she looks at me and then, phht, I am seeing the stage from the audience perspective, watching Herod and Herodias quarrel and cry and struggle to protect their love, watching John's patient fear as Herod's resolve slips away: watching Salome dance. When she dances, she brings us all with her, the whole audience living inside her skin for those moments. We all whirl and reach and bend, we all promise, we all twist away. We all tempt. We all rage. We stuff ourselves down Herod's throat until he chokes on us. And then we are all suddenly back in our own bodies and we roar until our throats hurt and our voices rasp. All the things that I have felt about this play, she will make them feel. What I am will be in them. What I have inside me will bring them to their feet and leave them full and aching. Oh god, it makes me weep, and then I am back with her, she still holds me with that monster hand and all I can do is cry with wanting so badly what she can give me.

Her eyes are too wide, too round, too pleased. "Oh," she says, still gently, "It's okay. You'll enjoy most of it, I promise." And she's gone, sauntering onstage, calling out something to Lance, and her upstage hand is still too big, still wrong. She lets it caress her thigh once before she turns it back into the Jo hand. I've never seen anything more obscene. I have to take a minute to dry my eyes, cool my face. I feel a small, hollow place somewhere deep, as if Jo reached inside and found something she liked enough to take for herself. She's there now, just onstage, ready to dance, that small piece of me humming in her veins. How much more richness do I have within me? How long will it take to eat me, bit by bit? She raises her arms now and smiles, already tasting. Already well fed.

About the Authors

Dorothy Allison is the author of the poetry collection *the women who hate ME* (Firebrand, 1991), the Lambda Literary Award-winning short story collection, *Trash* (Firebrand, 1988), the National Book Award Finalist for Fiction, *Bastard Out of Carolina* (Dutton, 1992), the Lambda Literary Award-winning *Skin: Talking about Sex, Class, and Literature* (Firebrand, 1994), and *Two or Three Things I Know for Sure* (Dutton, 1995).

J.M. Beazer received an MFA in Creative Writing from Sarah Lawrence College in 1993. From December 1994 to January 1995, she was a resident at the MacDowell colony, where she worked on her novel *The Festival of Sighs* and some ghost stories. She lives in New York City, where she's working on a second novel.

Lucy Jane Bledsoe is the author of *Sweat* (Seal Press, 1995) and a children's novel, *The Big Bike Race* (Holiday House, 1995). She is the editor of *Heatwave: Women in Love and Lust* (Alyson, 1995). Her novel, *Working Parts*, is forthcoming from Seal Press. Her fiction has appeared in numerous publications and anthologies, including *Newsday Magazine* (as a PEN Syndicated Fiction winner), *Women on Women 2*, *Afterglow*, and *Sportsdykes*. She also writes books for, and teaches creative writing to, adult literacy students.

Kate Bornstein is a Seattle-based performance artist and writer. She is the author of *Gender Outlaw: On Men, Women, and the Rest of Us* (Routledge, 1994), and the novel *Nearly Roadkill* with co-author Caitlin Sullivan. Her stage work includes the solo pieces, *The Opposite Sex Is Neither* and *Virtually Yours: A Game for Solo Performer with Audience*. When not writing or performing, Kate can be found cuddling with Gwydyn, following the adventures of Hothead Paisan, or prowling the Net in a never-ending search for blood, daddy, or X-rated Star Trek role-playing games.

Pat Califia is well-known as a sharp critic of repressive American attitudes toward sexuality and pornography, a long-time activist for gay rights and the right to free sexual expression, and a lecturer on sexual politics. She has authored twelved books including *Macho Sluts* (Alyson, 1988), *Doc and Fluff* (Alyson, 1990), *Melting Point* (Alyson, 1993), and *Public Sex* (Cleis, 1994) and edited *Coming to Power* (Alyson), *The Second Coming* (Alyson, 1996), and *Doing It For Daddy* (Alyson, 1994). She is currently at work on a novel, *The Code*, which will be published by Richard Kasak Books, and a history of transgenderism, *Sex Changes*, for Cleis Press. She lives in San Francisco where she recently completed her MA in counseling psychology.

Meg Daly is a poet and writer whose work has been published in several literary journals. She is the editor of the anthology *Surface Tension: Love, Sex and Politics Between Lesbians and Straight Women* (Simon & Schuster, 1996). Meg grew up in Wilson, Wyoming and now lives in Brooklyn, New York.

Mona de Vestel was born in Brussels, Belgium. She holds a MA in Interactive Telecommunications from the Tisch School of the Arts at New York University and works as a research analyst in multi-media communication. She lives in New York City and is currently at work on her first novel.

Kelley Eskridge lives in Seattle with her partner, Nicola Griffith. She won an Astrea National Lesbian Action Foundation Emerging Writers Award in 1992. Her short fiction has been published in the US and the UK, including *The Magazine of Fantasy and Science Fiction*, *Century Magazine*, *Pulphouse Magazine*, *Little Deaths* and *The Year's Best Fantasy and Horror 1995*. She is completing work on her first novel.

Jennifer Natalya Fink is a doctoral candidate in the Department of Performance Studies at New York University and an editor of *Women & Performance*. Her fiction can be found in *Global City Review*, *P-form*, *two girls review*, *Women & Performance*, *Windy City Times*, and *New Art Examiner*. Her book, *Performing Hybridity in the International Sphere*, will be published by University of Minnesota Press in 1997.

Sandra Lee Golvin is a native Los Angelena, queer cultural activist, dyke poet and lawyer. S/he is the co-editor of the 'zine *Diabolical Clits*. Her work appears in the anthologies *Hers*, *Ritual Sex*, and *Power Tools*, and the journals *Fireweed* and *Spoon River Poetry Review*. Her critically acclaimed one-woman show "Pumpkin Pie: A Story of Cross-Gender Transcendence" ran at Highways as part of Ecce Lesbo/Ecce Homo, the

Sixth Annual National Lesbian and Gay Performance Festival. Her thing is gender, language, and the belief in magic.

Gerry Gomez Pearlberg's writings have appeared in numerous literary magazines and anthologies, including *Women on Women 3, Sister and Brother, Best American Erotica 1994, X-X-X Fruit, Global City Review, Queer City,* and *Calyx.* She edited *The Key To Everything: Lesbian Love Poems* (St. Martin's, 1995) and *The Zenith of Desire,* an anthology of lesbian erotic verse (Crown, 1996). She recently completed her first poetry collection, *Botanical Gardens at Night.*

Karen Green's work appears in *Boji For The Mentally Ill, Princess, Pucker Up,* the anthology *Power Tools,* and dozens of self-published volumes. A favorite on the spoken word circuit in San Francisco where she studied under Kathy Acker, Karen now lives in New York. She works as a graphic designer and dances with the cult band The Voluptuous Horror of Karen Black. She's at work on her first novel, *flower.*

Nicola Griffith is the author of the novels *Slow River* (Ballantine/Del Rey, 1995) and *Ammonite* (Ballantine/Del Rey, 1993), which won both a Lambda Literary Award and the James Tiptree Jr. Memorial Award. Her collection of essays and short fiction, *Women and Other Aliens,* will be published by HarperPrism in October 1996. She lives in Seattle with writer Kelley Eskridge.

Corrina Kellam, a Southern Maine native, has recently relocated to Philadelphia in order to pursue a degree in poetry. Before moving, she completed her first collection of short stories entitled *The Quiet,* which features "Semiraw." She is currently going gangbusters on her next collection.

Linda L. Nelson is a writer and editor as well as Director of New Media & Technology for the *Village Voice* and *LA Weekly* newspapers. Her poetry, prose, and short fiction have appeared in several periodicals and anthologies. She lives in Brooklyn, New York with her dog, Tosca.

Jane Perkins has performed her collection of monologues, *Food, Clothing, and Shelter,* in theatres around New York City. She received an Emerging Artists Grant from The Field, and came in seventh place in the 1995 Writer's Digest short fiction competition. She is currently writing a novel.

193

Robin Podolsky is a writer who lives and works in Los Angeles. Her fiction and poetry are included in the anthologies *Blood Whispers, Discontents, Indivisible, Hers, Ritual Sex,* and *Grand Passion*. Her forthcoming book, *Queer Cosmopolis,* will be published by New York University Press. After a decade as an independent artist, she has surrendered to the academy and is working toward her BA at Pitzer College in Claremont, California.

Marian Rooney grew up in Virginia, England, and Ireland, and is still growing. She lives in Los Angeles with her baby daughter, Aoife, and Thom Calderón.

Linda Smukler is the author of *Normal Sex* (Firebrand, 1995), a finalist for a Lambda Literary Award in poetry. Her work has appeared in numerous journals and antholologies, and she has received fellowships in poetry from the New York Foundation for the Arts and the Astraea Foundation. Her new book of poems, *Home in Three Days. Don't Wash.,* with accompanying CD-ROM, is forthcoming from Hard Press in 1996.

Vanessian Samois is an Italian-Irish American with diverse interests. She holds an MA in philosophy from New York University, has a background as a visual artist, and recently devoted herself to experimental writing. In 1993, she won Honorable Mention in the Silver Quill Writing Contest. She has published graphics, poetry, and fiction in various literary journals and is included in the Marquis *Who's Who of American Women 1996*.

Wickie Stamps is a writer whose published works appear in numerous anthologies including *Flashpoint, Sister and Brother, Looking for Mr. Preston, Doing It For Daddy, Leatherfolk,* and *Queer View Mirror*. She has work forthcoming in *Best of Brat Attack* and *Switch Hitters*. She is the editor of *Drummer* magazine.

Nancy Stockwell has published in *Sinister Wisdom, The Washington Review, The Washington Post TV Magazine* and the anthology *A True Likeness*. She was awarded a grant for fiction by the Washington DC Commission on the Arts. She is the author of two volumes of stories: *Out Somewhere and Back Again* (Medusa Press, 1978) and *The Ruby Shoe Rebellion*. She writes and teaches in Kansas.

Trish Thomas is on a ten-year plan to live in ten states in ten years. Her first stop out of San Francisco is Portland, Oregon, where she's at work on a collection of essays about sex, writing, and popular culture. Her writing has appeared in *Frighten the Horses*, *Quim*, *Taste of Latex*, *On Our Backs*, and *Girlfriends*. Her essay "Thirty-Six Strokes" will be anthologized in *The Click*.

Alison Tyler is a San Francisco-based erotic writer whose short stories appear in *Playgirl*, *Herotica 4*, and *Pucker Up*. Her first novel, *Valentine* (Blue Moon Books, 1994) was produced as a book-on-tape by Passion Press in 1995. She has published three other novels: *The Blue Rose*, *The Virgin*, *Dial 'L' for Loveless*, and the short story collection *Blue Sky Sideways*, all for Rosebud Books. She recently finished *Dark Room*, a novel about on-line S/M, and she is currently at work on a horror novel.

Terry Wolverton is the author of the Lambda Literary Award Finalist for poetry, *Black Slip* (Clothespin Fever, 1993). Her novel, *Bailey's Beads*, will be published by Faber and Faber in 1996. Terry teaches creative writing and has edited several literary compilations, among them *Indivisible* (Plume, 1991), *Blood Whispers* (Silverton Books, 1991), *His*, and *Hers* (Faber and Faber, 1995). She lives in Los Angeles with her lover, artist Susan Silton, and is a recent recipient of a Movers and Shakers Award from the Southern California Library for Social Studies and Research.

ABOUT THE EDITORS

Heather Lewis is the author of *House Rules* (Nan Talese/Doubleday, 1994), which won the Ferro-Grumley Award, the New Voice Award, was a Lambda Literary Award finalist, and has been optioned for a film. Her fiction has appeared in the anthologies *Living with the Animals* and *Surface Tension*. She has completed a second novel, *Notice,* and is at work on a third novel. She lives in New York City where she teaches at The Writer's Voice.

Tristan Taormino is co-founder and owner of Black Dog Productions, a literary agency. She is editor of *Ritual Sex* (Richard Kasak Books, 1996) with David Aaron Clark, and *Power Tools* (Masquerade Books, 1996). Her work has appeared in numerous publications and anthologies including *The Femme Mystique, Heatwave: Women in Love and Lust, Virgin Territory II, Strategic Sex, While the Dancing Divas Were Out and About, On Our Backs, X-X-X Fruit, Venus Infers,* and *Blue Blood.* She is also Publisher and Editrix of the magazine *Pucker Up,* and is currently at work on a short story collection, *Bombshell & Other Stories,* a novel, an anthology of women's fiction, a book about girl 'zines, and an erotic audio project. She lives in Brooklyn with her dog, Reggie Love.

Books from Cleis Press

Sexual Politics

Forbidden Passages:
Writings Banned in Canada
introductions by Pat Califia
and Janine Fuller.
ISBN: 1-57344-020-5 24.95 cloth;
ISBN: 1-57344-019-1 14.95 paper.

Good Sex: Real Stories from
Real People, second edition,
by Julia Hutton.
ISBN: 1-57344-001-5 29.95 cloth;
ISBN: 1-57344-000-0 14.95 paper.

The Good Vibrations Guide to
Sex: How to Have Safe, Fun
Sex in the '90s by Cathy
Winks and Anne Semans.
ISBN: 0-939416-83-2 29.95 cloth;
ISBN: 0-939416-84-0 16.95 paper.

I Am My Own Woman: The
Outlaw Life of Charlotte von
Mahlsdorf translated by
Jean Hollander.
ISBN: 1-57344-011-6 24.95 cloth;
ISBN: 1-57344-010-8 12.95 paper.

Madonnarama: Essays on
Sex and Popular Culture
edited by Lisa Frank and
Paul Smith.
ISBN: 0-939416-72-7 24.95 cloth;
ISBN: 0-939416-71-9 9.95 paper.

Public Sex: The Culture of
Radical Sex by Pat Califia.
ISBN: 0-939416-88-3 29.95 cloth;
ISBN: 0-939416-89-1 12.95 paper.

Sex Work: Writings by Women
in the Sex Industry edited by
Frédérique Delacoste and
Priscilla Alexander.
ISBN: 0-939416-10-7 24.95 cloth;
ISBN: 0-939416-11-5 16.95 paper.

Susie Bright's Sexual Reality:
A Virtual Sex World Reader
by Susie Bright.
ISBN: 0-939416-58-1 24.95 cloth;
ISBN: 0-939416-59-X 9.95 paper.

Susie Bright's Sexwise by
Susie Bright.
ISBN: 1-57344-003-5 24.95 cloth;
ISBN: 1-57344-002-7 10.95 paper.

Susie Sexpert's Lesbian
Sex World by Susie
Bright.
ISBN: 0-939416-34-4 24.95 cloth;
ISBN: 0-939416-35-2 9.95 paper.

Lesbian and Gay Studies

Best Gay Erotica 1996
selected by Scott Heim,
edited by Michael Ford.
ISBN: 1-57344-053-1 24.95 cloth;
ISBN: 1-57344-052-3 12.95 paper.

Best Lesbian Erotica 1996
selected by Heather Lewis,
edited by Tristan Taormino.
ISBN: 1-57344-055-8 24.95 cloth;
ISBN: 1-57344-054-X 12.95 paper.

Boomer: Railroad Memoirs
by Linda Niemann.
ISBN: 0-939416-55-7 12.95 paper.

The Case of the Good-For-
Nothing Girlfriend by Mabel
Maney.
ISBN: 0-939416-90-5 24.95 cloth;
ISBN: 0-939416-91-3 10.95 paper.

The Case of the Not-So-Nice
Nurse by Mabel Maney.
ISBN: 0-939416-75-1 24.95 cloth;
ISBN: 0-939416-76-X 9.95 paper.

Dagger: On Butch Women
edited by Roxxie, Lily
Burana, Linnea Due.
ISBN: 0-939416-81-6 29.95 cloth;
ISBN: 0-939416-82-4 14.95 paper.

Dark Angels: Lesbian Vampire
Stories edited by Pam Keesey.
ISBN: 1-57344-015-9 24.95 cloth;
ISBN 1-7344-014-0 10.95 paper.

Daughters of Darkness:
Lesbian Vampire Stories
edited by Pam Keesey.
ISBN: 0-939416-77-8 24.95 cloth;
ISBN: 0-939416-78-6 9.95 paper.

Different Daughters: A Book
by Mothers of Lesbians,
second edition, edited by
Louise Rafkin.
ISBN: 1-57344-051-5 24.95 cloth;
ISBN: 1-57344-050-7 12.95 paper.

Different Mothers: Sons &
Daughters of Lesbians Talk
About Their Lives edited by
Louise Rafkin.
ISBN: 0-939416-40-9 24.95 cloth;
ISBN: 0-939416-41-7 9.95 paper.

Dyke Strippers: Lesbian Car-
toonists A to Z edited by Roz
Warren.
ISBN: 1-57344-009-4 29.95 cloth;
ISBN: 1-57344-008-6 16.95 paper.

Girlfriend Number One: Les-
bian Life in the '90s edited
by Robin Stevens.
ISBN: 0-939416-79-4 29.95 cloth;
ISBN: 0-939416-8 12.95 paper.

Hothead Paisan: Homicidal
Lesbian Terrorist by Diane
DiMassa.
ISBN: 0-939416-73-5 14.95 paper.

A Lesbian Love Advisor by
Celeste West.
ISBN: 0-939416-27-1 24.95 cloth;
ISBN: 0-939416-26-3 9.95 paper.

More Serious Pleasure:
Lesbian Erotic Stories and
Poetry edited by the Sheba
Collective.
ISBN: 0-939416-48-4 24.95 cloth;
ISBN: 0-939416-47-6 9.95 paper.

Nancy Clue and the Hardly
Boys in *A Ghost in the Closet*
by Mabel Maney.
ISBN: 1-57344-013-2 24.95 cloth;
ISBN: 1-57344-012-4 10.95 paper.

The Night Audrey's Vibrator
Spoke: A Stonewall Riots Col-
lection by Andrea Natalie.
ISBN: 0-939416-64-6 8.95 paper.

Queer and Pleasant Danger:
Writing Out My Life by
Louise Rafkin.
ISBN: 0-939416-60-3 24.95 cloth;
ISBN: 0-939416-61-1 9.95 paper.

Revenge of Hothead Paisan:
Homicidal Lesbian Terrorist
by Diane DiMassa.
ISBN: 1-57344-016-7 16.95 paper.

Rubyfruit Mountain:
A Stonewall Riots Collection
by Andrea Natalie.
ISBN: 0-939416-74-3 9.95 paper.

Serious Pleasure: Lesbian
Erotic Stories and Poetry
edited by the Sheba
Collective.
ISBN: 0-939416-46-8 24.95 cloth;
ISBN: 0-939416-45-X 9.95 paper.

Switch Hitters: Lesbians
Write Gay Male Erotica and
Gay Men Write Lesbian Erot-
ica edited by Carol Queen
and Lawrence Schimel.
ISBN: 1-57344-022-1 24.95 cloth;
ISBN: 1-57344-021-3 12.95 paper.

Politics of Health

The Absence of the Dead Is
Their Way of Appearing by
Mary Winfrey Trautmann.
ISBN: 0-939416-04-2 8.95 paper.

Don't: A Woman's Word
by Elly Danica.
ISBN: 0-939416-23-9 21.95 cloth;
ISBN: 0-939416-22-0 8.95 paper

1 in 3: Women with Cancer
Confront an Epidemic edited
by Judith Brady.
ISBN: 0-939416-50-6 24.95 cloth;
ISBN: 0-939416-49-2 10.95 paper.

Voices in the Night: Women
Speaking About Incest edited
by Toni A.H. McNaron and
Yarrow Morgan.
ISBN: 0-939416-02-6 9.95 paper.

With the Power of Each Breath: A Disabled Women's Anthology edited by Susan Browne, Debra Connors and Nanci Stern.
ISBN: 0-939416-09-3 24.95 cloth;
ISBN: 0-939416-06-9 10.95 paper.

Woman-Centered Pregnancy and Birth by the Federation of Feminist Women's Health Centers.
ISBN: 0-939416-03-4 11.95 paper.

Reference

Putting Out: The Essential Publishing Resource Guide For Gay and Lesbian Writers, third edition, by Edisol W. Dotson.
ISBN: 0-939416-86-7 29.95 cloth;
ISBN: 0-939416-87-5 12.95 paper.

Fiction

Cosmopolis: Urban Stories by Women edited by Ines Rieder.
ISBN: 0-939416-36-0 24.95 cloth;
ISBN: 0-939416-37-9 9.95 paper.

Dirty Weekend: A Novel of Revenge by Helen Zahavi.
ISBN: 0-939416-85-9 10.95 paper.

A Forbidden Passion by Cristina Peri Rossi.
ISBN: 0-939416-64-0 24.95 cloth;
ISBN: 0-939416-68-9 9.95 paper.

Half a Revolution: Contemporary Fiction by Russian Women edited by Masha Gessen.
ISBN 1-57344-007-8 $29.95 cloth;
ISBN 1-57344-006-X $12.95 paper.

In the Garden of Dead Cars by Sybil Claiborne.
ISBN: 0-939416-65-4 24.95 cloth;
ISBN: 0-939416-66-2 9.95 paper.

Night Train To Mother by Ronit Lentin.
ISBN: 0-939416-29-8 24.95 cloth;
ISBN: 0-939416-28-X 9.95 paper.

The One You Call Sister: New Women's Fiction edited by Paula Martinac.
ISBN: 0-939416-30-1 24.95 cloth;
ISBN: 0-939416031-X 9.95 paper.

Only Lawyers Dancing by Jan McKemmish.
ISBN: 0-939416-70-0 24.95 cloth;
ISBN: 0-939416-69-7 9.95 paper.

Seeing Dell by Carol Guess
ISBN: 1-57344-024-8 24.95 cloth;
ISBN: 1-57344-023-X 12.95 paper.

Unholy Alliances: New Women's Fiction edited by Louise Rafkin.
ISBN: 0-939416-14-X 21.95 cloth;
ISBN: 0-939416-15-8 9.95 paper.

The Wall by Marlen Haushofer.
ISBN: 0-939416-53-0 24.95 cloth;
ISBN: 0-939416-54-9 paper.

We Came All The Way from Cuba So You Could Dress Like This?: Stories by Achy Obejas.
ISBN: 0-939416-92-1 24.95 cloth;
ISBN: 0-939416-93-X 10.95 paper.

Latin America

Beyond the Border: A New Age in Latin American Women's Fiction edited by Nora Erro-Peralta and Caridad Silva-Núñez.
ISBN: 0-939416-42-5 24.95 cloth;
ISBN: 0-939416-43-3 12.95 paper.

The Little School: Tales of Disappearance and Survival in Argentina by Alicia Partnoy.
ISBN: 0-939416-08-5 21.95 cloth;
ISBN: 0-939416-07-7 9.95 paper.

Revenge of the Apple by Alicia Partnoy.
ISBN: 0-939416-62-X 24.95 cloth;
ISBN: 0-939416-63-8 8.95 paper.

Autobiography, Biography, Letters

Peggy Deery: An Irish Family at War by Nell McCafferty.
ISBN: 0-939416-38-7 24.95 cloth;
ISBN: 0-939416-39-5 9.95 paper.

The Shape of Red: Insider/Outsider Reflections by Ruth Hubbard and Margaret Randall.
ISBN: 0-939416-19-0 24.95 cloth;
ISBN: 0-939416-18-2 9.95 paper.

Women & Honor: Some Notes on Lying by Adrienne Rich.
ISBN: 0-939416-44-1 3.95 paper.

Animal Rights

And a Deer's Ear, Eagle's Song and Bear's Grace: Relationships Between Animals and Women edited by Theresa Corrigan and Stephanie T. Hoppe.
ISBN: 0-939416-38-7 24.95 cloth;
ISBN: 0-939416-39-5 9.95 paper.

With a Fly's Eye, Whale's Wit and Woman's Heart: Relationships Between Animals and Women edited by Theresa Corrigan and Stephanie T. Hoppe.
ISBN: 0-939416-24-7 24.95 cloth;
ISBN: 0-939416-25-5 9.95 paper.

Ordering information

Since 1980, Cleis Press has published progressive books by women. We welcome your order and will ship your books as quickly as possible. Individual orders must be prepaid (U.S. dollars only). Please add 15% shipping. PA residents add 6% sales tax. Mail orders: Cleis Press, PO Box 8933, Pittsburgh PA 15221. MasterCard and Visa orders: include account number, exp. date, and signature. FAX your credit card order: (412) 937-1567. Or, phone us Mon–Fri, 9 am–5 pm EST: (412) 937-1555.